CU00683735

Turkish Delight

Copyright

© 2024 Anjelica Søndergaard & Brændpunkt

Cover design: Søren Klok
Editor: Sidsel-Marie Holm
Translation: Anjelica Søndergaard

1st edition 2024

Paperback ISBN: 978-87-945344-0-6
eBook ISBN: 978-87-945343-6-9

All rights reserved.

No part of this publication may be reproduced, distributed, or transmitted in any form or by any means, including photocopying, recording, or other electronic or mechanical methods, without the prior written permission from the publisher or author, except as permitted by Danish copyright law.

Anjelica Søndergaard

Turkish Delight

NOVEL

BRÆNDPUNKT

Dedication

Turkish Delight is dedicated to all the family members and friends who, through the years, have helped to make my holidays both fun, cosy, festive and sometimes also completely crazy and surreal.

The pages of this book would be empty without you. So, thank you for lazy hangover-stricken days by the pool, late nights on the dance floor and lots of life-affirming laughs.

I owe a special thanks to my little sister, who, as a long-time travel companion and overall partner in crime, has been an invaluable help throughout this entire process.

Not only has she been ready with support, input and opinions on everything from wording in the text to the appearance of the cover.

She has also, on several occasions, "discreetly" reminded me that particularly helpful individuals always should be mentioned in a dedication.

Fortunately, I'm not completely hopeless at deciphering coded language, so thanks for the support, Susie. On our next holiday, the first round of strawberry daiquiris is at my expense!

Anjelica Søndergaard – 14. April 2023

www.turkishdelight.dk

Chapter 1

Maya turned critically in front of the mirror in the tiny fitting room. She studied her own body with an intense look from all angles, then sighed audibly.

"June, did Cecilia add cancellation insurance to our holiday booking?"

"What do you mean?" The voice came from the cabin next to her.

"I mean, is it still possible to say thanks, but no thanks, to show this pile of sadness to everyone in broad daylight?" Maya gave the mirror a frustrated glance.

"Two seconds, two seconds," the voice next door responded in a strained manner. "I just need to get my clothes back on. They don't exactly have a lot of space, these claustrophobic fitting rooms!"

Maya heard the curtain of the neighbouring cabin being pulled aside, and a moment later June poked her round face with the grey short hair into her cabin. "I succeeded in my quest of finding a bikini that can hold this Granny Smith-shaped body roughly in place, and in a lovely colour too.

So now, I'm pretty much ready to go!" she proclaimed with a big smile.

Then she saw Maya's reflection in the mirror. "Wow, Mau-Mau, you look amazing in that bikini! It just suits your eyes and hair so well! Turquoise is *so* your colour!" she clapped her hands in excitement.

Maya raised her eyebrows and looked at her sceptically. "I think that, maybe, you need to get your eyesight checked, my friend!"

She pointed down at her thighs.

"Look! I look like a freaking melted candle! And look here! How about this? Where the hell did that come from?!" she said with frustration, moving her arm back and forth so the loose skin dangled from the underside of her arm. "Bingo wings are what old people have! I'm only 44! It's far too soon for this decay, June! I didn't sign up for this, and I'm definitely not going on holiday when I'm so... Wobbly!" She sighed again and looked at herself disapprovingly in the mirror.

June's voice cut through in a calm but firm manner: "Maya, you have to speak nicely to yourself, and that has to start right now! I never allow anyone to talk nasty about my friends. That rule applies even if you're talking to and about yourself." She stepped further into the small fitting room and placed a hand on Maya's shoulder.

"And of course, you're going on holiday. We have been planning this for months, and we are all really excited about it. Don't throw that away just because you're frustrated that you don't look like a twenty-year-old when you *are* over the forty-mark."

She looked at Maya with a teasing look. "Let's be honest, no one is staring at your stomach rolls and your flabby thighs when you're running around with those boobs! They just need to be cramped into a good push-up bra, that's all!" she giggled.

Maya gave her a surprised look, but then she started to laugh. "Oh my God, June, you certainly have a way of saying things!"

"Hey, I never say anything I don't mean." She grabbed the curtain and looked at Maya with a smile. "Now, buy that bikini. It's so nice on you, and then get your clothes on! I'm hot and thirsty, and I can hear a cold pint shouting my name somewhere nearby."

Maya grabbed June's hand. "Hey, I know I have to get better at accepting that I look the way I look and all that." She shrugged. "But it's not that easy, and that kind of thing just takes time. So, thank you for reminding me of it."

"Of course, any time, and now, get a move on. I'm sweating like crazy!"

Maya quickly took off the bikini and put her clothes back on.

June was waiting for her outside the fitting room. They walked over to the checkout counter to pay for their new bikinis.

"Damn, June, I'm so glad you were here with me today. I would probably just have given up and gone back home if I was out shopping alone. And we're travelling very soon, so it really wouldn't have been the best of decisions."

Then she thoughtfully added, "Imagine being so influenced by what society has decided to deem attractive! After all, it doesn't matter, I *know* that... And I have to get a handle on it."

It was Maya's turn to pay, and she continued talking as she pulled out her purse. "It's pretty ridiculous, in a way. Because if something is unattainable for most people, most people will feel like losers, and that's actually not okay."

Maya was silent as she took her shopping bag, thanked the clerk and put her purse back in her handbag.

"Maya, I won't even pretend to understand exactly what you're babbling on about right now," June admitted as they walked towards the exit. "But that doesn't mean you're not right. If I have understood your many words correctly, then I think that there already are some recent waves around having a more positive ... body-image, or whatever it's called these days. But we probably need to start with ourselves and how we talk about ourselves and others, and then have some patience. Things take time. That's just the way it is."

She stopped on the street, pulled a pack of cigarettes out of her handbag, knocked one out, put it between her lips, lit it, and inhaled deeply.

"Holy shit, that's just what I needed." She slowly blew the smoke out between her lips.

Maya, who was about to close her coat, looked at her with a teasing look and waved the smoke away with a grimace. "When are you going to quit that shit? It's really unhealthy and stinks like crazy, and I don't want to be burdened with your smelly bad habit."

June just shrugged, inhaled deeply again, and winked at her. "As long as I enjoy smoking, I'm going to smoke. But I'll try to take your delicate lungs into account. But only because you're an old woman with a decaying body that we need to look after."

Maya lashed out at her while laughing: "Hey, you're older than me! Don't speak ill of my old lard-filled body. I'm perfectly capable of that myself!"

"If it's bothering you that much, I have a little ... Let's call it an advice, for you," June replied, as they started walking toward the lively Stork Fountain area further down the street.

She smirked at Maya, raised her index finger, and with a squeaky voice continued, "As my late grandma always said, "Brown fat is nicer than white fat, so get out in the sun, chubby!"

Maya started laughing. "Now, that is funny! She really said that?"

June nodded. "Yep, she was full of good advice and she was ice cold! If a child wasn't pretty, she would say; The kid may not be a looker, but you can always put some nice clothes on him!"

"She didn't say that!" Maya exclaimed with pretend indignation.

"She did. I'm not exaggerating," June insisted.

"I'm sure your grandmother was a popular lady in her time!" Maya shook her head in disbelief.

"I'm not sure it's well-regarded to be so brazen, no matter what time period you're from!" June replied, as she stopped briefly to extinguish her cigarette at a trash can and threw the butt away.

They continued strolling down the street toward the train station. The late summer sun was out, still throwing a bit of heat down on the people in the streets of Copenhagen.

"Oh, I can't wait to just chill out and relax in the sun!" Maya suddenly sighed. "It's just going to be so nice to get away with you guys, without husbands and kids. Where we can just swim and have fun and laugh and eat good food and drink wonderful wine and..." She stopped her stream of words when she noticed June looking at her with a big smile.

Maya threw her arms out and started laughing.

"Okay, okay, I guess maybe I'm a little excited after all, but is it really so strange? I haven't been on holiday in years, I'm going to travel with my best friends in the whole wide world, and we're going somewhere neither of us has been before. What's not to love?!"

June nodded. "You're right. It's going to be so much fun, and I'm really looking forward to it, too. Although I am a bit surprised that the suggestion came from Cecilia and not from you. Have you lost your touch?" she teased.

"Yeah, what is up with that?!" Maya agreed. "I didn't see that coming, but, hey! It doesn't matter to me who came up with the idea, and I guess it's time Cecilia started living it up a little."

They walked further down the street, enjoying the sun and blue sky, and looked at the many other people who had also chosen to take advantage of the nice weather.

"It will be exciting to find out where in Cennet we will stay," Maya continued, while stepping aside for a group of Asian tourists who came swarming out of a shop with souvenirs and handicraft.

"I spoke to Charlotte yesterday, and she is not thrilled, to say the least, that we have chosen a holiday with unspecified hotel. Where you risk being accommodated in a smelly and horrible place. Her words, not mine! But that's just what I can afford right now. My part-time job pays okay, but it's not overwhelming what I can put aside each month." Maya had a sad look on her face.

June slowed down and grabbed Maya's arm.

"Hey, stop talking nonsense. Charlotte may be used to travelling first class, but the rest of us aren't. This holiday-solution is not just because of you. Besides, the most important thing is that all four of us can go together, and Charlotte just has to survive a week on a budget holiday. Now, enough about that." She let go of Maya's arm and looked around with a searching look in her eyes. "Isn't there a pub around here? Let's go find a nice place. I'm still dying of thirst here!"

Chapter 2

"Come on in," Charlotte smiled as she looked up from her desk to see Sarah standing in the doorway into her office. She had a large cardboard box in her arms and an eager look in her eyes.

The always hard-working Sarah was head of the Product Development Department, in short PDD, at the popular skincare company called "*Shine Bright*" and was one of Charlotte's most trusted and well-liked employees.

"Come, let me help you with that. It looks a bit heavy." Charlotte hurried to help Sarah set up the box on the large conference table that was usually overflowing with products, documents with graphs, sales figures, drafts of new product ideas and launches and lots of used coffee cups.

"Wow," Sarah nodded approvingly. "I don't think I've ever seen what your meeting table actually looks like. It's so nice! So shiny and clean!"

Charlotte laughed. "Hey, you don't get paid for being cheeky!" She pointed to the box. "What are you bringing me today?"

Sarah pulled a box opener out of her pocket. "Yes, that's the big question. It is supposed to be our new series 'Get Young', but let's see what they've sent us."

With a quick hand movement, she swiftly ran the box opener over the top of the box.

"This is going to be exciting!" She opened the two cardboard flaps and immediately began pulling the content of the box out onto the table.

"Yes, this is amazing!" Charlotte studied the various products closely.

"The packaging is perfect! It just screams luxury product." She opened one of the cream product containers, took a little on her fingertip, and smeared it on the back of her hands. "Delicious, delicious texture and smell!".

She looked appreciatively at Sarah. "The finished product has become just as luxurious as I had imagined. I can't praise you enough for this!! You're incredible!"

Sarah blushed. "Thank you so much, Charlotte. Well, you know, it wasn't just me, and you've also been involved in all the steps in the process as well. But yes, my team is world class. So, I can't take all the praise myself. But I'll make sure to pass it on." Her voice filled with pride and her eyes beamed.

Charlotte was rummaging through the box and pulled up a couple of smaller plastic bags. "Hey, look. They have been really brilliant at production this time. They have sent some bags of samples without us even asking for them. I appreciate it when people think creatively and go above and beyond!"

She opened one of the bags. "This is perfect. There are samples of serum, day and night cream and eye cream. I know who's going to love it," she mumbled to herself as she looked through the content.

"I'll take one of these bags home with me. You can hand out the content of the other one around the office to those who want to try it," she added, as she packed the opened sample bag into her handbag.

Sarah packed everything back in the cardboard box, picked it up and walked towards the door. She stopped in the doorway and turned around.

"When are you going, and is it with the family?" She asked while resting the cardboard box against the door frame.

"We leave tomorrow night, so we are ready for the sun, the beach, and cold drinks on Sunday morning. It will be so amazing to get some sunshine and beach time again. And it's not with Kenneth and the kids this time. It's just going to be me and three friends. I've known them..." She thought for a moment. "Wow... It must be more than twenty years ago, since we got to know each other." She sighed and shook her head. "Yeah, time just flies so fast. But I'm truly looking forward to it! We haven't been so great at meeting up regularly for a few years. You know, because of husbands, kids and careers, the last part at least for me. But now it's like we all have some air in the program again."

"I'm quite envious, but you know what, Charlotte? No one deserves it more than you, so have an amazing holiday, and please send some sunshine back to us back in Denmark. God knows, we already miss the summer," she added with a look of resignation, and left the office.

Charlotte glanced at her phone and saw that there were three missed calls from Cecilia. She made a mental note to call her back on the way home in the car.

For a moment, she got lost in her own thoughts, thinking about when they had all met. They had been in their early twenties and their whole lives lay ahead of them. They have had so many good times together, their four-leaf clover.

But then came boyfriends who turned into husbands. Some of them also had children. The careers also had to be taken care of. As a result, they just didn't get to see each other that much anymore.

She loved her life, with three healthy children, a well-paid and exciting job, and a man who could still give her butterflies in her stomach, even after more than 16 years together. But she still was a little sad that she wasn't as close to her friends as she used to be.

She shrugged and shook her head again. Well, this was not the time to think about that. She just needed to activate her Out of office-reply, and then she was out of there!

***

Cecilia was standing with folded arms and frowned brows in front of her open wardrobe.

On the bed, her black newly purchased suitcase lay wide open and was still completely empty.

She bit her lower lip a little and began taking some clothes out of the closet, but then hesitantly put it back again.

The cell phone on the bedside table rang.

Happy to be interrupted, she hurried to answer it.

"Yes, this is Cecilia speaking."

"Hey you, it's Charlotte. I see you've called, but I couldn't call back until now. Had a really busy day at the office. The last day before a week away from my desk, I needed to sort out a thousand things and... You know what it's like..."

Cecilia could hear traffic noise in the background.

"Hi Charlotte!" she greeted in a cheerful tone. "Well, no problem, no problem. I know it all too well. That is also why I left earlier today, so I can get everything sorted out before we go."

"Good thinking!" Charlotte replied. "How far along are you? Have you finished packing yet?"

"No, that's actually why I called," Cecilia answered with a frustrated laugh. "I need your help. I've gone completely cold with the packing and have pulled clothes in and out of the closet for hours now." She cast a resigned glance at the packed shelves of the closet and then at the gaping empty suitcase.

Well, the problem is..." Cecilia began to explain, when Charlotte suddenly interrupted her and started to yell. "What the hell are you doing, man?!? Did your mom drop you on the head as a child or what?!"

"Um, huh? Is it me you're talking to or what?" Cecilia asked, a bit confused. She could count on one hand the times she had heard Charlotte swear like that.

"No, no, sorry Cecilia! It wasn't you," Charlotte answered quickly. "There was just some *idiot* in a van that drove straight across all lanes to get to the exit. Without blinking and without thinking about others. Insane way to drive!" She was clearly very annoyed. "Excuse me, dumbass! Some of us are going on a holiday tomorrow! So please mind others in the traffic!" she added in a loud voice. She took a deep breath, exhaled, and then chuckled. "Sorry, I'll be myself again in a second, Cecilia, are you still there?

Cecilia had been giggling over Charlotte's outburst. "Wow, people should definitely not cross you, huh?"

They both started laughing.

"Well, let's forget about him," Charlotte continued. "What was it you said before we were so rudely interrupted?"

"Technically, I didn't have time to say it," Cecilia chuckled. "But what I *would* have said was that I don't know what to bring. I have

16

stared at dresses, shorts and T-shirts for a while now, and I am completely lost.

"Hmmm, that scares me a little, Mammi," Charlotte said teasingly. "I don't know anyone else as organised as you. You are normally in total control of your things and mostly also our stuff as well."

"Yeah, yeah," Cecilia sighed. "I'm well aware of where my nickname comes from!"

"We mean it lovingly!" Charlotte quickly added, with laughter in her voice. "It's just because you're so good at keeping track of things... Even when no one asks you for it or wants it."

"I really don't understand what you're talking about. There's nothing wrong with reminding people to pee before heading out the door!"

"And we love you for that! Even though we are all grownups who have actually managed to navigate all that peeing-before-leaving all by ourselves for many years."

"Charlotte, I'm sure other groups of friends would appreciate my skills in structure and organisation more." Cecilia tried to sound insulted, but was not really feeling it.

"No, please don't leave us!" Charlotte quickly responded. "We would be completely lost without you! Just look at all this stuff with the holiday. If it wasn't for you, Mammi-mouse, we wouldn't be heading out tomorrow. Also, I will remind you, that you hold all the tickets and all the exchanged money, so your presence is very much needed! So, enough about that, let's get a little holiday mood going. What do you say to some work-music?"

A moment later, loud dance music blasted out through the phone.

"Now, Cecilia, I'm yours for the rest of the ride home," Charlotte shouted. "We have about twenty minutes to put something in your suitcase! Let's get started."

Chapter 3

June had been up early that day.

In reality, she had a distinct type B personality. And frankly, she wasn't normally really functioning until just before lunchtime.

Her husband, Bo, was the complete opposite and literally got up with the chickens every day to tend to his organic farm.

June had tried to go to bed at midnight the night before, so she could get about eight hours of sleep. Much to her frustration, she had been tossing and turning for hours. She wasn't super happy when the alarm went off at half past eight.

"For fuck's sake, it should be prohibited to get up at this unholy time of day, and on a Saturday!" she grumbled and reached for the phone on the nightstand. She turned off the alarm with an annoyed motion.

She lay for a few minutes with her eyes closed while she stretched her body and snuggled under the covers.

Then she remembered what day it was and quickly opened her eyes.

"Holiday time!" she mumbled to herself and

yawned loudly. "That's the only reason I choose to get up almost in the middle of the night."

She could vividly imagine both Cecilia and Charlotte rolling their eyes at the fact that she called half past eight in the middle of the night. They both got up very early on weekdays and probably also on weekends. Voluntarily!

In the kitchen, Bo had readied a pot of coffee for her. "Thank you, my darling, you are a lifesaver!" she whispered to herself in the cosy country kitchen, sending him a warm thought.

June got a large mug from the kitchen cabinet and filled it to the brim. She sniffed it, letting the aroma of the coffee embrace her, and then took a big sip.

"Now the day can just bring it!" With a content smile, she took another sip.

She walked towards the small dining area in the kitchen, placed the coffee cup on the table, pulled out a chair, and sat down so she could look out over the meandering fields around the house.

She could see a few deer grazing at the edge of the forest about a hundred meters away. Out in the courtyard, Henning and Meatball were barking and chasing each other for fun. The two idiots always put her in a good mood.

June had created her own little company, where she transformed problematic dogs into good, well-behaved family dogs, and occasionally she also helped the local animal shelter make the more difficult dogs ready for adoption. Like the two bozos out in the garden, who nobody wanted to adopt because they behaved like two very unruly bundles of energy. But after only a few weeks of June's intense training, she had two beautiful and happy dogs on her hands, who didn't know which leg to stand on to fit into the family, and she had fallen completely in love with both of them.

When she officially adopted them, the family held a small ceremony in the garden. June and Bo opened a nice bottle of wine, the twins had a glass of soda and some crisps, and the "Dynamic Dog Duo" got new Forever Home names; Henning and Meatball. The kids had come up with the names. It may not have been exactly what June herself would have chosen. But she had promised them that they were the ones who got to decide, and she always kept her promises.

It was still quiet in the house. She could hear Bo rumbling with something outside. Probably the tractor. There were some problems with the engine the day before.

The boys were still asleep. She knew that having children, who also enjoyed sleeping in, almost was like winning the lottery. As such, there was no guarantee that things would continue like this. But now they were seven years old, and they still loved to sleep until after nine o'clock. So maybe they just took after their mother?

June smiled at the thought of the two rug rats that she and Bo had struggled so hard to bring into the world. Andreas and David were extremely active and filled with sass *and* a little trouble. But they were good kids with big hearts, who found it easy to make friends, and they both loved animals as much as their parents did.

A sound of running feet came from the hallway, and loud voices hurried towards the kitchen.

"Well," June muttered to herself and got up. "Quiet time is definitely over now."

Andreas and David came galloping into the kitchen.

"Mom, I'm hungry!" – "Mom, can I watch TV?". The twins shouted at the same time.

"One at a time, gentlemen," June had a stern tone in her voice. "Have you made your beds and opened your windows so all the night farts can get out?" she asked, with laughter in her eyes.

"Yes, yes, we have!" they replied eagerly and in unison.

"Hmmm, I'm thinking that's a big fat lie. Shall we just check?" June walked over to the hallway door.

"No, no, Mom! You don't have to! We are telling the truth!" both chuckled and protested as they tried to block her way.

"Don't you trust us?" David pretended to be chocked.

June stopped and looked directly at him.

"Do I trust that you have kept your rooms tidy, as you have promised me? Although it has never happened yet without me having to ask you several times? The answer is a straight-up NO, young man! Of course, I don't trust your words! But if you both just rush down and get your beds made and air out – right now and without complaining and dragging your feet – then I'll find some breakfast in the meantime, and I'll allow watching TV while you eat. Deal?"

The boys looked at her, then gazed at each other, before they both hollered "Deal!" and dashed down towards their rooms at full speed.

June chuckled to herself. They were baboons, but they made her laugh every single day, and she loved them dearly.

She glanced at the clock. She had to leave in about one and a half hours at the latest, and still had some things on her to-do list before she was ready.

As she prepared breakfast for the boys, she muttered to herself: "Breakfast, shower, clothes, dry my hair, throw the suitcase in the car, check that I have my passport with me, kiss goodbye... Yes, I think that's it. I should be able to achieve that if I just get a little move on."

As she poured another cup of coffee, she could hear her sons heading back to the kitchen in full sprint.

"I'm going to take a shower, boys," she told them as they tumbled into the kitchen and began pouring oatmeal and milk. "Just put the milk in the fridge when you have taken what you need. I'll clean the rest up afterwards," she said, tapping the milk carton with a finger. "Is it received, mini-monkeys?"

"Yes, yes, Mom," they replied in unison and continued to pour.

"Then it's Vamos, old gal," June said to herself and walked with coffee in hand towards the bathroom.

Chapter 4

"Cat food, food bowl, tray, gravel, toys, poop scooper... The carrier is ready in the bedroom..." Maya mumbled to herself. "Wasn't there one more thing? ... What am I missing?"

She looked at the filled Ikea bag she had placed next to the front door in the spacious hallway and squinted her eyes while she was thinking.

"The pills!" she shouted and slapped her own forehead. "Jeez, I really can't forget them!" She ran into the living room and grabbed the white plastic tub that was standing on the coffee table.

She hurried back into the hallway and placed it on top of the bag of diet food that Freddy, her fourteen-year-old – and very overweight – cat, had been on for the past two years.

Unfortunately, with age, and aided by the considerable body volume, he had developed arthritis and had to have pills every day to help his joints.

Fortunately, he was not problematic in that direction. He inhaled everything indiscriminately as long as it was covered in wet food with salmon. It was as easy as putting the pill into that clammy and smelly jelly, stirring well, and then the furry animal was well running again.

It suddenly dawned on her.

Imagine that around this time tomorrow, she would most likely be lying in her new cool bikini with her best friends, enjoying life! She smiled from ear to ear at the bare thought and could almost feel the warm sun on her body.

Then she shook her head. "Come on, Maya, you need to get on with the program!" she ordered herself and glanced at her watch.

Shit!

It was almost twelve, and June could be here at any moment.

She was sure she had enough time to both pack and get ready when she got up. "But there was probably a little too much fun going on in project 'Pack your suitcase'," she said out loud into the empty hallway and laughed a little at herself.

Yes, living alone for so many years probably could make you a little weird. She was, without any doubt, some kind of unofficial champion at speaking out loud, even though no one was there to listen. Besides Freddy, of course, and he didn't really care at all about what she said. As long as she was available with endless amounts of cuddles, a cleaned litter box, and a filled food bowl, he was pretty much happy with life.

"Freddy-mousy, where are you? Our ride will be here any second, so we don't have time to play hide and seek," Maya called out. Freddy was nowhere to be seen, and the apartment was completely quiet.

She went into her cosy little guest room, where there were some filled bookshelves, an enormous wardrobe made of teak, and an extremely worn sofa bed that had once been dark blue. She had owned the sofa since her first apartment, and it had gradually faded in colour. The seating comfort also disappeared years ago, and she wasn't sure if she could still fold it out into a bed.

She cast a slightly resigned look at it. It wasn't pretty anymore, but she just couldn't bring herself to throw it out.

There were so many great memories associated with it.

Especially the many hours she had spent in the company of June, Cecilia and Charlotte, with cheap white wine, music on the stereo, and lots of half-burnt microwave popcorn.

27

They had talked about everything and nothing, often into the early hours.

She felt a small sting in her heart.

She missed those times. Like really missed them and the closeness they had enjoyed back then. Before boyfriends, husbands, children and everyday life were mixed into it all. She sat down on the edge of the sofa bed and lost herself in the memories for a moment.

It hadn't been easy being her when she was in her early thirties. It had felt like their group of friends almost broke up as June and Charlotte moved on to the next stage in life.

Maya was the only one of them that has never wanted to have children. She had always thought that she was completely okay with the fact that their lives, at some point, would look very different from each other in the future.

But no one could have prepared her for how abandoned and lonely she felt when her beloved friends, who were the most important people in her life, suddenly had other priorities. When she was no longer at the top of the list, as she had been before.

She understood it up to a point. Of course, it was logical that when you meet the love of your life, your priorities change, and even more so when you have children. But she had never understood how you could so easily move, genuine and truly close relationships, so far down the rankings because of a boyfriend.

She had always made a point of nurturing her friendships when she was in relationships herself. After all, they were the most important thing in her life. The ones she had chosen as her extended family. The ones who would always be there, no matter what happened. It had really hurt her deeply when she realised that not everyone thought like her.

She had felt betrayed, let down and alone for a long time, and that had led her to make some horrible choices. Among other things, with Michael...

She shuddered at the thought. No, she didn't want to think about him now. He had poisoned enough of her life already, and he belonged in the past.

Maya shook her head to turn off her stream of thoughts.

Her focus was only on the present and on being strong enough to handle things herself, even when life got difficult.

She subconsciously sat up straight when she thought about how she had fought to get out the other side of that nightmare as a stronger and more complete person.

Maya giggled at the bare thought of how Charlotte would roll her eyes if she could hear her inner pep talk.

Charlotte wasn't really feeling all that 'self-development and inspirational quotes hokey-pokey', as she called it.

An expression like *standing strong in your own light and letting it shine over the world'* almost spontaneously activated her gag reflex.

Maya didn't care, though. For the past six years, as she had struggled to recover from a massive downturn, both intense life coaching and mantra phrases like this had helped her out on the other side.

Maybe Charlotte wasn't exactly the target audience for self-help gurus and positive thinking, Maya thought with a smile.

Charlotte, with an exciting and well-paid job, a really sweet and handsome man, a large villa in an expensive area, a cool car, good health and three perfect children. On top of that, she was a truly beautiful woman who, despite three pregnancies, was still both slim and tight body-wise.

"I don't have any kids, and, even on a good

day, I look like someone who's squeezed at least five kids out through the undercarriage," Maya sighed and looked down at her belly, where two soft dough-like thick rolls clearly showed behind the t-shirt's fabric.

It was also frustratingly irritating that she hadn't managed to keep up her weight loss from last year. A lifetime of her weight going up and down like an elevator and trying out different crazy diets had almost destroyed her body's ability to regulate weight normally. Now she could only lose weight very slowly, but gained weight extremely fast again. It sometimes felt like she couldn't even walk past somebody, who knew somebody, who had once eaten a cake, without gaining a few kilos.

It didn't help that she was now in her mid-forties and truly loved eclairs.

She sighed again, shook off the negative thoughts, and reminded herself of her friends, with whom she was looking forward to go on holiday with, in a few hours. Yes, even Charlotte. Because, besides her annoying perfection, she was also an incredibly sweet, warm and positive person whom Maya loved dearly.

Stop with the thinking and locate Freddy! But where the hell could that bugger be hiding? He couldn't just disappear into thin air, she thought, looking at the time again.

At the same moment, the apartments intercom beeped.

She ran to the door and picked up. "Yes?" she practically shouted into it.

"Maya, is that you? Did I press the correct button?" A slightly confused voice came from on the other end.

"Hiya June! Yes! Yes, you have. Sorry, I'm a little flustered right now. Can't find Freddy, so my brain is melting a little right now," Maya sighed.

"How about letting me in? Then I'll help look for him," June replied calmly.

She was used to Maya being a bit overwhelmed when they had to do something that had a fixed time frame. Therefore, she had turned on her most relaxed disposition before she pressed the doorbell and was ready to act as an anchor for her good friend.

"Damn, I'm all over the place," Maya chuckled. "Yes, of course. I'll buzz you right in. Just come on up, my door is unlocked..." She pressed the button so June could enter.

June just faintly heard that Maya added, "And

if you can't find me when you get up, look for me in the bathroom. The next step from here is to take the 'Duck and Cover'-position in the bathtub, and then just quietly give up," before the door closed behind her.

June laughed to herself as she walked to the elevator.

She drove up to the 3rd floor, going mentally through her luggage again, just to make sure she remembered everything.

"I've found him!". Maya's voice came from the bedroom the second June walked in.

"That's great!" June took off her jacket and hung it on the coat rack. "Where was he hiding?"

"That little fat idiot is lying on top of my wardrobe behind my winter duvet! Can you please tell me how the hell he managed to pull his corpus all the way up there?"

Maya was standing on a chair and tried to pull the things on top of the closet aside so she could grab Freddy. But every time she moved something, the cat moved along with it.

"Maya, he's a cat. He probably jumped... or something..."

Maya looked at June with a sceptical look in her eyes. "Jumped? Have you seen him? You're

33

talking about the cat that's so fat he needs a helping hand to get up on the bed! He stands every night meowing like he's in agony until I lift him up!" She turned around and continued to rummage.

"Ha, got you! June, can you please open the carrier that's on the bed?"

June hurried to the bed and held the carrier door open.

"Fuck's sake, he's heavy!" Maya muttered, trying to get a better grip on the wiggling Freddy so she could step down from her chair without him escaping. She practically threw him into the carrier and quickly closed it behind him.

"Phew, I'm completely sweaty, and there's a *small* possibility that I may have forgotten to vacuum on top of the closet for a very long time." She brushed a handful of rather large dust bunnies off her clothes with a big smile. "I really need a cold soda right now, just to wash down the dust." She glanced at the time and opened her eyes wide up in disbelieve. "Shit, that will have to wait. We need to drop him off first." She pointed to the carrier where Freddy was sitting, meowing heartbreakingly.

"Let's go," June started walking out into the hallway. "I'll take the Ikea bag. You can haul chubby-boy yourself!"

Chapter 5

Cecilia jumped out of bed as soon as the clock radio turned on. She had already been awake for more than half an hour, as she was used to getting up even earlier on weekdays.

As usual, she made her bed and placed the two decorative pillows neatly against the headboard. When she pulled the curtains from the window and looked out to a windy, but sunny, day, she smiled to herself.

Cecilia loved her mornings and could usually never sleep in, even when she had gone to bed late the night before.

Her boss, Ole Svendsen, appreciated the freshness of the early morning and expected his employees to arrive no later than eight o'clock, a time he often referred to as well into the day. Cecilia lived only a quick bike ride away and was usually at work no later than half past seven.

But today was Saturday, the day she was going on her highly anticipated holiday. That made her feel both excited and a little nervous. She hadn't flown in many years and was eager to see how it would be.

After she got herself ready, she had breakfast in front of the TV, but couldn't concentrate on the program. It was about someone making ceramics and winning a prize. Maybe like those baking programs, she thought absently. She was again mentally reviewing what she needed to do before going on holiday.

As secretary to the director of a small publishing house, Cecilia usually had her weekends off. But she had promised Mr Svendsen, as the employees called him, to come into the office for an hour and make contract copies for the new writer he was meeting with next week. She should be able to get that done within an hour, transport time included.

Cecilia turned off her TV, carried the plate and cup into the kitchen, and washed both up immediately. She didn't want it sitting in the sink for an entire week, attracting those pesky little black flies.

She went out into her hallway, put on her shoes and jacket, and pulled out her keys.

On her way out, she stopped in front of the mirror, hanging on the wall next to the front door and, with a critical look, inspected herself.

She had always felt that she had a slightly mouse-like appearance. The dark brown hair, cut just above her shoulders did nothing to change that feeling. She casually ruffled her bangs a bit, but immediately smoothed them down again. She tilted her head and studied herself with frowning brows. Should she change her hairstyle? She had looked the same way almost her entire life. It was easy and convenient, but maybe also a little boring?

She spotted a grey hair and stepped closer to the mirror to inspect it. She sighed. "Well, I guess I can't run from it anymore. I'm getting old," she mumbled to herself. With two fingers, she pinched the hair and pulled it out.

That solution is short-lived, unless I want to choose between grey hair and baldness, she thought to herself as she grabbed the bike helmet and locked her apartment door behind her.

Less than an hour later, she was back home. Everything had been running smoothly, and her boss now had seven copies of the documents for next week's important meeting lying on his desk.

She glanced at the clock. She still had plenty of time. What was next on the list?

She packed the last toiletries, and then she

checked again that she had remembered to pack tickets, passport and the exchanged currency. Of course, she had already looked three times last night. But you can never make sure too many times, she thought to herself.

Cecilia had offered to exchange money for everyone, as Charlotte had an extremely busy life, June lived far away from everything and Maya most likely would forget it or exchange to the wrong currency.

She laughed a little at herself. She really was a bit of a mother hen! But that's probably just how it is. Your upbringing is part of your personality, for better or worse, if you like it or not.

Cecilia's parents had struggled to conceive for many years and, after endless negative pregnancy tests, had finally come to terms with the fact that they would remain childless. Therefore, when her mother suddenly started vomiting every morning, the doctors did not initially examine her for pregnancy. When the doctors finally realised that she was actually pregnant, everyone considered it nothing short of a miracle. When Cecilia was born, both of her parents were in their mid-forties, and she was their entire world.

Her mother, a warm and inclusive woman,

had spent her whole life helping others in her job as a nurse, and was always ready to help neighbours and friends if they needed a hand. Her father was a professor at Copenhagen University and was a skilled communicator of his vast knowledge, both to the students and his daughter. He passed on his love of books with passion and taught Cecilia to read even before she started school.

Together, they had given her a lot of good values, and she loved them very much.

As a teenager, like most of that age, she had had a period where she was embarrassed of them, and she still remembered the pain in her mother's eyes when, during a fit of a hysterical teen meltdown, Cecilia had called her a ridiculous old cow who should just lay down to die.

She had almost immediately regretted her words and had rushed to hug her mother tightly while crying, asking for her forgiveness.

Her mother had forgiven her on the spot, but Cecilia still hadn't forgiven herself, and she would still get red cheeks at the thought of it.

Shit, imagine still being be so ashamed of something that happened almost thirty years ago! She pushed the memory aside and reminded herself that she still had both of them in her life. Yet...

Cecilia felt a sting in her heart thinking about the fact, that in the foreseeable future she would most likely be alone.

She hadn't had children of her own, even though it had been her dream since she was a teenager.

Of course, it's also a little difficult to make children when you're never dating, she thought, rolling her eyes at herself. A few years ago, she had considered having a donor-conceived child and had even been to an interview with a clinic with expertise in this area.

But with her parents not getting any younger, and no other family who could help her with "project baby", she had given up on the idea again. Her friends made it clear that they were fully behind her and would do everything they could to help her.

She was grateful for their support, and she knew they meant well. But she was also a realist, and both June and Charlotte had families of their own. God knows that June herself had fought for her two boys, and Maya... Maya was not into the whole baby-thing. She always knew, from a young age, that she didn't want to get any kids herself. The funny thing was that children usually really liked her. Maybe because Maya, in many ways, still was a big kid who loved comic books, board games and play dress up. She also wasn't afraid to tumble around and make a fool of herself to make others laugh.

That side of Maya, Cecilia envied a little. She herself got almost spontaneous diarrhoea just at the thought of having to stand in the spotlight. *Attention, no thanks!* That was one of her unofficial mottos.

She rolled her eyes again and shook her head. "Wow, I guess you fell into your own little rabbit hole for a second. Stop with the overthinking!" she muttered to herself. In her mind, she went through her suitcase again and decided that everything should be in order.

She sighed audibly. She couldn't postpone it any longer. The last thing on the agenda before she could relax and start looking forward to the holiday.

She grabbed her phone and opened her Favorites in her contacts.

She hesitated for a moment, then pressed Call.

It rang five times before someone picked up.

"Yes, it's Jørgen."

"Hi Dad, it's Cecilia. I just wanted call and

41

hear how things are going before I leave. How is she today?"

Chapter 6

When Charlotte's alarm went off, she hurried to turn it off so her husband Kenneth wouldn't wake up. She slowly untangled herself from his arms, got up, and tip-toed off to the bathroom, where she made a half-tired grimace to herself in the mirror and splashed cold water on her face. She yawned loudly and stretched. Maybe she should go for a run? It always helped her clear her mind.

She walked back into the bedroom and towards their huge walk-in closet. She put on her running clothes, tied the laces on the new expensive running shoes, and quietly went back into the bedroom.

Kenneth opened his eyes immediately. His dark hair with the silver-grey touches was a bit unruly, and he looked tired.

"I'll go for a run so I can wake up properly," she whispered to him as she put her blond hair up in a perky ponytail.

"That's fine, honey. I'll get up in a little while, too. Just need to wake up first." He closed his eyes and pulled the duvet back up under his nose.

It was a few minutes to nine when she came back.

She went straight into the utility room to throw her running clothes in the laundry basket and put on a dressing gown, before continuing towards the double doors leading into the dining room. She could hear Kenneth talking to Oscar in there, and it sounded like they were enjoying themselves.

When she got there, it was obvious that they were working on both breakfast and a larger project. There were bricks in all shapes and colours, as well as a fairly large assembly guide, spread out between bread, butter, and cheese.

"Good morning, my darling," Charlotte said to her youngest child as she hugged him and kissed him on the hair.

"Look, Mom! See! Dad helps build a car!" Oscar squealed with pure joy.

"Yes, it looks super cool, mouse. It's very good of you to teach your dad about building like that. He's not good at that at all," she said teasingly, glancing at Kenneth.

"Now I never!" Kenneth answered with playful indignation. "I think your mother is teasing me. That's not okay, Charlotte."

44

"No, Mom. Don't tease!" Oscar agreed with a raised index finger, before he quickly turned his attention back to his blocks. He knew the tone between his parents very well and knew that they were just making fun.

"I actually think..." Kenneth continued, wiping his hands on a paper towel, "that she must go on a little timeout." He looked at her with a stern look as he slowly pushed his chair back and got up.

Charlotte looked at him warningly. "Forget it, Kenneth! I don't have time for that nonsense!"

"This is not nonsense," Kenneth replied as he crept towards her. "You have insulted my honour, and I cannot ignore that." He was now very close to her.

"Kenneth, drop it, now!" she said, grinning with her hands up in front of her, while moving backwards towards the door into the hallway.

"You might as well surrender," Kenneth growled. "You've been sentenced to death by *tickling*!"

"You'll never get me," she screamed, and started running with Kenneth hot on her heels.

Their eldest daughter, Hannah, walked into the kitchen at the same time. "Seriously, why do you have to be so embarrassing? Can't you just be like regular parents?!" she yelled at them, rolling her eyes like only a teenager can do.

They ran laughingly down the long hallway of the house and into their bedroom. That was the end of the road for Charlotte.

Kenneth walked slowly through the door and closed it behind him. "Now I have you, you sassy minx," he whispered with a triumphant look in his eyes.

"Bring it, pretty-boy. I know... Karate!" Charlotte replied confidently, doing a classic karate pose in the middle of the floor. She shouted "Hiyaaa!" and looked challengingly into his eyes.

This caused him to giggle uncontrollably, and they both broke down laughing.

Then he took three big steps and stopped right in front of her.

"You're so delicious, but you damn well can't do karate!" He pulled her in close, put his hands around her lower back, and kissed her softly on the mouth. He unfastened her dressing gown and let his hands slide onto the warm skin underneath.

"Honey, I'm all sweaty," she muttered, her mouth against his chest.

"It just makes you even sexier," he whispered, holding her out a little, opening her dressing gown all the way up so he could see her body.

Apart from a few stretch marks and slightly looser skin on her stomach, she looked almost like herself from when they met.

She had had her breasts done a few years ago. She had never had a big bosom, but after she finished breastfeeding Oscar, her once firm breasts looked more like two empty patches of skin with a coin in each. During that time, she had really gained a whole new understanding of the people who struggled with their body image.

However, she was a firm believer in that if you feel truly down about something, also regarding to yourself, and have the chance to rectify it, you shouldn't hesitate to do so. She definitely didn't plan on remaining unhappy like that.

Kenneth had supported her decision, but had stressed that she was just as attractive and feminine in his eyes, if she chose to live with the "skin patches".

She hadn't regretted it for a second. The first time she looked in the mirror and saw her new breasts, she felt like herself again.

Kenneth let his hands slide onto her back and

grabbed her tight buttocks with a firm grip.

He pulled her body really close to him and kissed her again. He had always been an amazing kisser, and she could feel that she wasn't completely unaffected by it.

His breathing quickened and she could feel how much he wanted her.

When she reluctantly pulled away, she saw the disappointment in his eyes. But only for a moment. Then he blinked and smiled at her again.

"I... I'd better take a shower. I also need to finish packing," she said, turning her back so he couldn't see her eyes welling up.

She walked towards the bathroom and blinked away the tears. She then turned around with a smile that she could feel must look fake. "What's your plan today? Were you going into the office?"

"Yeah, I'll have to work a few hours, but I'll come home and drive you to the airport," Kenneth replied as he straightened his clothes a little and started walking towards the bedroom door. "What time had you arranged with Cecilia?"

"We're going to pick her up around half past three. Then we have almost an hour to get to the airport. That's plenty of time, but then traffic is also considered." She quickly walked across the floor, held his face between her hands, and kissed him softly. "Hey, thank you, honey. You are the best. I love you mucho very much."

"I also love you mucho very much... Even if you're a weirdo who thinks she can do karate."

She stared at the door as it closed behind him.

She had to talk to him about ... all of it.

But not now.

It had to wait until after the holiday.

Chapter 7

"Woo-hoo, girls! Oh my God! You guys look *amazing*!". The voice echoed so loudly through Terminal 2 that people turned their heads to see what was going on.

Charlotte looked up from her phone and started laughing.

Cecilia was going through all the travel documents for the fifth time with a focused look on her face. She stopped in the middle of a movement and looked up. Her cheeks turned red.

"That's so typical Maya," she whispered, clearly annoyed.

"Come on now, Cecilia, it's hilarious!" Charlotte waved to Maya and June, who came trudging with suitcases, bags, and huge smiles. "And also harmless," she added.

Cecilia relaxed her shoulders a little. "You're right. Sorry, I just have travel jitters. I'm always anxious about forgetting something important." She returned to the stack of papers.

The others had now reached them.

Maya put down her bags and gave Charlotte a hug. "Hello, you two hot potatoes. Holy shit, how excited am I?" she exclaimed.

"Aloha, senoritas!" June said as she hugged Charlotte. "Has everyone remembered everything?"

"Aloha, aloha," Cecilia waved distractedly at them without looking up.

June and Maya both stared at her for a moment and then looked over at Charlotte with surprise all over their faces.

Charlotte took two steps forward and snapped her fingers right in front of Cecilia's face.

Cecilia looked up at her with a confused expression.

"Hey, Mammi-mouse. We are not going on holiday together without a welcome-hug, so please get your lovely nose out of the papers right now!" she said sternly.

Cecilia quickly folded up the papers and tucked them into the shoulder bag that rested on top of her suitcase. "Sorry, girls! I'll get myself together now... Hi everybody!" She had an apologetic expression on her face when she hugged first Maya and then June.

"I must say, you really know how to announce your arrival!" Charlotte whispered to Maya as they walked over to the departure screen to see if the check-in was open.

"Of course," Maya replied with a smile. "As you know, I'm working on becoming more visible. I'm giving myself permission to take up more space in the world, you know."

Charlotte rolled her eyes sarcastically, "Okay...?"

"But!" Maya whispered back with restrained laughter in her voice. "More importantly, I saw an opportunity to tease Cecilia a little bit. It was just too tempting not to do it."

"What are you two gossiping about?" June asked while stopping in front of the large departure screen hanging in the middle of the hall.

"Well, I'm just telling Charlotte that my mission on this holiday is to move Cecilia out of her comfort zone," Maya replied, looking teasingly at Cecilia.
"I knew all your yelling before, was only to embarrass me!"

"No, no, it wasn't *just* to embarrass you,"

Maya protested, "But mainly for that reason, that's true!"

"Hey, Maya and Cecilia, stop your bickering for a minute," June interrupted. "Our flight is already on here. Izmir Airport departing at 18:40. The counters are opening now, so let's go. March!"

It didn't take long before they were moving towards the stairs leading up to the airport security.

"I'll going to need a smoke before we fly. I promise to do it quickly!" June walked swiftly towards the exit while the others waited.

Cecilia suddenly began frantically rummaging in her bag while muttering something incomprehensible.

"Cecilia, are you okay? Did you forget something?"

Cecilia looked at Charlotte with a frustrated look. "I can't remember where I put my boarding pass, and now it's gone! I just had it! Now I can't go on holiday!" She had a hint of panic in her voice.

"Calm down now, Cecilia. I saw you put it in your front pocket. Check it again."

"Are you getting forgetful, old-timer?" Maya winked teasingly at Cecilia, but stopped when she saw an annoyed expression fluttering across Cecilia's face. "Sorry, I'm going to park my adult bullying. Well, at least for the next hour or so."

Cecilia gave her a little smile. "Apology accepted, Maya. I'm just a little thin-skinned today. I always get *so* much travel anxiety, and I'm not very fond of flying either. So just ignore my annoyance, and my forgetfulness." She shrugged apologetically.

Maya quickly grabbed her hand. "Cecilia, I will not ignore you or your feelings, in any way. I totally forgot that you don't like flying, and it's really not funny when you're forced into something you don't like. I know what that's like..." The last sentence she added in a lower voice.

She gave Cecilia's hand a small squeeze. "Consider me your personal support person for the entire trip, and just let me know if you need anything, okay?"

Chapter 8

"Cecilia, are you okay?" Maya said, worried.

Cecilia sat completely stiff with her eyes closed. She was white in the face, sweaty, and she held onto the armrests of the airplane seat with a tight grip.

Maya put her hand on top of Cecilia's.

"Cecilia, try to calm yourself down," she whispered as she gave her hand a little squeeze. "Just take a few deep breaths before you faint."

Cecilia did as Maya said and slowly regained control of herself.

"Thank you, Maya. It just spiralled for a moment, the stupid fear of flying. It has never been this bad before. I guess I drove myself all the way up the wall, by just thinking about it," she sighed, relaxed her shoulders a bit and moved a little in her seat.

She let go of Maya's hand.

The plane suddenly sped up and drove at a higher and higher speed down the runway.

Cecilia's body froze in her seat again. She quickly grabbed Maya's hand and closed her eyes tightly.

Maya whispered to her, "Just hold on, I've got you. It will soon be over. We'll be up shortly."

Cecilia didn't respond, but Maya was sure she could feel a little squeeze from her hand.

***

"Hey girls, look what I have bought!" Cecilia was still a little pale in the face. They had flown for half an hour, and she had used the time to shake off most of her anxiety.

"Damn it, Cecilia, I almost dozed off!" June, who had been sitting with her eyes closed and relaxed for a while, straightened herself up with a big sigh and looked at Cecilia with an annoyed look.

"Are you listening?" Cecilia tapped Maya on her shoulder.

Maya was deeply emerged in a book." "Yes, yes, two seconds. Is just really exciting right now," Maya replied, waving dismissively without looking up from the pages of the book.

"I'm listening." Charlotte sat with her computer in front of her on the folded-down table, but her eyes were fixed on Cecilia.

56

"Okay, now I'm ready," Maya said, pulling herself away from the book. "Fire away, mon ami. You have thirty seconds. And full disclosure. This disturbance better be important. The penalty is Death, if you come between me and Jon Snow with something non-important!"

Cecilia sent her an apologetic smile and shrugged.

"Then you'd better get out the guillotine. This can't compete with Jon Snow. But to be fair... Who and what can?" she laughed.

"That's very true, so you are off the hook this time, Cille-mommy. But get on with it then. What are you going to show us?"

"This." Cecilia pulled a worn version of Lonely Planet's *"Turkish"* out of her bag.

"Slightly anticlimactic, to be honest," Maya giggled.

"Seriously... Did you wake me up for that?" June growled, with narrow eyes. "I'm inclined to rethink that whole guillotine idea from before, Cecilia!" She let herself fall back into her seat and demonstratively closed her eyes again.

"Well, it's really remarkable, girls!" Cecilia ignored June's attitude. "There is a lot of practical information about the country, and about the culture, and about food and drinks. There are also phrases that we can practise if, for example, we are going to the market or something like that. That's really useful!"

"All right, let me see it." Maya pulled the book out of her hands and began flipping through it.

"I think it's going to be a big help for us," Cecilia added with a satisfied smile.

"Good thinking, mammi." Charlotte teasingly sent her a smile. "It's very... You. So well prepared. What would we do without our little helper?"

"Yeah, yeah, very funny," Cecilia smiled back.

"Um, Cecilia, how much have you actually read of this?" Maya asked with a suppressed laugh.

Cecilia stared at her for a moment. "I've only flipped through it. Why?"

"Because this," Maya began to read:

"*Hadi Yatalim*: Let's go to bed.
Dokun bana: Touch me here
And the very important:
Prezervatif var mi?: Do you have a condom?"

Cecilia immediately turned lobster red in the

face and reached for the book. "Maya, it doesn't say that! Give it back to me!"

Maya gave her the book back with a big grin. "Oh yes, it does, and I have to say I'm quite surprised, but definitely also very *impressed* that you're willing to do such thorough research for the holidays," she teased Cecilia. "I think *someone* expects some horizontal action within the next week. It's very atypical for you, and I love it!"

"Do shut up, Maya," Cecilia whispered with red cheeks, frantically flipping through the book.

"It's under the topic of sex," Maya added helpfully.

Cecilia finally found the chapter and blushed even more as she read the contents.

"Who chooses to include such a thing in a serious travel book?" she whispered in an indignant voice, looking at the cover with disgust. "I should have gone with *'The Trip to Turkey'* as I intended. But it was sold out. I could only get this one, and in a used version, even!"

"Mammi-darling, turn the prudish side of you down a notch. We are all adults, and it is perfectly natural for adult people to have sex. So why not lend a helping hand... So to speak!" Maya laughed loudly at herself.

Charlotte and Cecilia rolled their eyes. "You're so lame, Maya, really?". But they couldn't help but smile a bit, anyway.

"Who do you have to shag to get some quiet here?!" June demonstratively turned her back to the others as much as the seatbelt allowed.

"I don't know," Maya responded. "But you can probably find someone in Turkey. At least now we know how to ask for it!"

***

A while later, Charlotte's focus on her computer work was interrupted by a tap on the shoulder.

She knew that her decision to bring her work computer with her on holiday was not particularly popular with the others.

But as the CEO of a large company, she couldn't just disappear completely for an entire week. And it wasn't because she worked as such. She just looked at the new sales figures from August that she had just received before they took off.

It looked damn good. Shine Bright's market share had risen for the fourth month in a row, and she expected it to increase further when their new product hit the market in a few months.

At the same time, she also tried to concentrate on a podcast about how you, as a company, could ensure that you are still relevant in a digital market that was constantly changing.

The lecture *could* have been really interesting. Unfortunately, the speaker Tom Collins, who was recognised throughout the industry as an expert on the subject, was not a particularly inspiring communicator.

Someone lifted her sound proofing headphones out from her head. "You really have to see this". Maya's voice sounded strange, and she had a weird expression on her face. Her green eyes looked at Charlotte with excitement.

Charlotte quickly paused the podcast and removed her headphones.

"What is it? What's going on...?"

A loud growling noise filled the cabin. A moment later, a slightly fainter sound went off. Almost like a mix of a flat bike tire losing air and a hissing cat.

"Oh. My. Good!". Charlotte whispered with her eyes wide open. "It sounds like an angry bear and a... a... What is that weird squeak?!"

She looked puzzled at Maya, who was getting

more and more red in the face.

Now Charlotte noticed that the nearest rows were also looking around and wondering about the sound.

"Do you know where it's coming from?" Charlotte whispered to Maya.

Maya couldn't hold it back any longer. She exploded with build-up laughter and jumped up from her seat to walk back and forth in the aisle.

When Maya left her seat, Cecilia was suddenly visible. Tears ran down her cheeks and her shoulders were shaking with laughter. Cecilia, who hated too much attention and who became embarrassed if the others made themselves noticed at all. What on earth could make even *her* lose it?

Then Cecilia leaned back a notch, giving Charlotte a clear view of the window seat.

"Oh, my goodness," she whispered to herself.

Leaning against the window, at an awkward angle, was June. She was wearing bright yellow headphones, with her favourite band, Depeche Mode, still playing at full volume. A pink sleeping mask, on which was printed a pair of gigantic eyes with long black eyelashes, covered the top half of her head. Around her neck and half covering her face, she had a scarf that was bright orange.

She had clearly needed to sleep, because she was lying with her head tilted back and was completely turned off. The open mouth caused the fabric from the scarf to flutter back and forth as June was breathing in and out.

The grotesque sounds came from her.

Charlotte stared at the sight in disbelief. "Girls, we must..." she began, but then just gave up. She had no choice other than to surrender to the laughter.

There was now a lot of commotion in their part of the plane, and the flight crew, with big smiles on their faces, asked them to take a seat again and to please wake up their friend. The trolley with drinks would come out in a minute, and they could not block the aisle.

Maya made sure that before they woke June up, the other two agreed not to disclose anything to her until a later date, *and* that this situation should be recorded for posterity.

Cecilia and Charlotte protested, but not much, and not very enthusiastically. Both of them still remembered how grumpy June had been earlier. At the same time, they also felt pretty sure that June would be able to find it funny. When she was fully rested, of course.

June had been very far away in her sleep and was, for a moment, completely confused about where she was and why everyone smiled at her.

When she asked what she had missed out on, a grinning Cecilia just gave her hand a squeeze. "We'll tell you later, June-bug, we'll tell you later."

Chapter 9

"Which way?" Maya said with a frown as they stood with their suitcases at Izmir airport a few hours later, trying to locate the exit.

"I think I saw an exit sign right over there," Cecilia pointed, as they walked in unison towards the automatic sliding glass doors.

On the other side of the doors was the airport arrivals hall.

Everywhere there was a myriad of people who had just arrived or were leaving, airport staff, baggage helpers, large flocks of family members picking up travellers, and luggage in insane quantities. The noise was deafening.

"Wow, this is overwhelming!" Cecilia stopped moving.

Maya, who was walking right behind her, was about to stumble upon her. "Cille-mouse, you can't just stop here. Walk over to the side!"

They moved to the left of the doors and let the crowd behind them rush on.

"We need to get an overview," Charlotte looked around.

She spotted a blonde woman wearing a turquoise sweater with a sign up in the air that read Turkey's Sun.

"I've spotted one from the travel agency!" Charlotte grabbed her luggage. "Come on, girls, don't fall behind!"

They managed to get through the crowd and waited in front of a woman who smiled to the best of her abilities. The name tag revealed that her name was Sarah-Emilie. Hyphenated, of course.

"Hi, lovely ladies!" she greeted them with a loud and bright voice and showed them a dazzling white smile. Not only did she have an amazing tan, but she also had that annoyingly even and smooth skin that only young people have.

"Are you travelling with Turkey's Sun?" she asked, and all four of them nodded. "Super-duper, just a minute. Let's see if we can find you in my overview." With one smooth motion, she swung a clipboard in front of her and opened it.

"Which hotel will you be staying at?"

"We don't know, actually," Cecilia replied, pulling out the travel papers from her bag. "We have purchased an unspecified trip." She handed the papers to Sarah-Emilie, who quickly found the information she needed.

"Okay, ladies. I'm happy to tell you, that you will be staying in one of the nicest hotels in town, in my opinion. You're going on bus No. 3, and you'll find it by walking out the doors over there," She pointed to an exit a little further down the arrival hall.

"When you get out, cross the road where the taxis stop, cross the bridge on the other side of the road, continue straight for the bridge, and there you will find a big parking lot, and your transfer bus."

She quickly wrote *Bus 3* on a piece of paper and gave it to Cecilia, along with all their travel papers. "Have an amazing holiday, everyone. See you at the hotel," and then she turned to an elderly couple.

The girls looked at each other, a bit confused.

"Um, just a minute," June stammered. "It went a bit fast with that explanation... We haven't been here before and we're not quite sure where to go?"

"You can just follow us. We know where we're going." It was the older gentleman who had been waiting for the guide. "We've been here before, so just come with us."

"Thank you so much for that," Maya said and

started walking after them.

"Yeah, it's difficult, when you're new somewhere. Nobody wants to take a wrong turn and miss the bus," Cecilia added as they walked out the revolving doors.

"Don't worry," the man reassured her. "When it's a charter holiday, the transfer buses don't leave until all guests are located."

The parking area was filled with large and small tourist buses, as well as other travellers. They easily located bus 3, which was a small, cosy bus with room for less than twenty people. There was no queue, so they could hand over their luggage to the driver without waiting.

"Come, let's go in and find a seat!" Cecilia was standing with one foot ready on the first step.

"Just go in," June replied as she rummaged through her bag. "I'm craving a cigarette so badly right now."

The elderly couple sat down in the first two seats just behind the driver. The rest of the bus was empty.

Maya, Charlotte and Cecilia chose the back seats and they could see June out the window. The driver had joined her, and both were standing with a lit cigarette. They seemed to talk.

"Hey girls, look, I think she's flirting with the driver!" Charlotte whispered with a laugh.

Maya stretched her neck out to see better. "She's not wasting time, our lovely June! Hush! She's coming!"

"Hey girls, you got to hear this..." June, who was settling in, suddenly noticed that the other three were looking at her in a funny way. "Um, what's going on?" she asked suspiciously.

"Nothing, June, nothing at all..." Maya batted her eyes innocently. Charlotte and Cecilia giggled.

"Okay..." June turned in her seat. "Then why do I get the feeling that you're lying right to my face, Maya?"

"Okay, okay, it's just because we saw you standing there, hitting on the driver, and that's when we thought..."

June interrupted her. "Jesus Christ, Maya! I was smoking, and then he came over to borrow a cigarette. He said his name was Ali and that the weather was good... So, as you can hear, it's not exactly material for the next best-selling love story!" she laughed, placing her bag on the floor between her feet.

"Okay, so he didn't hit on you?" Cecilia asked with curiosity.

"Hard to say." June shrugged. "He was, to be honest, really not good at English. So, I mostly just smiled and nodded. And crossed my fingers, that I didn't accidentally say yes to something I would regret later! But I think he said something about our hotel being called Lokum something."

Charlotte's smile faded. "Come again?... Are we going to live somewhere called something with lokum? Lokum, like the word for a disgusting toilet in Danish." Her voice went up a few octaves at the word lokum. Before she had time to say more, the guide stepped onto the bus.

"Hello!" she still had a wide smile plastered from ear to ear. "I just need to count you all – and that was a very straightforward task," she added with a grin as she looked around.

"Now, listen up. In a moment, I will hand you some envelopes. It contains some brochures and some practical information. Most importantly, how you can get hold of us and also something about the welcome meeting at your hotel tomorrow morning. The trip to Cennet takes about an hour, and when you arrive, my colleague, Mia-Maja, will greet you and help you check in. What else ...?", she mumbled, mostly addressing herself.

"Okay, two more guests will come to your bus

in a minute and then your chauffer will drive you to the hotel. My colleague, Ömer, is on his way with them. I think they were lost inside the terminal and couldn't find the way out... How that is possible when there is only one exit, I don't know..." The last sentence was almost whispered, and it was obvious that Sarah-Emilie was not particularly impressed.

"But for now, and while you wait, you can look at our information." She handed the elderly couple a turquoise envelope, which the woman placed directly in her bag without looking at it. "This must be yours," she said, handing June an envelope with *Cecilia Berggren (4 pax.)* written on it.

"When the last two guests arrive, can I get you to give them their envelope?" the guide asked Charlotte.

"Yes, of course, no problem," Charlotte accepted the envelope that read *Thor Jensen (2 pax.)*

"Thank you so much for that, then I can get to bus 1. They are probably just waiting for me now. We have a lot of stops, so it's going to be a long ride..." She suddenly looked very tired. But it only lasted a few seconds, then her guide training kicked in and she smiled from ear to ear again.

"Well, then I just want to wish you a safe trip. See you tomorrow maybe, and remember, we're not further away than a text message!" and then she was gone.

"Can I see our envelope?" Maya asked curiously as soon as the guide had left the bus. "Girls, I think Ali was right." She showed them what was written in one corner of the envelope: *Hotel: Lokum Deluxe*.

"For God's sake, what is this? I'll tell you right away, girls, if it's a horrible hotel, we'll find something else tomorrow!" Charlotte exclaimed, looking very annoyed.

"Charlotte, can you just breathe for a second? Sarah-Emilie said that this hotel is really nice, so let's just wait and see what happens, okay?" June smiled at her calmly.

"Well, how can it be fine when it's called something with lokum!" Charlotte muttered and sat down with a very annoyed look on her face.

"I'm sorry, but I couldn't help overhearing what you were saying,". The voice was polite and belonged to the elderly man, who guided them to the bus area. "Well, it's really not any of my business..." he continued.

"No, but that doesn't stop him from interfering anyway," the woman sitting next to him added with a loud laugh.

"You're always telling me to be helpful, Nora, so this is me doing just that." He continued, addressing the girls: "Lokum in Turkish does not mean toilet as in Danish. Lokum is the Turkish name for the sweets you may know as Turkish Delight. So, you can rest easy." He winked at them. "Also, we have stayed at this particular hotel more than a dozen times during our holidays here in Cennet, so we are completely comfortable saying that you really *can* look forward to it."

"Oops, I guess I was a little too quick on the trigger, then. I'm sorry, everyone! I can only excuse myself with the fact that I'm tired after a long day," Charlotte laughed, but she looked embarrassed by her outburst.

"Oh, it's okay. Anybody could have made that mistake," Cecilia quickly said, trying to smooth things over.

Nora stuck her head up over the back of the chair. "I'm not much for admitting it, but I do, in this case, completely agree with Gert. Lokum Deluxe is, by far, the friendliest hotel we've stayed at in this town. The family who owns it is absolutely wonderful. So, my dears, don't worry, you're going to have a great..."

Loud voices outside the bus suddenly

interrupted them.

"My God, I can't even ... How embarrassing to be late like that. People just sit and wait for us. Forget it, I'm *not* going in!". The voice was bright and extremely high-pitched.

"Baby, we can't stay out here. The suitcases are on the bus and we have to leave. Come on, babe." The slightly deeper voice sounded almost pleading.

"I won't. It's too embarrassing!" The high-pitched voice turned up the volume and now had more than a hint of hysteria.

"Dear friends, this is not up for discussion. Either you get on the bus now, or you have to get to the hotel yourself. At your own expense," an even deeper and tired voice cut through.

Cecilia could see it all from her window and reported, in a low voice, to the others, who could only hear the conversation through the open doors of the bus.

"Okay, it must be the guests we're waiting for. Didn't it say Thor on the envelope? It's a young couple. Can't see them clearly, but I think they're some very good-looking younglings." She turned slightly in her seat so she could see who was talking to them.

"I guess it's him, the guide, I mean. Ömer,

wasn't that his name? He looks annoyed... Hey, here they come!" She quickly sat straight up in her seat, and the others pretended to be busy either with their phones or looking out the windows.

The young couple stepped onto the bus and Thor greeted them kindly. He was holding a blonde girl's hand. She looked down at the floor with a dismissive expression and said nothing.

Charlotte handed Thor their envelope. He said thanks with a confused look and put it on his lap without looking at it.

A moment later, Ali slammed the door to the bus. As they set off, he honked twice, waved to the driver of bus 1, who was almost done packing the luggage like a game of tetris, and drove off towards Cennet.

Chapter 10

"We're here!" Gert yelled with a cheerful voice when the bus stopped almost an hour later and the doors opened. The fresh night air poured in and filled the cabin with wonderful scents of warm asphalt, sweet flowers and exotic spices.

A smiling woman with brown hair stepped onto the first step of the bus.

"Hello, and welcome everyone! My name is Mia-Maja and I'm the destination manager here at Cennet. Remember to bring all your luggage up to the reception area and don't forget anything on the bus," she added with a smile and stepped off the bus again.

The young couple were the first to rush out of the bus.

The two of them had remained close throughout the entire journey and, except for a few kisses here and there, had been silent since the airport.

Even though it was past midnight, it was still pleasantly warm, and they could hear the singing of cicadas from the surrounding bougainvillea.

The hotel was a white building with five floors and big balconies. In the courtyard in front of the hotel, there was a selection of cosy tables, chairs, and umbrellas. The area was filled with neatly arranged flower pots in vibrant colours, and everything appeared clean and well-cared for.

On the other side of the courtyard was the pool area, complete with a pool bar, coloured lighting, tables and chairs. There was a man standing behind the bar, wiping glasses. He quickly put down his dishtowel when the guests arrived and hurried over to help with the suitcases.

At the hotel entrance, a well-dressed man with grey hair warmly welcomed them. With a kind look in his eyes, he emitted the energy of a loving grandfather.

"Hello everyone, welcome, welcome! My name is Alican and I am the owner of the hotel. If you need anything, just let us know." His English was rather good and with only a hint of a Turkish accent. Before they had a chance to inspect the area further, the girls' luggage vanished into the hotel.

Alican had now discovered that he recognised some of the arriving guests.

"So nice to see you again, my good friends

from Denmark!"

He greeted Gert enthusiastically and then turned to Nora.

"My God, you look younger and younger every time I see you, miss Nora. How is that possible?" he asked with a surprised expression on his face and gave her a big hug.

"Stop it, Alican, it's not nice to lie! How is your beautiful Ayşegül?" Nora laughed and followed him into the reception area.

The young couple had already received their keys and almost ran towards the elevator. "Wow, that looked urgent..." Maya whispered to June. "Do you think the speed of their feet has anything to do with getting to the room quickly, so they can do the sexy Hokey Pokey?"

June nodded: "Guaranteed. In less than five minutes, there will be a rumble in the jungle in that room. We all remember being young and in love, don't we? All the drama and romance, and lots of naked gymnastics on all surfaces that can support the body weight."

"Hey, what are you two giggling about?" Cecilia asked curiously. She had been pulling out their travel papers and hadn't seen the young couple's hasty exit.

"We'll tell you afterwards," Maya quickly

responded, because the woman at the front desk waved them over to her at the same time.

They got rooms next to each other and the beautiful young receptionist, Melek, had made sure to give them a good view as well.

"Breakfast is between 8.30 and 10.30, and is already included in your stay. My mother makes the breakfast herself and she is an excellent cook. So don't miss it!" She waved to the man from the bar, who was wiping his forehead with a handkerchief. "Please help these lovely ladies up with their luggage. They have to go up to rooms 407 and 408."

She walked them to the elevator and opened the door for them.

There was an awkward silence as they rode up. They were standing very close together, and all of them could smell that it must have been many hours since the barman had showered last.

The elevator stopped, and they all almost fell out when the door opened. The barman did not protest when they suggested handling the suitcases themselves.

"I wonder what we're going to see from our balcony," Charlotte said in a low voice to Cecilia. "The view of the pool is the other way... I hope it's not into a rock wall or anything like that."

"No, I don't think so," Cecilia replied with a smile. "Melek said she had given us a good view."

"We'll take the first room!" Maya shouted.

"Sshhh, Maya, turn down the volume, please! People are asleep now!" Cecilia hushed.

The barman opened room 407. "There you go."

Maya rushed in, with June following her. Charlotte and Cecilia's room was unlocked seconds later, and Charlotte gave the barman a tip, even if he did little to earn it.

The hotel room was, in fact, a small apartment. Inside was an elongated living area with a kitchenette to the left of the door. It was sparsely but practically furnished with a small round plastic dining table with chairs, a worn sofa bed, a landline phone that had seen better days, and an ancient 20-inch TV without a remote control.

To the right of the door was a slightly worn tiled bathroom, primarily kept in the green and brown colours of the 70s.

Next to the bathroom was the bedroom, which contained a wardrobe, a double bed, two bedside tables and a full-figure mirror on the wall directly in front of the bed.

"Kinky!" June laughed, winking at Maya, who stared at the mirror with a disgusted look.

The curtains were closed, so June walked over to pull them apart in the living room. "No way! ... Check this out, Maya!" she exclaimed with disbelief.

Behind the curtains, the balcony door was wide open, and the moment she pulled the curtains aside, even more of the fragrant night air poured into the room. They stepped out onto the balcony that ran the entire width of the apartment.

In front of them was the view of Cennet by night.

The city lights spread from the horizon like a glittering wave of diamonds up the mountain where they were located. In the distance, they could hear the honking of cars, music, laughter, and the faint sound of the ocean. It was the familiar hotchpotch of nocturnal sounds that characterise a place that never really sleeps. The moon shone from a black, clear night sky, making silver streaks on the ocean that they could see moving up and down behind the lights of Cennet.

None of them said anything. They just took it all in.

"Wow!" It came from the balcony to their right. Cecilia's face came into view as she leaned slightly over the edge.

"Have you seen it? Holy cow, I think it's going to be amazing when the sun comes up!"

"Okay, the room is nothing to brag about, but they get big points for the view, that's for sure!" Charlotte sounded somewhat impressed.

"Who cares about the condition of the room?!" June replied in a firm voice. "We have a place for our things, we have our own shower and toilet, the view looks absolutely phenomenal and we have good company. What else do we need? The only thing I can think of is a nice soothing cigarette."

"Girls!" Maya interrupted in a serious tone. "We have to celebrate our arrival properly."

"With what?" Charlotte looked at her with a smile. "We only have alcohol with nothing to mix with or bottled water – and neither is particularly exciting on its own!"

"Uno momento." Maya sneaked into the living room again. A moment later, she returned to the balcony. She had her hands on her back and a big smile across her face.

"Okay ladies, I have a little surprise for us. Yours truly has been so foresightful to bring the

Danish Hygge along, so... Tada!" With a smug look, she pulled out a box of rosé wine from behind her back. "And it's still cold!"

"Maya, you're a fucking genius!" June high-fived her and hurried inside. There was a rustle from the doors of the kitchen cabinets as she tried to locate the glasses.

A few moments later, they were all standing with a glass filled with cold wine, toasting over the edge of their balconies.

"Cheers to a wonderful holiday, girls," Charlotte said, taking a sip from her glass. "I agree with June, Maya. Absolutely brilliant move, this."

June had a lit cigarette between her fingers, and she slowly exhaled the smoke into the night. There was only a slight breeze, and the sounds of the night took over for a moment as they quietly enjoyed the wine.

"Well, girls, I have to surrender. I'm knackered," Cecilia yawned and emptied her glass. "Should we attend the welcome meeting tomorrow? I guess it fits nicely, time-wise, after breakfast, and it's right by the pool, anyway."

"Yes, let's," Maya replied. "It might be nice to get an overview of the possibilities in Cennet."

"I'm also ready to turn in," Charlotte said

while stretching her back. "Good night, everyone, sleep well. See you at breakfast."

Maya and June stood in silence for a moment.

June looked at her watch and opened her eyes up wide. "Shit, it's half past one. Maybe we should consider going to bed as well?"

"Yeah," Maya replied and yawned loudly. "This old body needs its rest."

She took the box of wine from the table and walked into the living room. "I'll just put this in the fridge and then I'll get ready for the night. The bathroom will be available again in about five minutes."

"Perfect. I'm just going to have one more quick smoke and then I'll come in too," June replied with a content sigh.

Chapter 11

A loud singing voice awakened Cecilia and Charlotte at about a quarter to eight. The unfamiliar sound had effectively pulled them both out of their sleep.

At first, Cecilia was confused about what was going on. But only until Charlotte reminded her about the multiple daily prayer calls in Muslim countries. Something Charlotte, who had travelled extensively, knew they would get used to quickly after a few days.

They decided to get up, now that they were awake, to see what it all looked like in daylight. They hadn't unpacked their suitcases yet, so they just wrapped their sheets around them and opened the doors out to the balcony.

They now saw Cennet in daylight for the first time.

The city was in a large bay surrounded by mountains on three sides. On the fourth side was the bright blue ocean as far as the eye could see. Lokum Deluxe was located well up the mountain, almost exactly behind the town centre. Because of that, they had a fantastic panoramic view of the entire sunny city from their balconies.

A warm breeze hit them, bringing with it the sounds of the city. The sky was clear and blue, and a few small fluffy clouds fought against the sun's rays but quickly had to give up holding themselves together.

The sight almost took their breath away.

Cecilia tied the sheet in front of her like a sarong. "I could stare the rest of my life at that view and still not get tired of it..."

"Yeah, it's beautiful," Charlotte nodded, rubbing her eyes. "Hey, how about a cup of coffee?" she asked with a yawn. "The others won't get up for an hour at the earliest, and I've had the great idea to bring instant along."

In ancient times, Cennet had been an important stop on the Silk Road's trade routes, both on land and by sea, Cecilia explained as they boiled water on the apartment's electric kettle.

She had, in usual Cecilia-style, done a lot of research before they left and she kept talking in an excited voice as they went out on the balcony again and sat down at the round plastic table.

They then sat in silence for a moment, enjoying the hot coffee and the view, before she continued.

"A few years back, the government passed a

law making it illegal to touch people to entice them into shops or restaurants. If you, as a business owner, do not comply with this legislation, your business will be shut down. Initially a few days, but in case of repeated violations permanently."

"That sounds great, to be honest," Charlotte nodded appreciatively, taking a sip of her coffee. "We were in Morocco a few years ago and I had to stay in the hotel for almost the entire holiday. Thank God it was an all-inclusive resort, so I had everything within reach. I was at the local market only one time, and that cured me from going on any more cultural adventures on that holiday! Besides the fact that street vendors in Morocco are allowed to grab people, and are not afraid to do so, I am also a woman with long blond hair..."

"A very *beautiful* woman with long blond hair," Cecilia interjected with a smile. "I can almost guess you couldn't walk in peace?"

"That's an understatement of the decade! If Kenneth hadn't been there, I don't think I would sit here today. I would probably just have... Disappeared... Sold to the highest bidder, maybe. It was a really scary experience."

She fell silent and emptied her cup.

"More coffee?" she asked while getting up.

"No thanks. I just get heart palpitations, so one cup is enough." Cecilia leaned back slightly in her chair so she could put her feet up on the edge of the balcony. "This is the good life!"

Charlotte came back out onto the balcony while stirring a fresh cup of coffee. She also brought her phone.

She put down the coffee cup on the table, went over to the balcony railing and began taking some pictures of the view.

Then she looked down. "Hey, there's a terrace and a kind of garden down there. Come and see!"

Cecilia got up, went over to Charlotte, and looked down.

"What do you know?" she said with a smile. "We were so busy looking out that we forgot to look down as well."

The garden was a lush green oasis with a big greenhouse. Charlotte took a few pictures.

"It looks amazing!" Cecilia exclaimed with excitement. "I bet they serve some of those fruits and vegetables here at the hotel. Yummy! Fresh sun-ripened deliciousness straight from the garden. I get hungry just by thinking about it!"

"And that must be where breakfast is served."

Charlotte pointed to a large tiled terrace that was a few levels above the garden. There were tables set up with white tablecloths on them, and a lady with dark, half-long curly hair walked around, putting flowers on the tables.

She looked up when she heard their voices and sent them a big smile.

Charlotte waved to the lady, who waved back and continued her work.

"I still feel a little tired," Cecilia yawned. "Maybe I should consider another cup after all... What's the time?"

"Quarter to nine. It will be almost 45 minutes before we have to meet the others, so you have time." Charlotte began swiping through the pictures she had just taken.

"I'd better not," Cecilia sighed. "I'd rather unpack a bit, then. You know I get uncomfortable if my belongings get too wrinkly and untidy in the suitcase." She winked at Charlotte.

"Yeah, that's true. We don't want you to have a complete meltdown. So please, go inside and unpack! While you do, I will enjoy the view a little more and also let Kenneth know that we have arrived safely. I will just unpack after breakfast... Then we won't get in each other's way either," she added, taking a sip of the coffee. "Just save some hanger space for me in the closet and I'll be happy."

"It's received, loud and clear," Cecilia replied while walking into the living room.

At the very top of her packed suitcase were a pair of shorts and a sun top, as well as a fresh set of underwear. She had purposely put a complete set of clothes on top of everything. Just in case it became necessary to change clothes in a hurry.

She went into the bedroom and got dressed. She then folded the used sheet neatly, put it on her side of the bed, and went back into the living room.

It was frankly a little silly to get stressed out by the thought that her suitcase might be messy. Because she always packed with military precision and she knew where everything was. Nothing was out of order or untidy with her.

She had enough self-awareness to know that it wasn't clutter as such that made her uneasy. It was more that she liked everything to have its place. Both possessions, people and situations. She had a really hard time relaxing if everything wasn't a certain way. When the world looked right, she didn't have to worry about it. Then it felt like she could breathe easier and more freely.

But it could be a little difficult to explain to others without sounding completely neurotic. She knew that. As a result, she tried to keep many of her thoughts to herself. Especially when she met new people.

Maya often tried to force Cecilia a little out of her comfort zone. As annoying and frustrating as it could be, she always meant well.

Cecilia got a lump in her throat. She truly loved her friends with all of her heart, even though they were very different people. That's also why it had been so important for her to suggest this holiday. She was fully aware of their astonishment when she made the suggestion. Since they knew that she typically never proposed anything more adventurous than dinner and drinks, and it was always in familiar places.

However, they had not commented on it. Maybe because they knew it was a big step for her. Or that she had a reason that she wasn't ready to share with them yet.

After the trip was booked, she had had some terrible nightmares about either getting on the wrong plane, getting lost in a world where no one understood her, or that the others suddenly didn't want to be friends with her anymore and turned their backs on her.

But she really needed them in the years to come, and she missed the closeness they shared when they were younger. She hoped that this holiday would give them the opportunity to really connect again.

Cecilia sighed, took a deep breath, exhaled slowly, and tried to snap herself out of the thought-stream. They were here, and the holiday was already in motion, *and* she was really looking forward to enjoying this week together with the others.

"Get your act together, girl!" she whispered to herself. "Stop your chaotic thoughts and begin handling the task in front of you."

She lifted a pile of the neatly folded clothes from the suitcase and placed it on the coffee table. Under her clothes was her toiletry bag, and she walked with firm steps towards the bathroom to put it where it belonged. Right when she opened the door, a lot of commotion and laughter sounded through the wall.

It came from June and Maya's room.

Chapter 12

A loud scream awakened Maya. Still half asleep, she looked at the time and sighed. Her alarm would go off in less than five minutes.

For a moment she had no idea where she was, but then she recognised June's voice. When she heard her yelling and swearing like a dockworker, she quickly became wide awake.

"For fucks sake! Now I've never... What a piece of old crap!"

Maya swiftly freed herself from the sheet and took a moment to inspect the waffle pattern imprinted on her legs. She shook her head in disbelief. Why would hotels in warm countries always use that type of sheets? It made you look like a freaking Belgian dessert for hours. She already had cellulite. No need to make it worse!

June's side of the bed was empty.

"June, where are you?" Maya called and walked into the living room.

"Here. In the bathroom." June's voice sounded slightly out of breath.

"Are you okay?" Maya asked through the

closed door. "I heard a crash, and then your colourful words ripped me out of my beauty sleep."

"Well, I'm okay, I just need to pull myself together," June replied with a laugh. "But I'll probably going to need a hand, so get in here and help me. The door is unlocked, and I am dressed... Well, sort of..."

Maya tried to open the door all the way up, but couldn't. Instead, she stuck her head in to see what was going on.

She found June sitting on the floor between the toilet and bathtub, red in the face with laughter. She was wearing a long T-shirt that barely covered her buttocks, and her panties were around her ankles.

"Oh my God." Maya quickly pulled her head back while covering her eyes. "What on earth are you doing? I don't have a desire for a live show before my morning coffee!"

"Calm down, honey." June sputtered with laughter. "My foo-foo *is* covered, so you can't possibly have seen anything! Now, come on, I still need a hand to get up."

Maya shook her head at first, but then also laughed, and with great difficulty, she pushed her way into the bathroom. There was just

94

enough room for them both in there.

"Okay, old lady, let's do this. What on earth happened?" she giggled as she helped June up on her feet.

"Well, this place isn't assembled properly!" June pulled her panties back up. "I needed to pee, as one does. So, I sat my lovely behind down on the seat, and then the toilet seat suddenly skated out to the right and took me with it!" June pointed to the floor behind her, and sure enough. There was the toilet seat. "It was pure luck that I didn't have time to turn on the waterfall. Then this scenario would have looked completely different!"

"Ha-ha... So, have you hurt yourself?" Maya tried to pull herself together between outbursts of laughter.

"No, no, luckily it's only my pride that got bruised. An advantage of being well-padded, my friend! Well, shall we put the seat back on so I can empty my bladder?"

There was a knock on the wall from inside Cecilia and Charlotte's room.

"What's going on? Are you okay?" Cecilia's voice was clear through the thin wall.

"Yes, yes, we're okay," Maya yelled back with a giggle. "It's just June who objects to the hotel being called Lokum DELUXE!"

***

At exactly half past nine, Charlotte and Cecilia knocked on Maya and June's door, ready for breakfast.

On their way down the stairs towards the ground floor, Maya laughingly told the others about June's morning, so it was a group in an excellent mood who sat down at one of the tables on the warm terrace.

There were no other guests out there, except for a slim woman with curly blond hair sitting at the opposite end of the terrace. A used plate and an empty glass revealed that she had been sitting at the table for a while. A nice brown colour on her body revealed that she had probably already been at the hotel for some time.

While they were admiring the view again, the lady they had seen from the balcony came over to them.

"Good morning, everyone," she said with a big warm smile. "My name is Ayşegül and I'm in charge of our breakfast buffet. Come, let me show you all the delicious things I have for you!"

Ayşegül proudly told them she made most of it herself from scratch. She especially recommended the different jams, made from the fruits of their garden and, of course, the freshly baked bread, which was still warm.

They could also get an omelette if they wished, she helpfully stated. All they had to do was let her know.

At the end of the table was a silver container on which was taped a piece of paper with the words "Turkish Coffee". Next to it was a plain white thermos. Ayşegül advised them to only drink coffee from the thermos and to not try the strong Turkish coffee, as it could cause a really upset stomach.

As she said "bon appétit" and disappeared into the kitchen, the girls were left speechless, their eyes fixed on the mouthwatering food.

"Where do you start?" Cecilia whispered, overwhelmed.

"From one end of the buffet, off course!" Maya answered with pure joy in her voice, while taking a plate from the large stack next to them. "Just stick with me, ladies. I have a black belt in eating at a buffet, and I know everything about how to pack a plate to optimise in the best possible way." She began stacking food on the plate with a trained hand and with a focused look on her face.

The other three looked at her in amazement, then looked at each other and started laughing.

"Hey Maya, you are aware that you can go more than one time, right?" June teased.

"Yes, but why go several times when you can make do with one?" Maya replied, without stopping loading food onto her plate.

The other three looked at each other again and then shrugged. "Well, shall we throw ourselves into it?" June started to fill up her plate as well. "It's all looking good and there's a lot, so dig in."

Chapter 13

They enjoyed the terrace, the beautiful view, and the delicious breakfast for almost an hour. Cecilia talked about the call to prayer earlier, but neither Maya and June had noticed it. They had slept heavily and had heard nothing, but both were looking forward to experiencing it later in the day.

Cecilia had finished unpacking before breakfast and sat down on the balcony with a book and relaxed while Charlotte put her things away. They were both very proper, and it didn't take long for Charlotte to get her belongings in order.

Their room was very tidy: shoes were in the closet, clothes were on hangers and shelves, and creams, perfumes, makeup and so on were neatly lined up on the table in the living room and bathroom.

June and Maya's room looked completely different. They were both more chaotic in their approach to unpacking, and there were clothes, shoes, makeup and bottles of sunscreen on all surfaces.

Charlotte came in at one point to give them some of the cream samples she had brought from Shine Bright's new collection, but she had quickly walked out again without them even seeing her.

"It was like getting into a tornado of personal belongings!" she told Cecilia and laughed. "It looked like there had been a burglary and the thieves had emptied everything out everywhere. I don't think they even realised I was in there!"

"I get quite stressed in my brain at the bare thought of it," Cecilia admitted. "Therefore, I'm truly happy that you and me are sharing a room! I love Maya and June very much, but I honestly can't handle the way they do things sometimes."

"Are you ready, girls? The welcome meeting starts in a minute," Cecilia called to Maya and June from her balcony.

Junes sweaty face popped out of the bedroom door. "Yeah, give us like... Five minutes? We are just about finished. Shit, I'm sweating!"

"Okay, but hurry up. It's embarrassing to be late!" Cecilia sounded a bit annoyed. "Me and Charlotte are ready now, so we'll just head down and save some seats for us."

June hung the last dress from the suitcase on a hanger in the wardrobe. "Maya, we should have been ready by now, so please move your ass a little faster, dear!"

***

It was a quarter past eleven before June and Maya came down to the welcome meeting, trying their best to sneak in without making a big deal out of it.

There were only thirteen guests participating, and Sarah-Emilie, the guide from the airport, was standing at the bar with a portable whiteboard, her indispensable clipboard, and a large stack of brochures. She was busy explaining Cennet's possibilities and was about to talk about the public transportation system and taxis.

Charlotte and Cecilia were seated at the table closest to the bar, right next to where the guide was standing. Cecilia had a notebook in front of her and a pen in her hand, and she was writing the guide's information down with a concentrated look on her face. Charlotte waved them over with a smile.

June and Maya quickly sat down at the table without rattling too much with the white plastic chairs. Cecilia sent them a quick dissatisfied glance but said nothing.

"Have we missed out on something?" June whispered to Charlotte.

"No, no, the guide has only explained a lot about the city. Cecilia has already been annoyed four times as the facts she gave were not entirely up to code," Charlotte whispered back with a laugh.

"It's entirely unprofessional not to have the correct information when you share it with others!" Cecilia hissed. "Then we can't trust anything they tell us, and now, please keep quiet! They are about to talk about the trips we can sign up for."

Charlotte and June simultaneously paid homage and clapped their heels together. Maya burst out laughing, and they got annoyed looks from the other tables.

A sour-looking lady sitting at the next table with an equally sour-looking gentleman, most likely her husband, hushed at them.

Cecilia got red cheeks from embarrassment, while Charlotte and June completely ignored it. Maya waved to the couple and sent them a big smile. They did not wave back, but looked even more annoyed and turned their gaze away demonstratively, as if the girls did not exist.

Maya had a hard time absorbing all the

information that was spewed out in a steady stream. She quickly agreed with herself that she could probably leave it to Cecilia. Instead, she wanted to use the time to get an overview of the area.

The welcome meeting took place at the pool bar, which was on the same level as the rest of the pool area. Around the pool were a lot of sunbeds with thin plastic mattresses in different colours and matching umbrellas.

The pool had a figure-eight shape, with the pool bar closest to the deep end. There were built-in steps on the opposite side, providing a safer and more comfortable alternative to the typical wobbly pool ladders.

Across the middle of the pool, a couple of meters above the surface of the water, was a green net that Maya presumed was for playing with balls in the pool. A couple of pool noodles in pink and blue floated around in the water.

The entire area looked inviting, and she was already looking forward to splashing around in the cooling water a little later.

On the other side of the pool, she could see the blond woman from breakfast. Wearing a white bikini made almost only out of strings, she reclined on a sunbed, leaving little to the imagination.

Near the bar, two women of substantial size, with sunburned shoulders and braided straw hats, were engaged in a game of Yatzy and conversation under a parasol.

At the pool bar, two very tanned men sat on their barstools, both with a half-drunk beer in front of them and a lit cigarette between their fingers. They had no shirts on, and their sizable bellies flowed over the edge of the khaki-coloured shorts, which also revealed a solid ass crack every time they leaned over just the slightest.

The ashtray in front of them was already half filled, so they must have been sitting there for some time. The men did not talk, they just sat and looked at a television screen mounted in the bar's corner. It showed football with the volume all the way down.

Inside the bar stood the barman who had helped them with their luggage last night. He looked tired and stared into space while he almost inhaled a large portion of chips. The sight fascinated Maya. The way he devoured his chips without even looking at the plate.

Suddenly, he blinked a few times and the trance-like state lost its grip on him. He continued to look in the same direction as before, but now with a smile across his face. Maya followed his gaze and couldn't help but chuckle to herself.

At the end of the pool, the blond woman had risen from her sunbed and was in a wiggling way, headed towards the pool bar.

The woman wasn't very tall, but she had a nice curved hourglass figure, with nice legs, firm thighs and arms, flat stomach, and plump breasts that were sitting, where breasts should sit, in Maya's opinion. A slim waist and proportions that matched both her top and bottom tied it all together.

At first Maya estimated her to be in her late twenties, but when the woman reached the bar and took off her sunglasses, she could see that she probably was older. She had long artificial eyelashes, painted red lips and long golden earrings in her ears. She also wore a lot of rings on both hands, and a cloud of fragrant perfume was hanging around her.

While her appearance might be a little exaggerated for a day by the pool, no one could deny that she was a good-looking woman. The two men in the bar tried with optimistic male naivety to suck in their bellies and shoot their chests out when she reached the bar, to make themselves more attractive.

It looked really uncomfortable! Maya signalled to Charlotte and June, but left Cecilia and her note-taking alone. "Hey girls, check that out," she whispered with suppressed laughter.

Maya quietly praised Charlotte and Cecilia for choosing a table that was so close to the bar that they could also hear what was being said up there.

The woman now leaned over the bar and smiled. With her sizeable chest resting on the counter, she asked for a menu.

The barman was visibly flustered when he discovered he had a view straight down the cleavage and initially did not respond to the woman's request.

The woman repeated her question.

He managed to break free of his stare, and quickly wiped off one of the laminated and worn-out menus, which he handed to her with a nervous laugh.

He dabbed his sweaty forehead with a napkin and frantically straightened his hair with his fingers. As she concentrated on the menu, the two male guests let go of their bellies for a moment and took a sip of their beers.

When she looked up again, they immediately sucked their bellies back in, trying to look relaxed. In reality, it looked very unnatural as they sat there with forcefully protruded chests and strained red faces, unable to say a word. They could only smile and nod as she glanced at them with a questioning look.

"Hmm, I can't decide what I want. What's good?" Her English sounded a bit broken and with an accent that, to Maya, who had seen many movies, sounded Eastern European.

"I... I..." the man behind the bar stammered, wiping the ever-increasing amount of sweat from his forehead with desperate movements.

"What would you choose to eat if you were the one who had a free choice on all shelves?" The woman had a soft voice and batted her eyes as she looked at him. She let a few fingers run slowly up and down the edge of the menu.

"Um... I... So... What do you mean?" he stammered frantically, as his face turned more and more red.

"What would you choose to eat... from the menu, I mean?"

The man behind the bar now looked like someone who could no longer think straight, and maybe that's why he half-shouted "Chips! I would choose chips," and then began wiping the bar with violent arm movements.

She thought for a moment and then caught his gaze again. "Okay, then I'd like to ask for a portion of chips and a Diet Coke. Thank you for your help." She sent him a big smile, lay down the menu at the bar, put her sunglasses back on, and sat down on a bar stool to wait for her food.

Maya, Charlotte and June were so engrossed in what was going on in the bar that they didn't realise the guide was about to finish.

"Hey, what are you guys doing? Earth to all of you!" Cecilia said, making all three of them look at her.

"What's the matter, Cille-mom?" Maya asked, still with half an eye on the bar. "We're just enjoying a big drama over here! I am sure that if we pay attention, we will soon be able to see a man implode right in front of us. This is excellent Live TV! Am I right, ladies?" she added, in a low voice but with great enthusiasm, looking around at the others.

June and Charlotte nodded and agreed. Cecilia didn't look like someone who could see any amusement in spying on others.

"Okay, fine," she then sighed and relaxed her shoulders. "But Miss Stupi... Um, Sarah-Emilie, I mean! She just informed us that a welcome drink will be provided for all of us to toast to our holiday. So maybe we could concentrate on our own table, just for a few minutes?" she added in a smoothing tone.

"You're right," June responded with a smile. "We are on holiday together, and there should always be room for Hygge. We will have plenty of time to spy on other people's lives. After all, we're here for an entire week."

Charlotte nodded in agreement.

"Besides..." Maya cheekily added, "I never say no to free alcohol, so I'm in!"

When everyone had got a glass with an indeterminate red content, which mostly tasted of pure grenadine, the guide finished by trying to teach the guests how to say "Cheers!" in Turkish.

"In Turkish, cheers are 'Serefé'," Sarah-Emilie said with a big smile, looking around at the guests at the tables. "If it's difficult to remember, you can try to recall it this way; It almost sounds like the word holiday. Well, if you're not too fussy about pronouncing the y. Maybe it will also help if you squint your eyes at the same time as well..." she added a little ironically. "But anyway. Holiday, everyone!"

All the guests yelled Holiday in unison, except June, who instead shouted *Celebrate* from the top of her lungs.

This caused all four girls to crack up, and the

angry couple who had hushed at them earlier sent them even more furious glances.

The guide ended the gathering by saying that she would stay a little while if anyone wanted to sign up for a tour or had questions, and then wished everybody a nice and relaxing holiday.

This allowed Maya to return to her soap opera at the bar.

Apparently, the guy at the bar had accomplished to call the kitchen and order the blonde's fries, because Maya heard the woman's response; "Just shout when they're ready and I'll *come*... To pick them up from you."

All the men in the bar stared after her as she wiggled back to her sunbed, showing off her tiny G-string bikini panty. Maya was certain she spotted a narrow strip of drool running from the corner of one of the male guest's mouths.

"Alright now, Henning. Please pick up your jaw from the floor and breathe out again," someone shouted sarcastically and with a thick Copenhagen dialect. It was one of the big ladies with the straw hats. "There's not that much suction in you anymore, anyway!" The two ladies were cackling loudly.

One of the men at the bar turned around, red in the face, and obviously really annoyed at being called out. "Close your eating slit, Jonna! You're not exactly a goddess yourself, are you?" he snarled back. The ladies just laughed even louder and returned to their Yatzy game. The men in the bar shook their heads, looked at each other with rolling eyes, and exchanged a few short sentences about how all this being married-thing might be something that needed to be reconsidered thoroughly.

Maya giggled and again turned her attention back to her friends and the surrounding tables.

It was almost empty now, and most of the guests had left the hotel just after the meeting was over. To their relief, the two angry people were among those who had hurried to leave, so the girls felt pretty sure that they had come from another hotel.

"Well, what do you guys say? Should we walk into town and have a look around?" Charlotte asked, looking at the time on her phone. "I need to move my body a little today. So, I vote for us to wander into town, sniff around a bit, find some lunch, and then head back to the hotel again. I could do with a dip in that one later," she nodded toward the pool.

The others agreed to the plan and to meet again in 15 minutes in front of the reception. Then everyone had time to pack a bag, change clothes, get some sunscreen on and use the toilet. The latter was suggested with a teasing smile by Cecilia.

Chapter 14

They met outside the glass doors shortly after. It was supposed to take less than half an hour to walk down to the city centre, and it should be easy to find. It was straight out all the way according to the map Cecilia had found at the reception.

"June, it's only middle-aged men with no fashion sense who look like that!" Charlotte exclaimed with a disbelieving look at June's choice of footwear. "Get those socks off! We won't go with you if you insist on having socks in your sandals!"

"I've already tried to get her to change. I've even tried to convince her all the way down the elevator." Maya threw her arms out in resignation. "But she won't budge. She doesn't care as long as she's comfortable." The last was said sarcastically.

Cecilia looked embarrassed but said nothing.

"Girls!" June interrupted in a firm voice. "If you don't like my style, don't look at my feet!"

She pointed down towards the hotel's exit gate. "I will change nothing, so shall we go? Or will you sit here and be outraged all day? Because then I might as well reveal right now that it's going to be a long holiday for all three of you. I intend to do exactly as it suits me with both my clothes and my shoes. The *entire week.* Okay, ladies?" she finished with a disarming smile and walked down towards the gate.

The other three looked at each other resignedly, then shrugged their shoulders and moved in the same direction as June.

They quickly got something else to think about other than June's footwear. Because the road that ran from the hotel and down the mountain was insanely steep, and there were large potholes where the pavement of the road had apparently just disappeared. They quickly agreed that they would not try to walk these hills, when it was dark or if they were wearing heels.

"The guide told us at the welcome meeting that it only costs about 5 euros for a taxi, from the city centre to our hotel, so that shouldn't ruin us," Cecilia reminded them.

"We can also try riding one of those city buses we heard about at the welcome meeting. Was it a Dolbus they were called? That could be fun," Charlotte suggested.

"Charlotte, it's not called a Dolbus, it's called

114

a Dolmus," Cecilia corrected her, "And yes, June, I know it's a bus, and it might make more logical sense for it to be called a DolBUS, but it's not," she quickly added as June began to protest.

There were primarily ordinary residences on the way down. Flocks of children were playing tag on the street and women were chatting over a cup of coffee on the terraces or hanging laundry on the balconies. Here and there, there were small local eateries, hairdressers and barbers, as well as a place that looked like a cafe, where only men sat at small tables and smoked hookahs and cigarettes while playing cards.

There was a cosy relaxed atmosphere everywhere, and the shadows from the buildings made it possible to move around without being completely burned by the sun.

Halfway down, they had to cross a major road with a lot of traffic. With no traffic lights, they patiently waited for a break in the stream of cars, to safely cross the street.

Finally, there was a brief pause, and they hurried to run across the road. They were just about to move on when a large pickup truck came running at full speed. In the back, a full-grown black and white cow was standing in the open air, seemingly without being strapped in. The man behind the wheel waved and grinned at them as they looked at him in amazement. They could hear the cow mooing, and the sound echoing between the houses as the truck continued further down the road.

The surreal sight made all four of them crack up.

"Jesus Christ, this place... What happened to common sense or logic? Don't anybody use that in this town?" Maya hiccupped, wiping her eyes with the napkin Cecilia had given her.

"I've never seen anything as crazy as this in my life," June stated. "I don't know what my full verdict on Cennet will be yet, but so far, it's been far from boring!"

They wandered on, and Cecilia told them about Cennet City Beach, which was artificially made in the early 1990s and built on top of an old cemetery.

"I remembered reading this, when you said the thing about common sense, Maya. Or maybe more the lack thereof," she added.

"Some years ago, there was an unusually big storm in the area, and there was a large flood. When the water fell again, most of the beach's sand also disappeared, revealing more than thirty coffins sticking out of the sand. There were also a few floating in the ocean. Several of them still contained dead people!" she said with a shudder.

"It was an enormous scandal in the city, because all the coffins should have been moved when they originally established the beach. But some wretched people in the mayor's office had apparently not wanted to spend money on it and had therefore only moved those closest to the waterfront. Some people, right? I mean, really?" She shook her head in disbelief.

"Are the coffins still there?" Charlotte asked, astonished.

"No, new orders were issued after the storm. Everything needed to be dug up and turned over, and they actually found more coffins still in the ground. All of them were, of course, moved to the current cemetery, and the townspeople insisted on a closing ceremony out of respect for the dead. Subsequently, the beach was re-established, so today it functions as an ordinary beach. We can go and see it if you want?" Cecilia suggested.

"Yes, we must definitely go down there and see if we can spot a coffin! That would be *so* cool!" Maya sounded a little too eager.

"Seriously?" Cecilia asked in an indignant tone.

"Girlfriend, no one can ever label you a normal person!" June laughed. Charlotte just shook her head.

"Well, it's not that I'm walking around here dying to see a corpse, no pun intended!" Maya explained. "But just think about it. Imaging coming home again with that story in your pocket! It beats everything!"

The other three went ahead without commenting further on it.

Maya retreated into her thoughts momentarily. She had grown accustomed to the fact that her way of viewing the world was not always understandable to others. The skill of unearthing intriguing stories and finding the silver linings, even in the strangest and hardest of situations, allowed her to navigate tough times in her life. Although others often found it weird, it had served as a life-saving solution for her on many occasions. Something she would be forever thankful for.

***

A walking promenade was created along the water and in the width of the Cennet, featuring small cafes, stalls with fruit and ice cream, playgrounds, exercise equipment, fountains, sculptures, and flower boxes.

Cosy benches and vantage points were scattered throughout the area, and there was a myriad of happy tourists, street vendors, local families with children and elderly men fishing from the edge of the promenade with some scrawny street cats as company.

Opposite the promenade, restaurants, bars and shops lay like pearls on a string. All the eateries had an outdoor area where their guests could enjoy the view of the promenade and the ocean behind it while consuming their tasty dinners and colourful cocktails.

Along the entrances to these small oases ran a wide sidewalk, where there was a constant stream of people in both directions.

It was, just like at the airport, a bit overwhelming to go from the quiet side street out into this bustle of life.

Cecilia swallowed audibly and took a deep breath. "Okay, what's the plan?"

"How about we just start by walking over to the promenade and then go for a walk back and forth?" Charlotte suggested. "Then we can get an idea about where everything is, and maybe we can also spot some places we would like to visit during our holiday?"

"Good plan, let's do it," June nodded and stepped out onto the sidewalk.

Chapter 15

They strolled along the promenade and chatted while enjoying an ice cream and the warm sun. They turned around when they reached the marina and walked towards Cennet City Beach at the opposite end of town.

The beach looked lovely and didn't show the slightest sign of having been a cemetery once. Much to Maya's disappointment but to the relief of the others.

On the way back again, they went to have lunch at a small cosy restaurant that had a not-so-Turkish-sounding name, *The Corner*.

All of them went with a Turkish pizza, a so-called Pide, and they were not disappointed.

"Dough and cheese baked in a stone oven are something you seriously can never go wrong with," Maya sighed, happy and with a full belly, as they sat and rested after the meal.

On the way back towards the hotel, they passed a lot of different restaurants and bars. Everywhere they tried to lure them in, and most of the greeting staff almost stuck their menus right in their faces.

Cecilia found it extremely uncomfortable, so when they got to a restaurant where there was no one standing out front, they stopped on the sidewalk.

"Holy shit, it's *so* stressful to walk here, it's not even funny!" Maya complained, shaking her head to release tension. "If this is the standard, then I can do without walking here for the rest of the holiday."

"Hello, ladies," a dark voice said behind them.

"No, we don't want anything!" Cecilia almost shouted to the nice-looking man who had appeared from the restaurant. "No, we don't want to see your menu, no, we don't want to see your drinks card, no, we don't want to see *anything*. Just stop, okay?!" She looked at the man furiously, with tears in her eyes, and breathed in small jerks.

"Cille-mouse... Come here for a moment," Maya said softly and wrapped her arms around her.

"Sorry, our friend is having a really hard time with all the... attention," Charlotte quickly explained to the man, who just shook his head and held out his hands in an understanding gesture.

122

"No, no, you don't have to apologise!" he replied with a smile. He looked Turkish but had a strong Irish accent when he spoke. "It's too much. I know all about that. Everyone is like vultures today!" He pointed towards the cruise ships docked down by the marina.

"When the cruise ships are here, it's absolutely terrible in the city. Everything becomes twice as expensive and the staff becomes more aggressive. Tonight, the ships are gone again and everything will be back to normal – and much better." Then he looked at Cecilia, a little worried. "I think you need some cold water. I'll just find you a bottle. Free of charge, of course!" he quickly added when he saw her irritated gaze.

He disappeared into the restaurant.

"Girls, he's very polite and pretty cute, too," Maya whispered to the others, letting go of Cecilia, who seemed a little better.

June looked up at the sign. *Lezzetli*, it said.

"Maybe we should consider eating here tonight? It's the only place that wanted nothing from us today." She looked questioningly at the others.

Everyone agreed.

A moment later, the employee returned with

a bottle of water, which he opened and gave to Cecilia.

"We just deliberated," June said, "and we'd love to eat here tonight if you have any tables available?"

"Well, of course. You are very welcome," the man sent them a big smile and pulled out a notepad from his back pocket. "At what time do you want to eat and do you want to be picked up at the hotel?" He asked.

"Um, what do you mean by being picked up?" Maya asked and looked cautiously at him.

"Well, we offer to come to your hotel and pick you up with a car. It's completely free. We can also drive you back home if you wish. It's also free," he replied and smiled warmly to her.

"Okay, good deal, we'll do that!" Maya quickly replied, feeling her cheeks blush. God, he was really attractive, this one! She quickly pushed the thought about him away.

June hurried to take over. "Shall we say nine o'clock? Then everyone will have plenty of time to get ready," she suggested with a telling glance at Maya, who just laughed it off. "We're staying at Lokum Deluxe. Do you know it?"

"Yes, of course. Lovely hotel! I also know the owners, they are very nice people," the man nodded as he wrote their information down.

Then he put the notepad back in his back pocket and held out his hand to June. "My name is Haci and I'm the manager here at the restaurant. What's your name?" he asked politely.

They all took turns shaking his hand and introducing themselves. He repeated each name with a concentrated look, as if he was memorising it all. Maya noticed that the touch of his hand sent a strange ripple through her body.

They said goodbye and were just about to leave when June remembered that they also had to buy groceries.

"Haci, can you tell us where we can find a supermarket nearby? We need to fill our fridges." He pointed in the same direction they were about to go.

"Take the second way on the left hand. There is a Migros. They have everything you need. But, girls, the hill up to your hotel is very steep. Are you going to *go* all the way up there with your shopping bags, or are you taking a taxi back?"

"We talked about taking a taxi. We'll see if we can find one after we've been shopping," Charlotte replied with a shrug.

"No, no, that won't do at all. Let me help you out. One second, I will fix this for you." He retrieved his phone from his pocket and dialed a number. The call was answered promptly, and he immediately began speaking rapidly in Turkish.

When he hung up, he was looking very smug. "Just wait a few minutes, okay? I just called a taxi for you. It's my cousin Bim, and he will drive you to Migros and then home to the hotel afterwards."

"So, how does this work?" June asked, a bit confused. "Will he just sit in the taxi and wait while we shop? After all, it can quickly cost a lot if the meter is running. Maybe this is not such a good idea?"

"No, no, don't worry," Haci interrupted with a laugh. "Of course, he turns off the meter while you shop. It's no problem." He looked very happy with himself once again, when a car at the same time stopped and honked on the other side of the road.

"There he is. Come with me!"

Haci got them safely across the street and into the taxi.

He explained to the driver where they were going, then said goodbye and waved at them as they drove down the street.

All four looked at each other a little dazed and then started laughing.

"What exactly happened here?" Maya giggled.

"Yeah, I'm still not sure," June replied while shaking her head and rubbing her forehead. "I have a bit of a hard time keeping up with the way they do things here. It seems a bit chaotic, but also much more... helpful, than we are used to?"

"It is freaking insane!" Cecilia suddenly yelled. She hadn't said much since they left The Corner. "This city is just insane! You can't count on anything at all. It's definitely not *at all* like in Denmark!" Her voice conveyed both frustration and delight.

The others looked at her in surprise. Cecilia sighed and shrugged. "I mean... Yes, today has been quite a challenge for me, dealing with all the hustle and bustle. Which I really hate! But..." She visibly relaxed her shoulders, and a big smile spread across her face. "At the same time, we have also been met with great kindness and helpfulness. Honestly, have you ever experienced anyone in Denmark, complete strangers, who just would help and find solutions for someone or something that had nothing to do with them at all?". She looked at the others questioningly.

All three of them shook their heads.

"No, that would be a shame to say," Maya agreed. "The vast majority of people at home have enough in themselves. I'm with you on this one. This place is equal parts madness and heart, and I can't wait to see what the rest of the holiday brings!"

"Hmm... Could this adventurous feeling possibly have something to do with a man whose name sounds like a sneeze?" June looked teasingly at her, and both Charlotte and Cecilia chuckled.

"What are you talking about?" Maya looked cluelessly at her for a moment. Then it dawned on her. June was referring to Haci. "My God, don't be stupid! I'm not interested in him. I just said he looked cute. That doesn't mean I'm going to do anything with him!" she refused profoundly, but she could feel the heat rising in her cheeks.

"If you say so..." June winked at her while grabbing the handle above the door as the driver turned sharply to enter the correct side street.

The taxi drove up the street and into a parking lot in front of a shop that had boxes filled with fruit and vegetables standing outside, and a large sign on the shopfront that said Migros.

"Well, here we are. Are you ready to go shopping?" Charlotte sat in the seat next to the driver. She opened her door and got out. Then she looked back at the driver. "Are you just waiting here, then?"

"I'll wait here," he replied with a big smile and turned off the meter. "You shop, I wait, no problem."

Chapter 16

When June and Maya came down to the pool in the afternoon, Cecilia had already settled in, completely engulfed in a thick book. Charlotte lay with her eyes closed and her headphones on.

It was obvious that September was a slow month at the hotel. There were only a few other people at the pool.

Henning, Jonna and their friends sat in their regular spots at the pool bar and under the pool umbrellas. Today, the ladies were not playing Yatzy. Instead, they sat and chatted about the book Jonna was reading.

The blonde with the amazing figure was again lying on a sunbed furthest away from the pool bar. She sat with her backrest up and a lit cigarette in her hand, which she slowly smoked on, indifferently turning pages in a magazine that seemed to be about fashion.

The young couple who had been on their transfer bus were in the pool. A moment ago, Thor had tried to splash water on his girlfriend but was quickly told that it wasn't funny at all. Now he was making it up to her, patiently carrying her around in his arms in the water while she lay with her eyes closed, enjoying the sun.

Directly across the pool, was a woman who looked to be about the same age as them. She was in the company of two young children and two teenagers. There were towels, bags, toys and rubbish all around them and it all looked quite chaotic.

The two teenagers played with the two small children while the woman lay half-asleep on her sunbed.

A man came up the courtyard and walked directly up to the family.

"Daddy, Daddy!" screamed the two little ones, while running towards him. He patted them a little disinterestedly on their heads and turned to the sleeping woman on the sunbed.

"It's half past three, so maybe it's time to go to our room?" he said and looked down at her with a tired disposition. She did not answer him and continued to lie with her eyes closed. "Hello! Wake up right now! It's half past three, I said!" he repeated in an irritated tone.

"Start packing!" he barked at the two teenagers, who immediately began throwing toys and towels into the bags.

The woman sat up and looked at him, clearly

annoyed. "You know what, Claus? You've been out looking at that boring train museum all day. While *I* have been in charge of all our children. It's your kids too, you know!"

He looked at her with an indifferent look. "You know I can't stand lying by a pool all day. I'm getting bored out of my mind. I thought this holiday was for me too, or am I wrong, Simone?" he replied with a shrug.

"This holiday is for all of our family!" Simone hissed back. "A family you obviously don't want to be a part of!" The last part was said with a loud and sarcastic voice.

All the children looked very uncomfortable, and the big ones tried to get the smaller children, and all their belongings, with them towards the reception while the adults finished arguing.

"Just stop, Simone. You've probably been lying there all day without moving a finger, so don't talk to me about family time!" Claus scornfully replied, turned on his heel and walked in the same direction as the children.

Simone sighed and looked confrontationally at Maya and June, who quickly pretended that they hadn't watched the entire show with much curiosity.

Then she got up, picked up her towel from the

sunbed with a furious motion, and stomped after her husband. They left a mess of dirty dishes, half-filled glasses and used napkins.

"Okay, happy days..." Maya said with a low voice and her eyebrows raised.

"I'm so relieved not to be in a relation like that!" June added while shaking her head. "I can feel myself getting completely claustrophobic at the bare thought!"

The barman had discovered that the family had left and started cleaning up after them while shaking his head and muttering to himself.

"CLAUStrophobic? Really, June?" Maya rolled her eyes and kicked her sandals under the sunbed.

"Hey, it wasn't on purpose, but it just shows that I have a natural comedic talent!" With one smooth motion, June pulled her striped sundress over her head so she was standing only in her new pink bikini. She spread out her arms and let out a content sound as a light breeze caressed her body.

Maya stood hesitantly for a moment with her hands on the sarong's tied knot, and June noticed it.

"Aren't you going to take it off? It's super-hot today, and it didn't help that we wandered around town for hours." She took a sip from her water bottle.

"Yes, but..." Maya sighed. "Okay, I'll have to ask you something," she whispered while waving June over.

"It's just because... I still feel really awkward about having to show off my body in front of others. I would like to be more like you. You don't really care what others say and do. What's the trick?". Her frustration showed in her voice.

"Aha, okay, I understand." June thought for a moment. "Okay, first of all, I get how you feel. It has also taken me years to get here. It wasn't until the day I discovered something essential that there was a mental shift inside me."

"Okay, and what was that?" Maya asked with genuine curiosity.

"It's very simple, Maya, it's all about perspective. You will always be too much for some, and too little for others, no matter what you do. That means that you, with a 100% guarantee, will fail if you try to make everyone happy. Everybody can see that those odds are ridiculous!"

June pointed at herself. "I am well aware that my body shape is objectively more *'shapeless bucket of vanilla pudding'* than *'a little junk in the trunk'* and that I, in no way or shape, fit into the conventual ideals of beauty. But you know what..." she continued with a proud voice and a big smile. "I have two healthy children, a house in the countryside with lots of nature around me, a lovely husband and some wonderful friends who love me as I am. My body size has never impacted any of those things."

Maya nodded, "I can see you have a point, June. But how do I get there?"

"First of all, and we've had this talk before, Maya, you have to stop trying to live up to an unrealistic idea of what beauty means. And then you have to start talking nicely to and about yourself. You are a beautiful woman with lots to offer, and you really need to get that into your thick head! So, lose the clothes and show the entire world that you can rock a bikini, even if your belly is flapping in the wind!"

Like a magic trick, she tied up Maya's sarong in one swift movement and pulled it off her.

Maya couldn't help but laugh, even though she had been a little taken aback by June's quick hands. She forced herself to calm her body and, with determination, dismissed the inner voice that frequently criticised her appearance and made her feel inferior to others.

June threw Maya's sarong on the sunbed and

looked at her again. "Maya, I told you already in the changing room. You look insanely good in that bikini. So, pull yourself together and get your ass in the water!"

June turned around and was about to walk over to the stairs at the end of the pool. But she stopped abruptly and whispered to Maya, "Okay, we'll probably have to make some noise when we go out there. I'm not completely sure, but I think the young ones are enjoying themselves over there, by the edge of the pool." Maya giggled and looked in the same direction June was pointing.

The young couple had somewhat discreetly pulled over to one side of the pool, with only their shoulders and heads sticking out of the water. The girlfriend hung on the front of Thor, with her legs wrapped around his hips and her arms around his neck, and they kissed intensely.

They were both covered in water, but it was obvious that his hands were under her buttocks and that he was slowly lifting her up and down.

Their movements made small waves out into the pool, and they were completely lost in their own world.

"I think you're right!" Maya whispered back and chuckled. "It's amazing what people choose to be blind about when they're in love."

June walked towards the poolside. "Come on, Maya, it's time for a swim!" she said in a loud voice that sounded a little artificial.

"Okay, I'll be right there, so we can swim. In the pool," Maya responded in an equally loud and artificial voice and went after her.

Cecilia looked up from her book. "What are you two up to now?" she looked very confused.

"Hey Cille-mouse, aren't you joining us for a swim too?" Maya asked, still in a loud voice.

"Yeah, okay, I can do that." Cecilia put the book down on the table next to the sunbed. "But do you have to speak so loudly?" She got up and walked towards Maya, who along with June had reached the steps leading into the water.

"Yes, it's actually very necessary," Maya whispered to her while laughing, nodding towards the young couple, who had now registered their voices and were frantically untangling themselves.

"Um, I think it's time to get up now. Do you want to come along?" the girl stammered with flushed cheeks.

"No, I think I'll have to swim a few laps first," Thor replied with a grin, looking down at himself tellingly.

137

"Ah, okay, got it," the girl replied, looking very embarrassed. "Then we'll just meet up by the sunbeds..." She turned her back on him, swam to the stairs, and hurried past the girls without looking at them. Thor started swimming back and forth in the pool and didn't look like it had bothered him at all to be discovered.

"Were they doing what I think they were doing?" Cecilia's voice was full of indignation.

"Yep. I think that's a certain. Why else do you think Mr Loverboy is cooling off with some front crawl right now?" Maya snickered as they walked down the steps.

"It's really not appropriate to do that when there are other people around you!" Cecilia's mouth completely curled up.

"Shit, it's cold on the foo-foo!" June squealed, while emerging the lower part of her body in the water. "Perhaps it's better to just get it over with!" she added, while quickly lowering the rest of her body under the water.

"What on earth is a foo-foo?" Cecilia looked confused again. Maya quickly pointed to the front of her bikini bottom.

"Okay... I hadn't heard that one before," Cecilia muttered, letting herself slide into the water.

They swam around in the cooling water for a while, and Maya and Cecilia ended up hanging on the edge of the pool chatting while June got up and had a nap in the sun.

"Hey, doesn't Charlotte want to go swimming?" Maya wondered.

"No, I think she's got her period." Cecilia shrugged.

"Okay, makes sense. Perhaps that's why she's wearing shorts as well instead of a regular bikini bottom." Maya nodded and looked up at the pool bar.

The barman was calmly walking down towards the pool area with a bright orange-coloured drink on a tray. He headed straight for the blonde, who now looked like she was sleeping.

"Hey, look at Mr Chippy," Maya sounded exited. "He's heading toward the hottie."

"Maya, you completely lost me here. Who the heck is Mr Chippy and who is the hottie?!"

Maya swiftly briefed Cecilia on the morning's drama, ensuring she was fully caught up on the backstory. "... I call him Mr Chippy because, well first of all, I do not know what his real name is, and second, it really fits him, I think. In general, it's not a bad idea to have code names for other people if you have to gossip about them without them understanding anything," she added with a sneaky look, again moving her gaze to the woman in the tiny bikini.

Mr Chippy had arrived and gently tapped the blonde on the shoulder. He placed the cocktail next to her on the table and was just about to leave again.

At that very moment, she opened her eyes, put on a big smile, raised her hand to him, and said something they couldn't hear. But she must have asked for a helping hand, because he hurried over to help her up from the sunbed.

She slowly adjusted her bikini, quickly purred up her hair, and said something they could just make out was about paying for her drink.

She turned around, and with her back to Mr Chippy, she slowly bent forward, still with her legs stretched out, to rummage in her bag that stood on the ground next to the sunbed.

Cecilia let out a weird sound and looked away in disgust. Maya began to giggle uncontrollably. "Shit, she's agile! I would have sprained at least my left hip with that manoeuvre!"

Mr Chippy's eyes were glued to the lady's buttocks. The two brown globes with only a thin strip of fabric in between quivered in front of him. His face turned bright red, and he swallowed visibly again and again.

The woman had seemingly finally found her purse and slowly straightened up again. She turned around with a big smile and took a few steps towards him, so she was standing very close to him. She looked up at him, let a hand slide down his arm, stuck a note in his hand, whispered something in his ear, laughed coquettishly, and turned her back to him again to put her purse back in her bag. In the same way as before.

Mr Chippy had a shocked expression on his face, and it looked like it took him a few seconds to reconnect with the real world.

Then he quickly turned around and rushed towards the bar, wiping his forehead again and again with his handkerchief while muttering to himself.

"Holy shit!" Maya whispered excitedly to Cecilia. "I've never seen a woman hit so directly on a man before!"

"It was just *so* embarrassing!" Cecilia rolled her eyes. "Imagine bending over like that when you're wearing almost no clothes! Why didn't she squat down with her back the other way? Or lifted the bag onto the sunbed? This is just *too much*!"

"Cecilia, she has a nice ass, so why not use it?" Maya laughed and lit up as a new idea took shape. "I got it now! The blonde's cover name is in place! I'll present for you..." Maya's dramatic arm gesture caused Cecilia to look at her questioningly. "*The saga of Mr Chippy and The Egg Slicer*!"

Chapter 17

"Maya, you've changed your clothes five times. Make a damn decision and let's go! The car will be here in five minutes!" June yelled, irritated.

She had been ready for more than half an hour and had spent the wait with a cold Diet Coke and a few cigarettes on the balcony. Meanwhile, Maya had tried on all her clothes at least once. But each time she looked in the mirror, she sighed resignedly and pulled it off again. The untidy pile of clothes on their bed was steadily rising.

"I can't decide," Maya complained from inside the bedroom, pulling a dark green top with sequins up over her head for the second time. "It's like nothing is sitting nicely right now. I don't feel comfortable in any of it. I have a total wardrobe crisis, June! So please, stop rushing me." Her voice rose a few octaves, and she sounded stressed out.

June walked to the bedroom door, leaned against the door frame, and threw out her arms. "Mau Mau, I'm not trying to be annoying, but the restaurant is picking us up in about..." She looked at her watch. "Three minutes now. We simply can't be late when we've booked someone to pick us up."

At the same time, there was a knock on their door and a voice called out to them, "Are you ready to go, girls?"

June opened the door for Charlotte and Cecilia. She nodded appreciatively and wolf-whistled when she saw them. "You clean up nicely, you two. Totally hot potatoes! All we need now is for Maya to pull herself together," she added with a sigh.

"I'm ready now," Maya responded and walked out of the bedroom with a triumphant look in her eyes. She was wearing a black low-cut dress that showed off her legs.

"Excuse me, isn't that exactly the same dress you started out with?" June said in a resigned voice.

"Yes, but that's just how it is," Maya replied with a grin as she quickly packed her bag. " Occasionally, you need to try on your clothes multiple times for them to fit and sit properly. Now, shall we go, girls? It's exactly nine o'clock, and we shouldn't keep the driver waiting, should we?" she winked at June and walked over to the open door where Charlotte and Cecilia were waiting.

"Sometimes you are really not normal, Maya!"

144

June sighed and walked after her while shaking her head.

***

It was quite dark outside, so they were relieved when a minibus arrived a few minutes past nine.

The driver politely rushed out to open the sliding door on the side of the bus, while stating that he was coming from Lezzetli. Four women, possibly in their sixties, wearing lovely dresses, were already on the bus. As they entered, everyone nodded in a welcoming manner.

It didn't take long to get from the hotel to the restaurant. The driver drove furiously down the mountain, accompanied by loud thumping music. Perhaps not the most appropriate music choice, considering the company on the bus, but when the drive was so short, they laughed it off and added it to the list of oddities in Cennet.

They arrived in one piece, and the driver turned the music down just before parking in front of the restaurant.

It was a completely different experience to be in the city center in the evening, now that the sun had set and the cruise ships had sailed off. All the lights were on, both street lamps and the many neon lights that were on all the facades, and there was a very calm atmosphere everywhere compared to earlier in the day.

Haci stood in front of the entrance to Lezzetli, dressed in a white shirt and a pair of black trousers. He greeted them all with a big smile, and to their surprise, he remembered all their names.

"Cecilia, are you feeling better now that the whole town has calmed down a bit?" he kindly asked. She blushed and looked a little embarrassed. She quickly apologised for her behaviour earlier. He immediately told her to forget all about it.

He took them to a table he had reserved for them. It had a beautiful view of the promenade and the sea.

Haci and a colleague who introduced himself as Umut gallantly pulled out the chairs for them and handed out menus. They ordered four beers, four Cola Light and some water right away, after which they started inspecting the hefty menu, where there were hundreds of dishes to choose from.

"Jeez," June mumbled. "They have Turkish, Italian, Mexican, Indian and English cuisine in here. I don't even know where to start?!"

"Yeah, it's very possible to be so overwhelmed by too many choices that you can't choose at all." Cecilia thought for a moment. "I think it's called... Choice paralysis or something like that," she added, while looking around the restaurant curiously.

"Hey, they have a Dish of the Day on that sign," she pointed to a handwritten sheet of paper taped on a pillar in the middle of the restaurant. She squinted her eyes and read out: "Dish of the day: Seabass with salad and lemon. Oh, freshly caught fish, that sounds delicious. I think I'll have that." Satisfied with her choice, she folded her menu and placed it on the table.

Charlotte did the same. "You know what? I'm going with you here. I'm not sure what fish Seabass is, but it sounds nice, regardless."

Haci came back with their drinks and distributed them on the table.

"Have you decided on food yet?" He took a notepad out of his back pocket.

"No, not yet." June looked frustrated up at him. "You have too much to choose from!"

Haci nodded. "I know. It's far too much. But my boss loves to have an extensive selection, so what can I do, right?" he whispered and shrugged.

"Okay, but then maybe you can recommend something? What's good?" Maya asked and looked up at him with a smile.

He looked at her with a mischievous look. "Well, besides me?" he replied cheekily, winking at her.

She could feel her cheeks burning and, in that moment, she was extremely thankful for both the makeup she was wearing and the dim lighting. Hopefully, that combination was enough to hide it from the others. Charlotte, Cecilia and June started laughing, and Maya did the same and did her best not to show how awkward she felt.

"No, no, I'm just kidding," he quickly added while he giggled. "I would recommend the lamb steak. Our chef is superb with lamb."

"Okay, then I'll have that." June looked relieved to have decided on something.

"Hmm, the problem for me is that I'm not that crazy about lamb, so is there anything else you can recommend?" Maya frowned and flipped through the menu once again.

"You know what, I'm ready to bet on, that if you don't like lamb, you haven't tried lamb. It must have been an old sheep or something," Haci replied to her with laughter in his eyes.

Then he leaned forward a little and pointed at her.

"I'll make you an offer. You choose the lamb steak, and then if you don't like it, you just send it back and order something else, and you don't pay for the lamb. What do you say?" He looked at her with a challenging look and a big smile.

Maya closed up the menu and gave it back to him with a grin. "That is a good deal, I'll take it!".

"Excellent choice and don't worry, you're going to love it!" He turned to Cecilia. "Have you decided?"

"Yes, Charlotte and I would like to ask for the Dish of the day, the one with the Seabass."

"Good choice, ladies. Anything else?" he asked as he gathered their menus.

Before they had time to answer, his colleague, Umut, came to their table and rapidly said something in Turkish. He was pointing at the sign saying Dish of the day, pointed at the order form and then looked at the girls.

Haci looked a little annoyed and replied something very short and sharp in return. He waved Umut away again.

"What was that about?" June asked Haci.

Haci sighed and quickly explained. "He just

reminded me, that we only have one Seabass left in the kitchen. Therefore, one of you should choose something else from the menu..."

Cecilia interrupted him. "Oh, not a problem. I'll just find something else then." She stretched her arm towards the menus.

"No, no," he replied and removed the stack of menus from her reach. "Here at Lezzetli, our customers come first. So don't worry. You'll get your fish, both of you." He smiled and left the table with brisk steps.

"Okay... I wonder what's going to happen next," Maya mumbled. Then Charlotte started giggling.

"Oh my God, Haci just sent away Umut on a scooter, look!" she pointed, and now they could all observe a very annoyed-looking Umut racing away on a scooter heading for the harbour.

"Surely they don't send anyone away to buy just one fish?" Cecilia asked the others and suddenly looked mortified. "Oh no, now I feel completely guilty! I could easily have chosen something else!"

"Hey, please don't kick yourself over this. They do it the way they do it here. Neither you nor I can change that," June replied calmingly while lighting a cigarette.

"Also, it's kind of cool!" Maya added with excitement. The other three looked at her questioningly. "How often do you experience such service? Well, maybe you do..." She nodded with a cheeky grin towards Charlotte, who rolled her eyes in return.

"But the rest of us mere mortals almost never get business-class treatment. And I got to say... I don't hate it!" She leaned back in her chair with her arms crossed and a big satisfied smile. June looked at her for a moment, then shrugged her shoulders and reached for her beer. "I can't say I completely disagree. This VIP-something-something has its charm, girls. So, cheers to us and more VIP experiences!"

Not long after, Umut came back on the scooter. He looked a little less irritated now, and he even smiled at them as he got off and triumphantly showed them a bag containing a fish.

They had almost emptied their beer when the food arrived on the table, so they ordered another round.

The fish was served whole, so Haci offered to de-bone them. Both Charlotte and Cecilia happily agreed.

As Cecilia whispered after he left the table, she had great difficulty eating food that looked at her. On top of that, she had never before in her life tried to have a fish served with both fins and eyes intact.

Both June and Maya's lamb steaks were cooked to perfection, and Maya had to grudgingly admit, that she actually really liked the meat.

Everyone's plates were more than empty, when they a little later sat full and happy, enjoying the view and atmosphere.

Umut cleared their table after the food, and they thanked him for buying the fish for them. He passed it off as nothing, but they could see that he appreciated the kindness.

Charlotte and June both ordered a cappuccino, while Cecilia and Maya went with Turkish tea. The tea was served in a small glass with pieces of sugar next to it, so they could determine the sweetness themselves.

"This! This is the good life," June sighed contently and leaned back in her chair. She rubbed her stomach, which looked somewhat bloated. "Even though my stomach isn't happy with this heavy lamb meat at all, and I look like a balloon right now, it was worth it. "

"This tea is really strong, but it's not bad after an excellent dinner." Cecilia stirred her glass thoughtfully.

"Am I the only one who could also drink something cold and alcoholic?" Maya, who had already drunk her tea, looked around at the others expectantly.

"No, I could do with something sweet." Charlotte immediately waved to Umut, who was passing by. "Hi Umut, can we ask to see your drinks card, please?"

A moment later, a laminated menu was in front of them, and Maya immediately grabbed it.

"Well, at least it's not as confusing as the food," June said with relief as she tried to see from the other side of the table.

"Hey, they have Frozen Strawberry Daiquiris! That's what I want!" Maya quickly decided and passed the menu on to June.

"Yeah, I'm with you on that one!" the other girls agreed in unison.

The time was approaching midnight, and the restaurant was now half empty. All around them, bars and dance halls turned up the music. There was an expectant atmosphere in the air, and several groups of younger people, laughing, and with very little clothes on, came rushing past the restaurant and further into the night.

Charlotte looked longingly at them. "Sometimes I wish, I was that young again. Completely free and carefree, dancing through life."

Maya looked at her sceptically. "Uh, I think maybe you forgot what it was like to be young, my darling."

"What do you mean?" Charlotte looked genuinely confused.

"Well, as I remember my youth, it was crisis upon crisis upon crisis. Everything was a drama, and all of my emotions were on my sleeves." Maya took a sip of her daiquiri and continued. "You live your life without nuances at that age. It's all black and white. Either everything is great or everything is shit. No grey areas. The slightest change in your circle of friends or your status can cause one's entire universe to collapse instantly. At least that's how it was for me."

She threw out her arms and sighed. "I seriously remember my younger years as one long feeling of constantly having to balance on a tightrope strung over a bottomless gorge, where I had to hold my breath at the same time so I wouldn't fall down!".

"Great ... Thanks for killing the mood, Maya," June muttered and took a deep puff of her cigarette.

Maya sighed again and then smiled. "I'm sorry, guys. I'm just saying that if given the choice between being me at 17 and me now, I'd definitely choose me now. Even though I was considerably firmer body-wise back then than I am today!" she laughed, and the others visibly relaxed again.

"It's just that on the inside, I feel so much better where I am in life now. More at rest. The time back then was ... painful and energy-draining... Hey, I think our drinks are coming now!". She nodded at Haci, who was heading over to their table with four huge glasses filled to the brim with what looked like red slush ice.

"They're quite sizeable," Cecilia giggled as he put them on the table, and she pulled out her phone to take a picture of them.

Maya was the first to taste it. "Oh my God, this is amazing, girls!" She took another long sip with the straw. "Oh, my brain hurts," she suddenly groaned, pressing her hands into her temples.

"Then slow down a bit!" Charlotte laughed and took small sips herself.

"Very difficult to remember when it's so delicious," Maya complained, still rubbing her forehead.

"Can I join your party, ladies?" Haci stood at the end of their table with a drink in his hand.

They immediately welcomed him to take part, so he pulled a chair from the vacant table next to them, and sat down.

"So, where are you guys from... Sweden?" he asked curiously, taking a sip of his drink.

"No, no, Denmark," Cecilia replied. "Close to Copenhagen, if you know where that is?"

"Ah, yes, I know Copenhagen. I have lived in Dublin for some years and have travelled a lot in Europe. I never made it to Copenhagen, but it's on my bucket list. But I've gathered enough knowledge along the way, to know the word 'cheers' in Danish," he replied with something resembling pride in his voice. "It's SKÅL!".

"Absolutely correct," June hold out her glass. "SKÅL, everyone!"

"Dublin... So that's why your accent sounds Irish. Why did you live in Dublin? Do you have family there or something over there?" Maya asked curiously.

"It's a bit of a long story," he replied and smiled at her.

"Well, then it's lucky that we're not in a hurry. You can tell us... If you want to?" Maya pushed with an expectant look in her eyes.

Haci looked at her contemplatively for a moment before breaking into a smile.

"Okay, but it has to be the compressed version then, because my boss probably wants me to work just a little now and then as well."

They got comfortable while Haci took another sip from his glass.

"My story is, unsurprisingly, about a woman," he began his tale. "When I was in my mid-twenties, like many others, I met a girl and fell in love. Ciara was from Ireland and was here on holiday with a bunch of friends. Just like you are. We met at the bar I was working at back then. Both of us were young and very much in love. After several years of long-distance-relationship, we finally got married.

Now, we had agreed from the beginning that we would live the first year in Ireland and the following year in Turkey. So that together we could decide which country we wanted to live in when we wanted to have children. So, I moved to Dublin, found work and tried to settle in.

When the first year ended, it was time to change countries, but Ciara had a sudden change of heart about leaving her life and family behind to live in Turkey.

I loved my wife and didn't want to hurt her feelings, so I stopped pushing for a move. But that didn't change the fact that I still missed my family, my friends and my culture every single day."

He took a sip from his glass before continuing.

"After three years in Ireland, I gave up. It was too hard to be so far away from everything I know. So, I went back to Turkey. Alone. And since then, I've focused on healing my heart and building my life up again."

He emptied his glass. "That was, however, several years ago, and my life is on the right track now. I have a good job, I have a roof over my head, and I've just met some wonderful women who are fantastic company," he concluded, letting his gaze rest on Maya, who blushed deeply. Again.

He got up and insisted with a smile that he would get them a round of drinks at the house's expense. Then he went over to the four older ladies who had also been on the "party bus" a little earlier and sat down with them.

"Wow, he's a nice man, huh, Maya?" Cecilia whispered with an eager look. "Even I, who is almost completely blind about everything, can see that he is interested in you."

"What? No, he isn't. He's being nice to all of us!" Maya replied dismissively, but she could also feel a small jump of joy in her stomach.

"Yes, *nice* to all of us. But his gaze is completely different when he looks at *you*, honey-bunny," Charlotte winked and made kissing sounds. "I wonder if he kisses well? That *has* to be your mission this holiday, Maya. Finding that out." she giggled.

Cecilia and June laughed loudly and were completely on board with that plan.

"Hush, all of you!" Maya shushed and felt like her face was burning up. "Do shut up now! No one at this table is able to whisper right now, okay? So just drop it!" she hissed while looking around to make sure no one else had heard them. "At the very least, make a codeword so no one knows who we're talking about, for God's sake! Are you all novices in life, or what?" she asked, now a little less annoyed, and she couldn't help but laugh as well.

"Okay, okay. Simmer down, simmer down. We'll leave it alone for now," June agreed. "But! Tomorrow we will have to work on a codename for... Him, who shall not be ..."

"Stop! You make him sound like Voldemort, and *no*, that will *not* be the code name for him!" Maya quickly interjected when she saw June's face light up, as if she suddenly had a good idea.

"Well, it doesn't matter, anyway." June shrugged and pointed at the bar. "Because here comes the next round of drinks, and it looks just as good as the previous one!".

Approaching two o'clock, they all decided it was time to locate their hotel. All of them were exhausted and definitely felt the effects of the drinks they had consumed.

They waved at Haci and asked him to be driven home. He immediately called the driver from earlier, and he came racing in the minibus a few minutes later.

Haci followed them across the street to where the bus was parked. When they held out their hand to say thank you for a great night, he laughed and shook his head.

"No, no, when you are in Turkey, you also have to learn the Turkish way of saying hello and goodbye." He then explained that in Turkey you greet others by giving a kiss on each cheek.

They stood completely still while he laid one cheek against their left cheek and then his other cheek against their right, while making a kissing sound. He got to Maya last and looked deep into her eyes while smiling. Then he kissed her on the left cheek, right cheek... And then on the left cheek again. She looked up at him in surprise as he whispered to her. "If someone is a really good friend or is very special to you, you can kiss them three times..." He winked at her with a mischievous look and helped her into the taxi where the others were already seated.

"See you tomorrow?" he asked, as Maya squeezed into the back seat with some difficulty.

"Maybe, we haven't made plans yet," June replied, smiled at him. "But we'll be back another day. Your place is great!"

"That sounds good," he replied happily, sending a long glance to Maya. "I will see you, when I see you, then."

Then he closed the door to the back seat and asked the driver to get them safely to Lokum Deluxe.

"Shit, I'm tired now," Cecilia yawned for a moment, looking at her watch. "I usually lie in a deep sleep now," she laughed. "But it's been such a good day, so it's okay."

"Agreed," June nodded. "Fantastic day, and you know what? We still have six of them left. Only God knows what will happen!" she said with excitement, as they arrived at the hotel. "Then it's out, ladies," she announced to the whole car. "Remember bags, phones and knickers!"

The reception was empty, but they could hear someone rattling with papers in the office in the back. They sneaked over to the elevator and drove up to the fourth floor.

"Good night, everyone," Charlotte yawned while opening their door. "Breakfast at half past nine tomorrow?"

"Okay, if we can't have it any other way," Maya muttered. "But then I'm going to have a nice nap by the pool tomorrow afternoon"

"That's entirely up to you, Mau Mau. Sleep well, girlies." Charlotte smiled, walked after Cecilia and closed the door behind her.

While June brushed her teeth, Maya stood on the balcony and enjoyed the warm night.

She lifted up the shoulder area of her dress and sniffed in. She could still smell Haci's cologne on her clothes. She smiled at the thought of his cheek kisses and felt a shudder of anticipation run through her body.

She registered this both so strange, yet so recognisable sensation, with a sense of wonder. Then she sighed and went inside to get ready for the night.

Chapter 18

June growled when the alarm rang. "Why the hell do we have to get up already? Aren't we on holiday, or what?" she moaned, snoozing the alarm with an experienced hand motion without even opening her eyes.

"You can just sleep in, but then you'll miss breakfast..." Maya yawned and stretched. "I don't know about you, but I'm hungry and I'd really like a different taste in my mouth." She grimaced and reached for her phone on the nightstand.

"Hey, Cecilia has written something." She rubbed her eyes and sat up in bed with the sheet wrapped around her.

"She's saying that Charlotte had spoken to Melek at the front desk, who told her that there will be a storm later today. As in rain, wind and thunderstorms. So, are we still having a pool day? Maybe just for a few hours?". She looked questioningly at June, who in the meantime, had hauled herself up into a sitting position.

"I'm up for anything as soon as I get coffee on the inside and sunscreen on the outside." June untangled herself from the sheet and swung her legs out of bed. "But first, I have to pee a lot. Uh, I'm filled to the brim, so I'd better move fast!" she exclaimed as she stood up.

"Thanks for the unnecessary information, June!" Maya shook her head as June rushed to the bathroom.

During breakfast, the four of them agreed that Melek's weather prediction had to be inaccurate. They sat under a clear blue sky, where only a few fluffy clouds made the trip over their heads. It was already very humid, so they were happy to sit in the shade.

They switched into their swimwear and headed to the pool after breakfast. They picked four sunbeds that were placed in the shade.

"Phew, it's hot today," June huffed. Her thin sundress was already clinging to her back and her stomach.

"Yes, so off with the clothes and into the pool, that's my plan for today!" Maya replied as she spread her towel out on the sunbed. Then she walked towards the tempting blue waters of the pool.

"Are you coming?" she asked the others as she walked by them.

"Yes, please, I will be there in a moment!" June struggled to pull the damp dress over her head.

Cecilia and Charlotte wanted to wait a while and settled down with their books and an extra parasol.

Maya sat on the edge of the pool with her legs down in the water. Her face turned towards the sun. She sat with her eyes closed and a big smile on her face, enjoying the sun's rays against her skin.

June sat down with a heavy thump next to her. "Whoops, the edge was further down than I expected," she laughed and splashed her legs a little in the water. "Oh yeah, this! This is amazing!" she sighed and let herself slide into the water with a big splash. For a moment, she disappeared completely beneath the surface of the water.

"God damn it, June," Maya squealed. Her eyes were now wide open. The splashing cold water provided by June had ripped her from her relaxed state of mind.

"Sorry," June laughed, spitting water out of her mouth and shaking her head so that more water splashed from her.

"Holy Shit, it's cold," Maya shrieked while she quickly got up and moved away from the edge of the pool. "I'll get you for that! Payback time!" she shouted while pointing directly at June.

Then she set off at full speed towards the pool. "Cowabunga!" she shouted loudly as she jumped into the water, rolled up like a cannonball.

Maya hit the water right next to June, who momentarily disappeared in the cascades. They were both completely drenched and almost died laughing as they swam to the edge of the pool again.

"Have you heard about just paying a little attention to the other guests?" a low voice suddenly sounded behind them, and a shadow fell over them.

"Relax, Mammi. We're on holiday and we are allowed to have some fun." Maya didn't even bother to open her eyes when she responded. "Move it, honey, you're blocking the sun! And I desperately need some colour on all this blubber!" she added with a laugh, trying to wave Cecilia away.

"You are also adults and should know better than to... be so noisy and obnoxious! Look! There's water everywhere!" Cecilia replied sharply.

"Now, listen," June smiled and looked up at her. "You can't stop playing games and goof around, just because you're an adult. Life sucks if you don't remember to let your inner child out to play regularly. Also, water in and around a pool is to be expected. Besides that..." She looked around and shrugged, "then *are* no one else right now that we could bother, even if that was our intention."

"But..." Cecilia's cheeks blushed.

"Sweetheart, look around. Who are we bothering?" June pointed up towards the pool bar.

"Look. Henning and Bjarne are sitting all the way up at the bar, and their lovely wives are sitting under the bars canopy, also all the way up there."

She pointed the other way.

"In the corner over there, Thor and his girlfriend are practically inseparable on a sunbed. Trust me, they wouldn't notice if the world collapsed around their them!".

She threw out her arms and looked questionably at Cecilia. Cecilia's shoulders lowered, and she sighed. "Yeah, okay, I see your point. Sorry, I'll try to be less... *Me* for the remains of this holiday. Maybe I'm just a little tired today, too." She smiled apologetically at both of them and looked a little embarrassed.

"Cecilia-mouse, it's okay," Maya assured her. "We all have bad days. I think we can survive your uncalled-for scolding this time."

Cecilia laughed, made a funny face and then walked back to her sunbed.

"Well, maybe it is time anyway to get up and dry off a little," June said shortly after.

"Yeah, good plan," Maya replied and swam over to the steps at the end of the pool. "I actually have a very naughty date with Mr Snow this afternoon. I really don't want to miss that! He's actually waiting for me right now, up by my sunbed."

"Not bad," June replied in a dry manner, as she walked up the last steps of the stairs. "Maybe you could ask him to run to the bar and get some drinks for us then? I feel a little thirsty today."

Chapter 19

Around half past one, grey clouds appeared in the sky, and the humidity rose even more.

Maya was worried that her hair would start to frizz. High humidity and natural curls aren't always a good combination, she told the others as they got dressed and walked over to the pool bar for lunch.

It was Ayşegül who looked after the pool bar today, and she welcomed them with a big smile.

Maya quickly decided on a cheeseburger and was sitting with her phone in her hand when it began spewing out a long series of loud dings. The others looked up from their menus and stared questioningly at her.

"Rookie mistake, guys," she sighed and rolled her eyes. "I wrote to my mother to hear how my little fat boy was doing. Clearly, things are going fine as she's currently sending me a million pictures of him in different scenarios, all captured in the last couple of days. I *know* that it always gets out of hand when they babysit him. I should have known better, so I have only myself to thank for this..." With a resigned motion, she put the phone on silent and threw it into her bag.

"But at least now you know he's doing great." Charlotte winked at her, trying to decide whether to choose an omelette or a sandwich.

As they patiently waited for their meals, the sky darkened with an increasing number of clouds. Just as they were finishing with their lunch an hour later, the first raindrops fell.

"Well, I guess I'm done with sunbathing for today," June said, a little irritated, while tucking her towel into her bag.

"Yes, it looks like it. What's the plan now that we can't be outside?" Cecilia asked as they quickly crossed the courtyard between the pool area and the hotel.

"How about hanging out in our room? We have lots of candy and crisps," Maya suggested as they waited for the elevator. "We also have plenty of drinks, even the kind that have percentages," she added with a grin, "and fancy face masks."

"I could do with a facial and some vodka and Coke," June nodded.

"Guys, it's the middle of the day, and we also drank yesterday!" Cecilia sent them a look of resignation.

"And so, what?" Maya looked at her with a smile. "The forecast is bad and it should only get worse during the day and evening. We might as well drown our sorrows while we wait for better weather?"

"It so happens, that we have a relatively okay minibar in our room. It just needs to be set up," June added as she put the key in the door.

"Okay, I'm game," Charlotte said, rummaging through her bag for the room key. "Just give us a few minutes to change clothes. Let us know if we need to bring something to the party."

"Maybe bring some extra soda, so we have something to mix with? I think that should do it," Maya yelled just before both doors closed behind them.

***

The storm intensified over the next few hours. The girls had initially sat down on the balcony, but had to move inside when the rain started hitting them.

It was hot and extremely moist, and Maya had completely given up doing anything about her hair, and had put it up in a messy bun on top of her head.

171

They sat around the dining room table and enjoyed themselves with card games, candy, and crisps. Once in a while, they could hear a faint rumble through the balcony door that was ajar.

At first, only Maya and June drank from the bottles set up on the narrow kitchen table. But as the hours went by, both Charlotte and Cecilia realised that the weather was only getting worse. Therefore, when Junes offered them her *special vodka and coke* later in the afternoon, they both said yes.

However, June's *special drink* seemed to have mostly to do with the amount of alcohol in it. As a result, the drink turned out to be more than ordinarily strong, and it gave them both a tingling sensation in their bodies after drinking just half a glass. Which made Cecilia switch to wine after just one drink.

At one point, they had ditched the card game and swapped to one of those drinking games they "remembered from their younger years," as Maya had said with a sigh. This had triggered loud booing from Charlotte, and June had thrown a handful of crisps in her face. Cecilia had considered, for just a moment, to clean it up, but decided to leave it alone. She was already half drunk and didn't quite trust her own ability to do any cleaning right now.

172

"Okay, okay, okay... My turn ... *Never have I ever*... had a one-night stand!" Cecilia giggled. She looked around at the others with excitement.

Both June and Charlotte laughingly rushed to drink, but then looked at Maya.

"Hello, Mau Mau, I think you just forgot to drink!" June yelled, and laughed loudly.

"Have you forgotten the rules again? You have to drink if you've done something the person asking hasn't. And girlfriend..." She snapped her fingers in front of her, "There's *no chance in hell* that you haven't shagged some random lizard in the heat of the moment, at some point in your life!" She pointed directly at Maya and looked at her challengingly.

"Okay, Okay," Maya grinned back. "I just want you to define a one-night stand first!"

"Oh my God, now she's starting again with her calculations," Charlotte muttered, emptying her glass.

"No, no. No calculations. I just want you to clarify what you think is a one-night stand." Maya sat straight up in her chair, looking very concentrated. "Okay. Do we agree that a one-night stand is usually that you meet someone you don't already know? A complete stranger. You have sex with him or her, and then you move on. Maybe you don't even know the person's name or anything. Do we agree so far?" she asked the others.

"Yes, so far we agree..." June replied with a sceptical voice.

"Aha! Okay! But what if you actually *know* the person in advance? Well, as in, not a complete stranger. Maybe someone in the circle of friends or a colleague? Or a guy at a bar that you've talked to several times? Is it still a one-night stand?" Maya looked at the others with anticipation.

"Yes!" they almost shouted in unison.

"You can't bend this out of shape. If you hook up with someone one time, it's a one-night stand. No matter how much or little you knew them first!" Charlotte said, looking at her expectantly.

"Well, okay..." Maya looked disappointed for a moment. "Okay, I surrender then. Cheers!" she said with a smirk and emptied her glass, accompanied by lots of laughter and applause from the others.

"Okay, okay, I have a good one, okay, are you ready? Okay... *Never have I ever*... been with a woman sexually." Maya looked around at the others excitedly. No one moved.

"Okay, then I have one too..." Charlotte didn't

get to finish her sentence, when Maya suddenly noticed June slowly taking a sip of her drink.

"Hold on, Charlotte..." Maya interrupted while staring at June.

June took a deep breath and then grimaced, "That amount is probably not quite sufficient," she laughed and emptied her glass.

Charlotte, Cecilia and Maya sat with their mouths wide open and stared at June, who looked back at them with a smirk. Maya was the first to break the silence.

"What?! You really need to elaborate right now!" she yelled, half standing up from her chair. "When have you been with a woman, and apparently not just once? You haven't told us anything about that! Does Bo know it? Tell us, tell us!" She began jumping up and down in her chair with sheer excitement.

Both Charlotte and Cecilia laughed at Maya's reaction. "Well, I think a story like that needs a refill!" June smiled and got up to make another drink.

She returned to the table and calmly sat down again.

"Okay," she started, hesitating for a moment. "I can't just skip to the end, so you'll have to get the backstory as well, okay?"

175

The others nodded while taking sips from their glasses and looked at her eagerly.

"To start from the very beginning, you all know that I've struggled with my internal lady parts since I was a teenager. Insanely long periods with insane cramps, explosive diarrhoea and so on. And then the horrible migraines joined the party as well."

Cecilia wrinkled her nose. "Excuse me, but does it have to be so disgustingly graphic when you tell something? Too much information, June!"

"Yes, I'm afraid it must," June replied with a mischievous look in her eyes. "Should I continue my story or not?"

"Yes, you damn well should!" Maya waved dismissively to Cecilia. "Shut up, Cecilia. This is probably the juiciest news we have heard so far this year!".

June continued with a smile. "You also know that I struggled to get pregnant, and that I was undergoing fertility treatment for several years. It took years before we finally had Andrew and David. The thing is, while I was pregnant, I hardly had any problems with my body, which was excellent! Unfortunately, it wasn't long after the boys had arrived before it all flared up again. So, a couple of years ago, I got a full

176

hysterectomy. You already know that as well."

She cleared her throat and took another sip of her glass. "Damn, my mouth is getting dry from all this talking... Okay, relax girls, I will try to get to the point a little faster," she swiftly added when she saw the others moving impatiently in their seats.

"For many women, such an operation would mean feeling like losing some of their femininity, and I understand the notion. But for me..." She paused for a moment as she slowly rolled her drink between her hands. "For me, it was a liberation. No more painful periods, no more days where I would feel like dying slowly, because of that debilitating fucking migraine and..." she looked at Cecilia with a smirk, "No more explosively emptying my bowel while I almost fainted from the pain. And, with that, no more problems with the bathroom being labelled a toxic waste site for at least two hours every time, because of the unbearable stench. A stench very much resembling a neglected and filthy monkey enclosure!"

Maya and Charlotte burst out laughing, and Cecilia, who had just taken a mouthful of her wine, spat it all out on the table and Maya.

"You are *so* incredibly disgusting! It's *so* not okay to create these kinds of images inside my head." Cecilia coughed and laughed simultaneously, as she got up to find something to wipe the table with. "I'm feeling more and more glad that I'm sharing a room with Charlotte!" she chuckled, while wiping off both the table and Maya with a dishcloth, which had definitely seen better days.

When they had settled again and refilled their glasses, June continued her story.

"Well girls, where was I? ... Oh yeah, monkey enclosure," she teased.

"June, come on, get on with it! When is all the naughty stuff starting?" Charlotte complained impatiently.

"Calm down, I'll get to that in a minute! Okay, I now almost have a new body. A body who is actually not bad to be in, and then something strange happened. Because, from what I could see on the internet, many women, both my age and younger, have completely lost their sex drive after such an operation." She looked thoughtfully into the air for a moment.

"Therefore, I had mentally prepared myself because it could be the consequence for me as well."

She shrugged and laughed out loud. "But ladies, I'm telling you... This old vessel had *completely* other plans. Because my sex drive *exploded*! Yeah, it came as a bit of a shock for both me *and* Bo!" she added with raised eyebrows.

The others began to giggle.

"For years he has been used to his wife being in pain half the time, and the rest of the time I still had massive bowel problems... Yes, it's extremely sexy, I know," she winked at Cecilia, who wrinkled her nose again.

"But there you have it. This is June, version 2.0, and she doesn't want to sit at home and watch Barnaby while knitting woolly socks!"

She slammed her fist on the plastic table, making glasses and crisps bags bounce around. Cecilia hurried to make sure nothing fell over. June didn't seem to notice it at all.

"No thanks! For the first time in my life, I had a body that worked, at least most days. Where I didn't have to worry about getting pregnant, or being out of business for at least a week every month..."

She looked at them intently and leaned forward, "I don't think you can fully comprehend what freedom it gave me. I had suddenly been handed over the driver's seat of my own body! ..." June leaned back again with a thoughtful expression and relaxed her body a little more.

"The issue at hand was that Bo had always had a relatively low sex drive. Maybe that's why we always worked so well together sexually, before my surgery." June shrugged. "He was really doing what he could to keep up, but this... Volcano?" She pointed at her lower body. "He had no chance to match that!"

Then she looked at them seriously and, with a hint of pride in her voice, she continued: "But my husband Bo is a solution-oriented superman, and he is in no way or shape jealous. He knows I love him passionately and was willing to sacrifice my own physical needs for his happiness. But he didn't want me to live half a life now that I was finally feeling good physically. He wanted me to seize the opportunity and live life to the fullest. So, he actually asked me to find a lover." She fell silent as she took a sip of her glass.

"And? Did you do that then?" Cecilia asked, astonished.

"No," June shook her head. "I wasn't crazy about the idea of having to be with just one person. I know that sounds a bit backwards," she quickly added when she saw their wondering glances. "But Bo is the one and only for me, and if I were to live out my... physical potential...

Then it shouldn't be in a way that could jeopardise our relationship. Emotions can quickly arise if you're with the same person every time. At least, that's my thinking..." She shrugged again. "I actually don't know if it would be a problem, but I'm not willing to take the chance," she admitted.

"What did you do then?" Charlotte asked curiously.

"I did the only thing I could do. I made a profile on Tinder and started looking for one-night stands in there. I can reveal that it's surprisingly easy, and yes, Bo has approved it. So, a couple of times every month I go on a 'sexy date' instead of playing golf or something boring," she added with a smile and a shrug.

Maya, Cecilia and Charlotte had stopped giggling and were now just staring at their friend.

"Seriously?" Cecilia stammered with a shocked expression on her face. "Do you just go out and... Have sex with strange men every week?"

"Yes, or women. Or couples. It varies." June leaned back casually in her chair and ignored Cecilia's judgmental tone.

"Are you going to go on dates while you're

here?" Charlotte asked curiously.

June shook her head. "I have promised Bo to keep my activities within Denmark, and I had a date last week, so it should be enough until I get home... Besides, there's always the shower head in case I'm heating up," she added with a cheeky smile.

"June, please don't defile our shower like that!" Maya shouted, looking disgusted.

June got up. "Dear friends, I can see that you have tons of questions, but I am honestly tired of talking. So let me just end my long story by saying that I'm okay, Bo is okay, and my marriage is intact. Okay? New subject, please!"

The look on their faces made it evident that their minds were overflowing with countless questions. But they also knew June well enough to know that if she didn't want to elaborate further, there would be no additional information.

They shrugged their shoulders with disappointed faces and somewhat reluctantly accepted June's decision.

June grabbed her half-empty glass and held it toward the centre of the table.

"Well, cheers and bottoms up, girls! Fantastic holiday so far. *I love it*! As skincare expert, Ole

Henriksen, would say!"

Maya got up, clanged her glass and cleared her throat loudly. "Dear June-bug, holy shit! Where do I start...? First of all, I don't think I've ever heard you say so much about your sex life at once before. I also have to admit that I'm extremely curious about more details. However, I respect that you don't want to talk about it anymore right now. Even if it's super annoying!" she added in a slightly critical voice. She was silent for a moment and then started laughing. "I also have to admit that I'm actually a little shaken to my core... Who the hell saw coming that you were going to be *Slutty McSlut* in your age?"

Cecilia and Charlotte laughed too, and Maya let herself fall back in her chair while sceptically shaking her head.

"Yeah, I was a bit surprised by myself as well!" June giggled. Then she looked inquiringly at Charlotte and Cecilia. "You two still haven't said anything... The cat is out of the bag now... What do you say to it all, my lovely senoritas? Am I voted completely of the island?" She looked at them and smiled.

"Well... Okay... I don't quite know what to say, but you are my friend, and hey, it's your life. If it makes you happy, more power to you,"

Charlotte smiled, holding out her glass.

Cecilia hesitated a little, but then also raised her glass. "I don't want to claim to understand it, June. Nor do I particularly like the whole idea of sleeping around like that. Just the thought of you throwing yourself at a bunch of strangers makes my toes curl up completely. But..." She paused and looked around at the others with a crooked smile, "Even though you guys are completely and utterly insane, at least some of you, I still love you all. Cheers!"

"Cheers to our friendship," Charlotte replied quickly, letting her glass hit Cecilia's.

"Cheers to a great holiday," Maya continued, doing the same.

"Cheers to Slutty McSlut!" June laughed as she straightened up in her chair.

"Cheers to Slutty McSlut!" they all shouted in unison and emptied their glasses.

"Well, hunny bunnies, I think that's enough talk for now. This party needs to get up in gear. I'm voting that we open the bottle of Danish Pepper Drops I've smuggled with me, and then I think we need some party music as well." Maya jumped to her feet. "I have just the right playlist on my Spotify!"

"Great idea!" June shouted and got up at the

same time as loud rhythmic music blasted out from Maya's travel speaker. "I'll get the shot glasses, and after that I think it's time for a cigarette in the storm!"

"Oh no, not Danish Pepper Drops and Maya's party music," Charlotte moaned, but couldn't help but laugh as Maya at the same time bounced through the room to the beat of the music. "This will not end well," Cecilia sighed and groaned as a black bottle was placed on the table in front of her. "I'm really not good with shots...."

Chapter 20

It was four tired-looking women who came down to breakfast the next day. With slow movements, they ate their food and laughed as they reminisced about the Tour de Day Drink the previous day.

They hadn't gone to bed too late, but the bottles were almost empty, and Maya and June's room both smelled like, and looked like, an abandoned pub.

The storm had lasted all evening, and it was only the fact that the rain had turned the road outside the hotel into a roaring river that had kept them from walking down to the city center for dinner.

This morning, they were happy that they had ordered room service at the hotel instead. They had been very far from sober and all of them ran out of energy quickly after sharing five large plates of chips, four cheeseburgers, and a pizza.

June vaguely remembered something about someone knocking on their wall at some point during the party. She had, as she remembered it, just knocked at the wall herself while she shouted "Cheers"

It was around the same time, that Maya had pulled out four sheet face masks of the type with something printed on the front. For the next half hour, they had been stumbling around in their room, completely devastated with laughter, because they all looked like pandas. There was also a big possibility that they might have let out some wild panda howls after Cecilia found a video on YouTube of pandas emitting a resounding "*Arruuuuuuuhh*" as part of their mating game.

They had also played loud music and had sung along to all the songs, whether or not they could remember the lyrics. She was fully aware that the hotel's walls were as thin as cardboard, so she could easily imagine how irritating the noise coming from their room must have been. And how much of a relief it must have been when they turned everything off around half past nine.

She made a mental note about apologising to their neighbour if she had the chance. Anything else would be plain rude.

Luckily, none of them had a terrible hangover today, which was fortunate. Because they had agreed the night before that today was a beach day, if the weather was nice. The first thing they had checked when they got up was to see if the sun was out, and today the weather did not disappoint.

The storm from yesterday had washed away the dust and the humidity, leaving behind a clear sky with scattered white fluffy clouds that disappeared as the sun gained power over the day. It was not as moist as yesterday, and therefore much more pleasant.

Melek recommended they go to Star Beach, just outside Cennet. She ordered a taxi for them and explained to the driver where they were going. Half an hour later, they were dropped off at the end of a cul-de-sac, where a narrow gravel path disappeared in between some low buildings.

"This was well worth the drive," Maya nodded as they stepped out onto the footpath at the end of the gravel path. "My God, this is beautiful!"

The others could only agree with her.

Spread out in front of them was the Mediterranean Sea. Its sparkling blue waters mirrored the sky, while the soft, white sand beckoned them closer.

They could clearly hear the waves moving over

the sound of people's chatter and laughter, and the music that came from the small cafes along the footpath.

"It looks like the beach is divided into different areas. Can anyone see Star Beach somewhere?" Charlotte asked while looking around.

"There! That must be it!" Cecilia pointed to an area on their right where all the sunbeds had large pillows instead of the usual thin plastic mattresses. There was a big sign with the words *Star Beach* written on it.

Many visitors were already in this section of the beach, but there were still some empty sunbeds in the back row, furthest away from the water.

"Oh yeah, that looks just right! Let's hurry and get sunbeds before someone else rents them!" Maya hurried towards the sign.

A very tanned man, around thirty years old, stood at the entrance to Star Beach. He had short hair, wore black swimming shorts, and had a bare chest. Additionally, a black fanny pack was securely fastened around his waist. His well-trained body was accentuated by the numerous tattoos that decorated his arms. His slightly close-set, brown eyes were complemented by his pearly white teeth and a charming smile.

"Hello, beautiful ladies, welcome to my beach!" he greeted in a loud voice, while clearly letting his eyes running up and down their bodies. "Four sunbeds with umbrellas?" he asked and without waiting for an answer, he walked across the sand towards a couple of available sunbeds.

"Yes, please, but there are only three sunbeds here." Charlotte pointed to the sunbeds he had stopped in front.

"No problem, no problem," he said with a big smile, winking at her. Then he went to the next sunbed in the row and said something in Turkish to the young man who was half-asleep on it. He pointed towards an empty sunbed a few feet away and began moving the young man's ashtray and beer bottle away.

To their surprise, the young man just shrugged, quickly gathered his things, smiled at them, and moved.

"There you go, ladies. Four sunbeds. Would you like me to set up the umbrellas?" he asked as he moved their sunbeds a little closer together and placed a low plastic table between each of them.

"No, just leave them down for now, that's fine" June replied and pulled out her purse while the others put their towels on the big soft pillows.

"A bottle of water is also included for each of you. I'll get them for you, and an ashtray for you," he said, addressing June, who had sat down on the edge of the sunbed and was already lighting a cigarette.

"My name is Gio, and if you need anything, just call me or wave at me. I can also help put on sunscreen if you like," he said with a smirk to Cecilia, who had just pulled her sundress over her head. He glanced uninhibited at her body and then nodded appreciatively. "Just call me if you need a hand." He boldly winked at her and walked towards the restaurant.

Cecilia had turned lobster red in the face and held the dress up in front of her like a shield.

"Oh my, Cecilia, I think you've got an admirer," Maya teased her as she straightened the pillow on her sunbed. "What an offer. Help with applying sunscreen... You can't say no to that, Cille-mouse! I wonder what areas he wants to focus on?" she asked, imitating hands smearing sunscreen out, and it was clearly taking place on the upper part of a woman's body.

Charlotte and June were laughing out loud and agreed that there would undoubtedly be areas of the body that would get more sunscreen than others.

Cecilia threw her dress in Maya's face with a grimace. "Hey! Stop yourself. It will be a no thank you from this panel of judges!" But she giggled when Maya handed her dress back to her. Then she folded it up and placed it in her bag.

Cecilia sat down on the sunbed, adjusted her bikini and sighed contentedly. Just sitting and looking out over the sea was really relaxing.

She smiled at the thought of the holiday so far. It had already been very different from what she had imagined, and they weren't even halfway through yet. This country was kind of crazy in itself. So, when the others dropped bombs, such as June and her Tinder escapades, she couldn't help but wonder if they were really here or if she was trapped in some strange dream. But she also had to admit that she really enjoyed herself, and it had been a long time since she had laughed so much.

Just look at this guy, Gio. The whole situation with him was so surreal to her. She had never met a guy who was so direct in his flirting, and she wasn't sure what to think about that. At the same time, she couldn't help feeling just a hint of joy about being the one noticed in the group. She was so used to being overlooked by men when she was with the others.

It had really bothered her when she was younger. "Why do the others always have to take up so much space, and why aren't they making room for me?" she had complained to June, again and again. Normally, June just shrugged it off, but at some point, she had done something else.

She had told Cecilia, very directly, that she no longer wished to listen to her complaining about always getting lost in the crowd.

"Listen, Mammi-mouse. I'm about to say something very important and I want you to listen carefully! You know I love you with all my heart. But you really need to learn to take responsibility for yourself!"

The words had hit Cecilia like a slap in the face, but she still listened. Mainly because she knew June well enough to know that she possessed a remarkable understanding of the human psyche, and her words always came from her heart. Her scolding was never used to criticise, but to offer guidance and support, and help others grow as people.

In a gentler tone, June had explained how individuals occupy varying amounts of space in the world and how everyone has the power to regulate the energy they send out when encountering others.

"So, when you ask others to turn their energy down and take up lesser space, instead of turning yourself up, you put the responsibility for you on them. Is that reasonable?"

Cecilia had never thought of it that way before, and it had been a bit of an eye-opener.

She didn't start working on taking up more space in social settings after their talk. But it helped her to let go of the feeling of not fitting in more easily.

Because she just had to admit that she didn't actually *want* to turn herself up to get a lot of attention from strangers. She thrived on being around people she knew well. Where she could relax and be herself, and where she was loved, although she was sometimes a bit odd.

Like when she was with Charlotte, Maya and June.

They knew her inside out and still wanted to be friends with her, despite her slightly quirky sides. She felt her eyes getting wet just thinking of her friends and their friendship. They were invaluable to her!

She was pulled out of her thoughts when Gio came back with four bottles of ice-cold water, which he placed on the table between Cecilia and Maya and asked if they needed anything.

When they said no, he sat down on the edge of Cecilia's sunbed and smiled at her.

Cecilia cast a desperate sideways glance at the others, who just giggled and quickly looked away.

"Hello again, beautiful woman," he smirked, while nonchalantly brushing some sand off his leg. "What's your name?"

Cecilias started to get red spots on her neck. "Um, Ce... Cecilia," she stammered, sending him a nervous glance.

"Beautiful name, beautiful name... To a very beautiful woman... So, where is your husband?"

"My... My husband?" Cecilia replied confused, while registering a half-choked sound from Maya, who was lying on the sunbed next to her. "Well, I'm not married."

Gio stared back at her sceptically. "That can't be true! I don't believe you!" He shook his head in disbelief. "Such a beautiful woman can't possibly be single. You must be married. How can you not be married? Tell me, where are you from?"

"Denmark..."

"Okay, then men from Denmark are blind!" Gio said with a big smile and pointed to himself. "My name is Giovanni, but you can call me Gio, and I'm not blind. I would be so lucky if you were my girlfriend!"

Cecilia stared at him, but said nothing. She looked at her friends again for help, but quickly realised she was on her own. All three of them lay shaking with pent-up laughter. Maya even still had her own sarong in her hand, which she pressed against her mouth as tears ran down her cheeks.

Gio didn't seem to notice, but continued on. "I'm half Italian, and Italian men are known to be good with women. So why not give me a chance?" He smiled charmingly at her.

"Um... I... I don't know?" The latter was said a little questioningly, and Cecilia was now officially in a state of panic.

"Okay, maybe we can have a drink together one evening then?" Gio asked and continued, not waiting for her response. "Here, give me your phone. I'll add you on Facebook so we can talk online, okay?" He held out his hand.

She reached into her bag a little hesitantly, found her phone, unlocked it, and handed it to him with a bewildered look.

He routinely searched for himself, and while sending a friend request to himself, he pulled his own phone out of his bag and approved the request right away. The whole thing took less than thirty seconds.

"So, now you can contact me whenever you want," he winked, handed her the phone back and got up from the sunbed. "I have to go back to work, but just call if you need anything." He smiled with great self-confidence, and once again let his gaze run up and down her body. Then he bit his lip in a way that probably was supposed to look sexy and walked towards the cafe while whistling.

Cecilia sat with her phone in hand and stared after him. She looked completely stunned.

He had only just left when Charlotte, Maya and June exploded into loud laughter.

"*OMG!* Jesus Christ, a creepy crawler!" Maya got up from the sunbed and walked back and forth while she laughed. "No, no, no, and now you are *friends*, Cille-mouse! What the hell happened here?" she asked before breaking down again with laughter.

"I... I'm not quite sure what happened, to be honest... I was totally taken by surprise," Cecilia

197

said in a low voice, still looking very confused.

"Yes, that was obvious," June laughed, now standing up as well. "He was also very persistent in his behaviour. He's probably used to ladies throwing them self at him."

"No, but seriously?" Charlotte had sat up on the sunbed to wipe the tears of laughter from her cheeks. "It was the most awkward thing I've ever seen. Are you okay?" She looked at Cecilia, who had finally managed to put her phone back in her bag.

"Yeah, I'm okay. It was just a little overwhelming. I can just delete him again, so no problem." Then she giggled. "I'm serious, girls. This place is really so different, and that guy honestly made me feel a little sticky. So, how about a swim in the sea?" She got up and looked at the others expectantly.

Both June and Maya were ready right away, but Charlotte said no again.

"It's must be so annoying to get your period during a holiday," Maya said compassionately to Charlotte as June and Cecilia walked ahead towards the water.

"Yeah, it's super annoying, but there's not much to do about it," Charlotte shrugged and smiled at her. "But pads and water are a terrible combination," she added with a laugh.

"Can't you use a tampon when swimming?" Maya asked, placing her sunglasses on the small table next to the sunbed.

"No, I'm not bleeding that much right now, so it's really uncomfortable to use them. Unfortunately, that doesn't really leave me with a choice." Charlotte shrugged a little resignedly.

"Yeah, that true. Well, let's hope it stops before you go home so you get to dip your carcass, too. See you in a minute!" Maya waved and walked hastily towards the others who were already out to mid-thighs.

"Uh, it's a bit cold, huh?" she shivered, standing at the water's edge, letting her feet sink into the wet sand.

"Yes, especially around the foo-foo!" June, who was already completely below the surface, yelled back.

"For fuck's sake, shut up about your foo-foo!" Maya shouted back at her. "It's enough that you share it with everybody on Tinder. The rest of us don't have to hear about it all the time!" she added, while hurrying through the water. When she reached June and Cecilia, she submerged herself into the water with a big squeal.

"Yes, that was really a bit of a surprise, June-

Bug," Cecilia giggled as they floated around in the clear water. "I'm still not quite sure how to file it in my head. I don't have a folder set up for something that... Smutty," she added with a smile.

"Cille-mouse, I'm sure there are a lot of things you don't have folders for," June said matter-of-factly. "So maybe you should just file it under Miscellaneous. That folder must be almost filled by now, anyway!" she teased.

Maya giggled. "Yes, especially after this holiday. Holy shit, a lot of strange things have happened already!"

"So true. It's a bit like being in The Twilight Zone." Cecilia added, but before she could utter another word, a wave slammed right into her face.

She quickly lodged her feet on the sandy bottom and stood up so she could rub the water out of her eyes. She coughed up some water and breathed deeply a few times.

"Hey, are you okay?" Both Maya and June got on their feet and looked at her worriedly.

"Yes, yes," Cecilia said, half-choked. "I just need to get this water out of my lungs... A word of advice: Don't talk while swimming without keeping an eye on the waves!" she added with a small laugh.

"Maybe it's time to go back up anyway, so we can get dry before lunch," June suggested as she squished water out of her bikini top and started walking towards the shore.

"Good idea," Maya nodded, and started walking after her together with Cecilia, "and let's try to get through the rest of the day without drama with slimy Don Juans and killer waves, Cecilia!" she said teasingly, and jumped aside as Cecilia splashed water at her.

Chapter 21

"Ahh, I could easily get addicted to this." Maya stretched her body on the sunbed with her eyes closed and a satisfied look on her face. They had eaten a wonderful lunch at the restaurant belonging to Star Beach and were now relaxing with full stomachs.

The insecurities about showing herself in a bikini had almost disappeared from Maya's mind. Not that she was suddenly overly happy about how she looked. But everyone had already tanned a bit, which, in her opinion, always made people look both healthier and more attractive.

All around her, men and women of different ages and sizes laid on the sunbeds. The thing all of them had in common was that they had come to the beach to have a good time with family and friends. Because realistically, the size of one's thighs and stomach should never affect neither relationships nor one's ability to have fun.

Besides that, Maya thought to herself, she was definitely not that big when she compared herself to some of the other women on the beach. She was ashamed to think like that, so she didn't say it out loud. Even if the thought wasn't really judgmental of everyone else, but had everything to do with herself.

She chose to focus on the improvement, she had made the last couple of days, and embraced the feeling of lying in her bikini without the constant worry of being judged on her appearance.

Maya heard her phone beep and opened her eyes in disbelief. She was sure she had put it in silent mode. She found the phone at the very bottom of her bag and dusted some sand off the screen.

"What. The. Actually. Fuck!" She sat up abruptly and swung her legs over the edge of the sunbed. The other three girls opened their eyes, got up on their elbows, and looked perplexed at her.

Maya quickly tapped the screen a few times and put the phone to her ear, before they could say anything.

"Hello? Yes, it's me. Why do you ask what size Freddy uses in clothes? What are you up to?" An eager voice interrupted at the other end, and Maya looked puzzled.

"Mom... Mommy... *Mom*! Listen to me!" Maya interrupted abruptly. "Have you gone completely batshit crazy? Do not, I repeat, do *not* knit a sweater for Freddy out of his own fur!"

She could hear Charlotte, Cecilia and June giggling in the surrounding sunbeds.

The voice on the other end started talking again. Maya took a deep breath and looked like a thundercloud.

"Mom! Stop talking and listen to me..." Maya interrupted again with all the self-control she could manage. "I can give you two really good reasons why you should stop yourself right now! One: Freddy is a freaking cat! He's wearing his own fur! Two: It's really just super cray-cray behaviour!"

The voice on the other end spoke excitedly again, and Maya kept rolling her eyes. "Yes, I know Freddy is sort of your grandson... But listen, Freddy doesn't deserve nice clothes!"

[...]

"Why? Because all cats are assholes, it's in their nature. If you and Dad died tonight, he'd start snacking on you before you were even cold!"

[....]

"Yes, I agree, that was a seriously grim example, but Mom, please, listen to me!" Maya begged and shook her head in disbelief.

[....]

"Mom, you're losing it! You're just one step away from collecting Daddy's clipped toenails so you can make *such a nice homemade collage for the dining room wall!*" Maya hissed and slapped her hand into the sunbed.

[....]

"Fine! Do whatever you want." Maya now sounded resigned. "If you want to be weird, be weird. But you get to deal with the damage from Freddy yourself if you try to put it on him! I will have nothing to do with that project, and it has to stay in your house at all times!"

[....]

"Huh? Yes. Yes, Mom, we're having a good time," Maya sighed in a calmer voice. "I'll say hi to the others from you. Say hi to dad and kiss Freddy from me. Bye, bye Mom, you crazy woman, you!"

She ended the call and glanced at the others, who were all in fits of laughter.

She shook her head resignedly. "The woman has now officially completely lost her marbles!" she sighed while gesturing with a rotating finger in front of her temple.

Maya got up and, with another sigh, she threw her phone on the sunbed. "I love my mother, but Jesus Christ, she's frustrating sometimes!" She took a sip from her water bottle. "Is it normal for women to go mental when they reach a certain age?" she asked, looking at them dumbfounded.

"I'm probably not the right person to ask," June replied in a dry manner. "My mother was always completely off the rails, no matter what age, so I can't help you with that question."

Suddenly Maya's phone beeped again. She unlocked it with an annoyed look, which was quickly replaced with a small smile on her face and a bubbly feeling in her stomach.

"Oh, I guess that message wasn't from your mother," June said teasingly.

"It's Haci from Lezzetli... He has sent me a friend request on Facebook..." Maya looked like she didn't quite know what to do.

"Well, approve it then!" June exclaimed. "You think he's cute, right? Then why not?" Charlotte and Cecilia nodded in agreement.

Maya thought for a moment and then approved the request with a crooked smile.

A moment later, a message appeared on her screen. It was from him.

Maya could feel her cheeks getting a little extra colour, and a funny feeling spread throughout her body. She wondered what was going on with her.

Haci had brought out some sensations that she hadn't had a visit from in a long time, and it knocked her a little off kilter.

"What does he write?" Charlotte asked curiously.

"He asks what I'm doing today and how my holiday is going." Another message ticked in. "Now he asks if we are going to have dinner at his place tonight?" Maya looked questioningly at the others, who quickly agreed that they might as well do that.

Maya ordered pickup for nine o'clock again. Haci wrote back that he was looking forward to seeing her and that he would make a special table for them.

Her face lit up as she repeated his words to the others. When they started making kissing sounds, she defiantly flipped them the bird.

"You guys are so fucking childish," she sighed dismissively, but couldn't help but laugh as well. "Come on, girls, let's change the subject. Who wants to go swimming?" she asked and got up.

"I'm with you," June replied and rose from the low sunbed with some difficulty. "It's probably not a bad idea for you to cool down your funhouse before we go out tonight either," she added with a laugh, while ducking from the sandal Maya threw at her.

"Stop your vulgarities, June. We're not all a Slutty McSlut like you!" she laughed, looking at her tellingly. June just shrugged and winked at her. "No, but you'd damn well could benefit from it. There's nothing like a proper shagging to release all tension," she exclaimed and laughed loudly, while walking towards the water.

The other three looked at each other and couldn't hold back their laughter. Then Charlotte shrugged. "Well, she's not wrong, although most normal people might not speak so loudly and bluntly about it!"

"No, that's..." Cecilia added, still hiccupping with laughter. "This holiday, friends... I'm not sure I'll last another four days..." She put on her sandals and wrapped a towel around her. "I just have to go pee first. See you in a couple of minutes."

"I'd better join June, so she has some company. Are you still okay here on land?" Maya asked Charlotte.

"Yes, yes, it's no problem. I'm just about to take a test to determine if I'm doing enough to be a good wife for my husband." Charlotte rolled her eyes sarcastically at the women's magazine she was holding in her hands.

"Sounds not at all like a complete waste of time," Maya replied sarcastically with a grimace. "Well, have fun with it. I'll go swim." She turned on her heel and walked towards June, who was already floating around with a satisfied smile.

Chapter 22

"Holy Moly, I look like a lobster!" June exclaimed, looking in the bathroom mirror with a surprised look. "I've been wearing sunscreen today. How the hell did this happen?" she muttered and walked into the bedroom. "You are pretty red on your back and shoulders too, huh?" she added, pointing to Maya, who was standing in her underwear in front of the bedroom mirror putting on makeup.

"Yeah, I've put Aloe Vera on at least three times, but it absorbs right into my skin and I just feel so warm," Maya puffed, waving her hands in front of her face, which looked a little red, too. "Damn, it's impossible to put on a proper foundation when my face is sweating like that," she complained, looking at June resignedly.

"Wow, yours are worse than mine" she laughed when she saw June's fiery red face, neck, chest, shoulders, and arms.

"*You think*?!" June said ironically. "I've been wearing factor 20 all day. This sun must have been burning ridiculously today!"

"June, honey, you have to use factor 30 when you are going into the water as well. And did you put something on during the day?" Maya asked with a giggle and put on a summer dress with a flowery motive over her head. She walked over to the curtain that had been drawn and pulled it all the way aside so that the evening air would come in. She breathed in deeply, and a satisfied smile spread across her face. Then she turned around and, with confidence, walked up to the mirror again. "Alright then, it's going to be a light makeup today, that's just how it's going to be," she muttered to herself, rummaging through her toiletry bag.

June went outside and looked in at Charlotte and Cecilias balcony. They both sat with a cold soda and chatted.

"Hello in there. How are you two doing? Are you burned too?" June asked over the railing.

"Yeah, you might say that," Charlotte laughed and pulled the collar of her striped t-shirt down from her shoulder. You could clearly see where her bikini strap had been sitting.

Cecilia was using a brochure as a fan. "I'm boiling up," she complained, "and I'm sunburned on top of my feet. It hurts just to wear sandals, so I'm really glad we're being driven back-and-forth today," she added with a relieved expression on her face, taking a sip of her soda.

"Are you almost ready?" Charlotte asked, looking at her watch. "We'll be picked up in ten minutes."

"Yes, I actually think Maya is ready ahead of time today... Apparently, the time of miracles is not over!" June joked, winking at Cecilia and Charlotte.

"Hey, I can hear you!" Maya stuck her head out on the balcony and pointed at June with a phoney angry expression. "Don't gossip about me when I'm not there!"

"Well, Mau Mau, if we do it when you're here, it's not really gossiping, is it?" June responded with a big grin on her face.

"Whatever! I'm ready now. Shall we go?" Maya smiled and grabbed her handbag.

They were picked up by the same young man who had picked them up a few days before. They once again shared the bus with the four older well-dressed ladies, and everyone greeted each other with genuine smiles.

At the restaurant, a happy Haci, who looked both freshly cut and shaved, greeted them. He gave them the same table as last time, but this evening he had decorated it with rose petals and neatly folded napkins. There was clearly more effort put into their table than the surrounding guests. A large sign with the word *Reserved* was placed on it as well.

The girls giggled and took pictures of the table, and once again they felt very VIP-like. "This is perfect, Maya," June whispered. "You flirt, and we all gain something from it."

While waiting for the food, they sat and chatted and sent greetings home to their families from their phones.

"Um, guys..." Cecilia suddenly interrupted with a confused look in her eyes. "Do any of you remember anything about a boat trip we might have booked?"

June and Maya looked at her incomprehensibly, while Charlotte looked like something was dawning on her.

"Now that you're mentioning it, I might remember something about us talking about a boat-trip the other day. During the storm. Because the bad weather really annoyed us... Have we seriously drunk-booked a boat-trip?" She laughed and shook her head with a sceptical look.

"Yes, I'm afraid so," Cecilia giggled, showing them a text correspondence with the destination manager, Mia-Maja. According to the conversation, they had booked four seats for the boat trip on Wednesday and had agreed to pay cash on the day.

"But, Wednesday... That's tomorrow!" June sighed and looked completely defeated. "I can't go on a boat trip tomorrow, when I look like this. I'm a freaking red shrimp!" she exclaimed, flailing her scorched arms.

"Then you can sit in the shade," Maya replied firmly. "What time are we leaving?"

"We will be picked up at half past nine at the hotel."

Charlotte looked at her watch. "So, I guess we should go back to the hotel before midnight tonight then, right?

"Yeah, that's fine by me," Cecilia replied, suppressing a yawn. "I'm kind of exhausted after all that alcohol yesterday and the beach trip today."

"It can also be *quite* tiresome to be non-stop slammed with messages from youngsters in heat," Charlotte added with a teasing look.

Maya and June looked questioningly at her.

"The guy from the beach. Cecilias new friend," Charlotte explained with a smirk.

214

"My God, did he write you?" Maya almost yelled, looking at Cecilia expectantly. "Do tell!"

Cecilia blushed and sighed loudly. "There is not much to say. He's been writing this afternoon and tonight, mainly about how delicious he thinks I am, that he's never met anyone like me, and that we need to meet for a drink." She rolled her eyes and looked kind of annoyed.

"Okay, and are you going to meet him?" June asked excitedly.

"No thanks, he's not my type at all!" Cecilia declined with a smile. "Besides, I'm pretty sure he's a bit of a player."

"And?" June has a mischievous smile on her face. "You're not going to marry this dude. You can just have sex with him and then get on with your life!"

"June, that's never going to happen!" Cecilia replied with an indignant look. "I could never be with someone I don't know, let alone someone like him. Just imagine what he is carrying around in terms of nasty diseases! I'm not like you, I can't just throw myself at anyone ..." As she finished the sentence, her voice dropped slightly.

June's smile had disappeared. "Cille-mouse,

215

of course, you are always in charge of your own decision. And only you get to choose which way you want to go with all this. But I would appreciate it if you just turned down the judgmental tone a notch regarding my lifestyle. The two of us are not the same person, and we do not live the same life. I am well aware that my life choices would not suit you. But shouldn't we be able to accommodate our differences in this circle of friends?" she asked while looking directly into her eyes.

Charlotte and Maya said nothing and pretended to be very preoccupied with their phones. It wasn't the first time Cecilia's box thinking clashed with June's very broad way of navigating the world. Although there had been a few more clashes on this holiday than they had experienced in years. But they also knew that these conversations were necessary to nip any tensions in the bud and were best handled without interference from others.

Cecilia had turned fiery red in the face and looked very uncomfortable. "June, I..." she began, looking at June with a hint of regret. "I'm sorry, June, I didn't mean it that way! I... I just felt pressured, and then... Then sometimes something stupid comes out..." she finished quietly, looking down at the table.

June reached across the table and took her

hands. "Cecilia, I know. Your claws come out when you feel cornered. And you have every right to feel the way you do. That being said, we are your friends, and there is no need for you to lash out at us like that." She smiles at her. "If our banter becomes too much, just say so. But preferably, without it being about how the rest of us are wrong, okay?"

Cecilia's eyes welled up, and she blinked a few times to get the tears away. "I'm really sorry, June. I don't think you're a bad, or wrong, person," she whispered while squeezing June's hands.

"Maybe not bad or wrong, but I live in a way that goes against everything you stand for," June replied understandingly. "I know you're having a bit of a hard time dealing with it. But you have to find a way to move passed it. Because my reality is what my reality is, and I'm not planning to change anything about it."

June shrugged, smiled and gave Cecilia's hands a squeeze before letting them go.

Cecilia sighed and relaxed her shoulders. "I hear you. I'll pull myself together, June-Bug, I promise," she said with a slight smile. She looked relieved when the food was served a moment later. "Oh, I am starving!" she exclaimed, a little too excitable, obviously to compensate for the slightly awkward atmosphere around the table.

The other three smiled and sent each other a quick glance. The conflict was over and everyone could feel comfortable again.

"Bon appétit and call me if you need anything," Haci said to Maya with a warm smile.

"We'll definitely do that," June replied in a teasingly tone, winking at Maya, who sent her a deathly glance back.

Charlotte raised her glass. "Cheers, ladies, and thank you for a wonderful holiday so far. Best entertainment in years!" she chuckled and took a sip of her wine. "Um, not bad at all, not bad at all... Let's try the food. My steak looks absolutely perfect!"

Chapter 23

When the alarm went off, Cecilia, for once, was still sound asleep. Hearing Charlotte in the shower, she snoozed the alarm, knowing she couldn't leave to use the bathroom just yet, anyway.

They had agreed to have breakfast an hour earlier today so they could be ready to be picked up at half past nine.

When the phone buzzed for the second time, she turned it off with a sigh and sat up with a pillow in her back. She could hear that the water had stopped running in the bathroom, so it would probably be available soon.

She checked her phone and sighed again. Fourteen messages from Gio last night! She rolled her eyes. The man was absolutely insane! Besides five noisy video recordings from various bars and nightclubs, he had sent nine messages asking if she was coming to town. The last message was an audio recording sent at five o'clock this morning, and she suspected that alcohol had been involved, because it was almost incomprehensible. She recognised only enough English to understand that he wanted her to come and meet him so she could go home with him.

She put down her phone without replying to the messages. It was simply too much! To her own surprise, she kind of liked that she got some attention, even if it was from someone like him. But this amount was far too pushy and far too overwhelming.

"Good morning. The bathroom is all yours now." Charlotte looked very fresh and immediately marched over and pulled the curtains. Daylight poured in, and Cecilia let out a complaining sound while covering her eyes.

Charlotte looked at her in surprise. "Are you okay? You usually never have a problem with sunlight."

"No, I'm just tired today and have only just woken up. But I'm getting up now, so it's fine." She squinted her eyes at the bright light.

"Uh, yeah, you do have dark circles under your eyes today," Charlotte nodded and thought for a few seconds. "Hey, I have brought the eye serum from our new product line with me. Just a moment. I'll get it for you."

Cecilia swung her legs out of bed and got up. Then she stretched, yawned, and smiled at the view. It's hard not to be happy when getting up to this, she thought to herself.

Charlotte tossed some small samples on her bed. "Here, try this. Just dab it on like an eye cream. Only under your eyes, and before your day cream, okay?" she smiled and pulled out her hairdryer.

Cecilia picked up the samples and went to the bathroom to get ready.

When she stood in front of the mirror a little later, she could see a distinct difference around her eyes. "It's almost a miracle cure, this eye serum, Charlotte, very impressive!" she smiled and began to get dressed.

"Yes, it's going to revolutionise the market," Charlotte replied with pride in her voice, sending her a smile. "You can truly see a transformation of the skin, Cille-mouse. You look so much fresher now. How are your burned feet doing today?"

Cecilia looked down. "Thankfully, they're feeling way better, but I really have to slather them in sunscreen and cover them up today," she said, tossing the sunscreen in her bag so she wouldn't forget it.

"Are you awake?" a low voice sounded outside.

Charlotte walked out onto their balcony and

found Maya's tired face lurking in.

"Yes, we are almost ready for breakfast. What about you?" Charlotte asked as she shook sand from her towel and folded it up.

"June stays home today. She's still very sunburned, so she just wants to take a day in the shade and get some sleep," Maya yawned and had obviously just woken up.

"We'll go down for breakfast in five minutes. Are you able to get ready that quickly?" Charlotte asked, looking tellingly at Maya's messy hair.

"Yeah, yeah, I'll just slap some clothes on. I can do the whole sunscreen-thing and packing afterwards," Maya replied, rubbing her eyes and yawning again. "Just go down. I'll be down in a couple of minutes," she added, before disappearing back into her room.

***

June had turned off her alarm and woke up on her own when it was way past ten. She had heard the others leave, but had quickly returned to dreamland afterwards.

Her skin felt very warm and when she looked in the mirror, she still had all kinds of shades of

222

red. Fortunately, it was better than yesterday, so the Aloe Vera cream Maya had forced her to apply last night, before going to bed, must have helped. However, she was still absolutely sure that she had made the right decision by staying home and give her skin a break from the sun.

Realising she couldn't make it down to breakfast in time, she boiled some water for a cup of coffee herself. She felt grateful for Charlotte's thoughtfulness in leaving the instant coffee on the kitchen table.

They still had some bread and cheese left in the fridge, so she could make herself a few sandwiches as well.

June went out onto the balcony and enjoyed the view and silence while eating her breakfast. She loved being on holiday with her friends, but breakfast in peace and quiet also had its charm. She smiled to herself. It wasn't often that was possible, so she had to enjoy it when the opportunity was there.

She took a long shower, applied sunscreen, and packed her things before heading down to the pool.

On the way down, she noticed that the door to the neighbouring room 406 was open. She looked in and could see a room similar to her own, just mirrored, like Charlotte's and Cecilia's.

There were piles of bed linen and towels lying on the floor, and an elderly Turkish lady was tidying up and cleaning. There was clearly no longer anyone living in there, as there were no private belongings to be seen.

The lady looked up when June looked in, and with a friendly smile said something in Turkish. June presumed it meant something like good morning or hello, so she just waved, smiled back and quickly moved on. She was a little upset that she would not be able to apologise for their loud behaver, to those who had stayed there a few days ago. But she couldn't do anything about it now.

It was another quiet day by the pool. The bar played pop music from the 80s at a low volume and again there were almost no guests to be seen.

Henning and Bjarne were sitting in the bar glaring at sports on TV as usual, but their respective wives were not to be seen.

The young couple lay across from her on separate sunbeds. The girl, who they had found out was called Lulu, had her arms crossed and looked demonstrative the other way. Thor had an equally dismissive body language and flipped frantically through a magazine with cars on the cover.

Okay, June thought with a wry smile. Trouble in paradise! This is going to be interesting to observe.

She chose a sunbed in a quiet corner. She put op two umbrellas so she could sit completely in the shade, reading her book.

As she sat down, another couple arrived and waved at her before lying down on a couple of chairs close to the edge of the pool. It was Gert and Nora, the elderly couple who had arrived at the same time as them.

I wonder what they've been, June speculated. They hadn't seen them at all since they had arrived.

For the next hour, she relaxed with her book and, at the same time, she had half an eye on Thor and Lulu.

After a while, when Thor hadn't given in to her sulking, Lulu had started sniffing loudly as she turned her back on him. Thor reacted to her sounds fairly quickly and got up with a guilty conscience painted all over his face.

"Lulu, baby, are you okay?" he gently asked while placing a hand on her shoulder.

Lulu shook off his hand and let out a dismissive sound as she sniffled on, still with her back to him.

He sighed and sat down on the edge of her sunbed. "Malou, we're on holiday and we're supposed to have a good time, right? So come on now, turn around," he pleaded while stroking her back gently.

Lulu reluctantly turned around and sent him a hurt look. June noticed the dry eyes and cheeks and shook her head at the fact that Thor was apparently completely blind to Lulu's games.

"You say it's supposed to be a good time. But it doesn't feel that way when you don't care about me or my feelings," Lulu replied in a dismissive tone and sat up with an angry movement. "You always put yourself first, and I'm just not okay with that, you know!" she added in a high-pitched voice. "I thought you liked me, but apparently you don't give a shit at all. Oh, how stupid am I for believing your words?" She sent Thor another wounded look and even managed to squeeze out a few tears this time.

Thor looked like someone who had been slapped in the face. "Lulu, baby, you know I'm absolutely crazy about you, and you know I can't stand it when you're sad. So please, stop saying things like that!" he exclaimed, pulling her close to him.

June could see Lulu's face over his shoulder and how it, in a split second, changed from upset to triumphant as Thor clearly gave up the fight. "You know what, my choice of lunch isn't that important anyway," he smiled. "If you'd rather we share a pizza, then I'll just wait with that cheeseburger I've been dreaming about all day for tomorrow or something. Okay, honey?"

He looked at her with a questioning look, and Lulu sent him her most endearing smile as she nodded. "Oh Thor, you're just the best boyfriend ever!" she answered while batting her eyes. Then she gave him a big wet kiss on the lips.

June could see the relief spread across Thor's face. The fight was over and they were on good terms again. They lay close together on Lulu's sunbed, whispering and kissing intensely.

June had observed it all from her sunbed, over the edge of her book. She found it quite interesting how Lulu wrapped Thor around her little finger. She blatantly used emotional blackmail to get her way. June, who had experienced this kind of thing in her childhood, could almost feel her skin crawl by the bare thought. This is such an unhealthy relationship, she thought, while shaking her head. Hopefully, they will become wiser with age. Hopefully, they would both learn not only how to speak up but also how to see through other people's bullshit and gaslighting. She knew from her own experience how much other people's manipulation could harm in the long run, and she would put her foot down immediately if anyone tried to mess with her, her family or friends.

June glanced again at Thor and Lulu, who had now hurriedly risen from the sunbed and quickly packed up their things. Lulu giggled with red cheeks, and Thor tried to hide the front of his tight swim shorts with his towel.

They walked close together and at high speed towards the hotel, where they disappeared through the doors by the reception.

June couldn't help but smile to herself. She could easily understand what it must feel like to be so turned on by another person all the time. She felt the same way about Bo. If only he had the same needs and desires as her, she would have deleted her Tinder profile immediately.

She pulled out her phone to send him a text. She discovered that the others had sent her some silly selfies and pictures of Cennet from the waterside. Maya had also recorded a sweet audio message that they missed her and that she would have loved to be on the boat with them. For a moment June felt a little sad not to be with the other three. Then she sighed and shrugged. She only had herself to blame for not being a grown up about putting on sunscreen. And this was the price to pay for that error of judgement. Besides, she thought with a shrug, it was actually not that bad to lie here with her book and relax completely for a few hours.

Early in the afternoon, June started to feel hungry, so she packed everything except her towel and walked up to the pool bar. She sat down at a table, and Mr Chippy immediately came running with a big smile and a menu.

She ordered a mixed pizza and a cold Efes beer, and scrolled through Facebook while waiting for her lunch.

When the food was being served, Gert and Nora came and sat down at the table next to hers.

"Hello there! Are you alone today?" Gert asked, sending her a big smile as he pulled out the chair for his wife.

"Yes, the others are on a boat trip. I should have been there too, but... Lobster party." June pointed to her red arms and shrugged smilingly. "So, I'm having a day in the shade instead."

"Well, that's probably not a bad idea," Nora nodded. "Do you have aloe vera with you? If not, just let us know. I never travel without it, and it's just amazing for sunburns," she kindly added while receiving a menu from Mr Chippy.

"Oh yeah. Maya, who I share a room with, has been covering me in it since yesterday. But thanks for the offer." June replied and put her phone back in her bag. "We haven't seen much of you two. Have you been away on a trip or in your room a lot?" she asked curiously.

"I can tell you this. We are *not* in our room much," Gert said with a weird look and a crooked smile. "The neighbours make a lot of noise."

June immediately felt embarrassed. "Wh... What number do you live in?" she stammered.

"402," Nora replied, giving Gert a little whack with the menu, "and it's not that bad, Gert. They're just in love. We were probably just like that when we were young and crisp," she laughed and winked at June. "Now we are only crisp and everything makes crackling sounds when we move," she added with a small laugh.

June felt relief flow through her and laughed loudly at Nora's joke.

"I don't quite agree with that, Nora," Gert

continued, shaking his hands dismissively. "I recognise some of the noise from ourselves way back, but I don't think we ever argued that much about everything." He grinned and sent Nora a mischievous look.

"Let me guess. You have Thor and Lulu as neighbours?" June asked with a giggle. "The young people who are either attached by the hip or arguing over small things?"

"Bingo! The girl drags him around the arena like a circus horse!"

"Gert! That wasn't very nice!" Nora exclaimed, with an indignation in her voice that didn't sound quite genuine.

"You can say what you want, my darling. But the kid is very good at taking orders. We have heard that... Over and over every night, and she's clearly happy with the effort," he added, a little lower and again with a cheeky look.

June nearly choked on her beer from laughing and had to wipe her face with a napkin.

"Gert! Stop, you big chatterbox! It's not nice to talk like that about others!" Nora exclaimed again. "I must apologise on behalf of my husband. He doesn't always think before he speaks."

Nora looked at her husband with a reprimanding look, but the warmth in her eyes was still there. Gert just laughed and accepted the two club sandwiches and the two Efes beers, Mr Chippy brought to the table at that moment.

"You don't have to apologise at all. I am not that sensitive, and I actually fully agree with your observations." June smiled and raised her glass at them. "I consider myself lucky not to live next to them. Because I've seen them here by the pool, and that alone tells me that you're not exaggerating."

"We'll be fine. Young people who are in love, we can manage. I'm feeling more blessed that we don't have to live near that horrible family with the children!" Gert said matter-of-factly.

"Gert! I'm telling you right now. Stop with the gossiping! It's really not nice to talk about others like that!" Nora put down her cutlery on the table with a clonk.

"Nora, I don't care! They are terrible! I'm usually very open about other people. But *this* family?! They don't care about other people at all!"

Nora sighed and reluctantly agreed with him. "Okay, that's true, but I also think that no one is happy in their family. Imagine having a life where you are never happy?"

Gert looked warmly at his wife. "You're a

good person, Nora, and you always make excuses for people. But these are just totally out of reach."

"Excuse me, but is it the family with the four kids, you're talking about?" June interjected.

Nora nodded.

"We have also seen them here by the pool. Terrible vibes around those parents, that's for sure. But they really just kept to themselves when we saw them. Have they made any trouble with anyone else?" June asked curiously.

"Yes, that's safe to say," Gert replied with a laugh, ignoring Nora's piercing look.

"But I haven't seen them since Monday. Are they still here?" June took a sip of her beer that was already getting a little lukewarm.

"No, they left last night after ten days here at the hotel." Nora replied. "I think many people were happy about that," she added with a small laugh.

Gert ate the last of his sandwich, moved his chair back a little and sat a little more relaxed.

"They lived in two rooms opposite each other on the third floor.

Every single day when they got up, they opened the room doors and let the kids run around in the hallway. Something that you might be able to tolerate if it wasn't at 7 in the morning! As if things weren't already annoying enough, their communication consisted solely of yelling to and at each other."

Gert took a sip of his beer and continued: "Last week there was also a younger couple living in the same floor. One morning, they kindly asked the family to turn down the volume, as they were still sleeping. This caused the dad to explode and behave threateningly towards them."

June stared at him in disbelief. "Seriously?"

Gert nodded. "Unfortunately, yes. Of course, they had hurried to slam the door shut, but the dad had been yelling and screaming and knocking on the door for a minute or so. It wasn't until his wife came out and screamed at him to get back there, that he stopped. The young couple had not dared to leave their room until it was quiet again and had immediately reported it to the reception. Alican had directly offered them a new room on a different floor and had helped them with both packing up and moving rooms."

"That's just insane!" June exclaimed, wide-eyed. "What happened then?"

Gert shook his head with disbelieve. "Alican

tried to talk to the family, but they hadn't opened their door when he knocked. He could clearly hear them in there. He had to slide a note under the door instead, asking them to respect the other guests and not to play and be noisy in the hallways."

"Did that help?" June asked.

"Yes, apparently. There were no more complaints, but there were also no other guests in their hallway either. So maybe that's why," Gert shrugged and smiled at Mr Chippy who had begun to clean their table.

"But the most disgusting thing happened yesterday," Gert continued after Mr Chippy had left again. "The wife and all the children were by the pool, and she was lying as usual with her book or her phone, letting the big kids take care of the little ones."

Nora mouth tightened. She was clearly not impressed with the parents' involvement in their own family.

Gert smiled almost imperceptibly and continued: "We were in the pool and suddenly we heard the little boy loudly proclaim that he was about to poo. His older sister told him to hold on while she rushed over to wake his mother up, so she could take over. The kid then shouted in a desperate voice that he couldn't hold it in and started pulling down his diaper. Mommy dearest was visibly annoyed by the disturbance and reacted very slowly. Because she took her sweet time, the kid started to... defecate *right* next to the pool." Gert had equal parts disgust and laughter in his voice.

"You are joking!" June was horrified.

"But that wasn't even the worst part," Gert continued. "The worst part was that the mother came over, clearly saw the boy's shit on the ground and then apparently decided to do nothing about it. She just ordered everyone to pack up, and then they rushed up to their room."

"I... I don't know what to say to that... I'm speechless!" June stammered.

"Well, listen to the end." Gert eagerly moved to the edge of his chair. "The poops stank was all over the pool and it was located pretty close to the water. If it came into contact with the water, the pool would have to be emptied and cleaned completely, okay? Really not a desired scenario for the hotel. So, we immediately told Alican, who furiously marched up to the room, where the mother was staying, and knocked on the door. She opened up this time, and he asked her if she was going to come down and clean it up. She promised to come down in a moment and then she closed the door in his face. He waited for about five minutes, but the lady, of course, did not show up. Poor Alican had no choice but to clean up the lady's mess. It goes without saying that the family remained unseen until they swiftly checked out and left in a hurry."

He leaned back with a big grin.

"How can people be so indifferent? I mean. Yes, kids have accidents, but then surely it's the adults' job to clean up after them." June shook her head and looked perplexed for a second. Then she raised her glass towards Gert and Nora. "Well, at least they're gone now, and the hotel is peaceful again. Let's drink on that!" She emptied her beer and signalled Mr Chippy to bring her the bill.

While June was paying, Gert and Nora told her that the reason they hadn't been at the hotel a lot actually had nothing to do with noisy neighbours. They were just always out hiking a lot when they travelled. They had become very fond of the areas national park, which was only a few hours' drive away from Cennet. Besides that, they had a long list of friends to visit as they had been coming to Cennet for many years.

Gert and Nora also asked for the bill. While all three of them were packing up, Thor and Lulu came back from their tête-à-tête and put their bags on the same two sunbeds as before.

237

They both had red cheeks and looked very relaxed and happy.

June sent Gert and Nora a telling look, and they all giggled.

June thanked them for a pleasant lunch, wished them a good day, and went back on her sunbed in the shade, with her book. She was already looking forward to telling the others about the drama at the hotel.

Chapter 24

Charlotte, Maya and Cecilia returned just after five, happy and again, well-tanned, on their noses.

June was sitting in her room with the balcony door open and a cold soft drink when she could hear them out in the hallway.

"June-Bug!" Maya happily exclaimed as she opened the door. "You missed out on an amazing trip!" She threw herself down next to June on the sofa.

Charlotte and Cecilia also entered the room and waved at her.

"Yeah, I could see from the pictures that you were enjoying yourselves. I look forward to hearing all about it later. And I've also picked up some gossip today," she added with a knowing smile.

"Hey guys, can we wait until later with the stories?" Cecilia interrupted while jumping up and down. "I really need to pee, and I also need a long bath." Charlotte immediately retrieved the key from her bag and dangled it in front of her. Cecilia grabbed it, ran out, and quickly opened the door into her own room.

Charlotte grinned. "Yes, she wasn't happy with the condition of the toilet on the ship. And to be honest, it wasn't super delicious. So, I think she must have held it in all the day."

"That's her choice, okay? She should have just done like I do. I swim away from others, and then I just pee in the ocean. You just have to move your legs at the same time, then no one notices," Maya laughed, while tellingly fluttering her legs in the air.

"Yeah, because it's really nice for others to feel a warm current out on the open sea." Charlotte rolled her eyes.

"I'm seriously not going to swim from now on if you're in, that's for sure!" June added with a wrinkle on her nose.

"Don't worry, I'll just warn you before I shoot off the yellow stream. And, speaking of urine. I'm going to go potty now." Maya laughed out loud and headed to the bathroom.

"Really, Maya?! That is disgusting ... The yellow stream..." Charlotte shook her head, but giggled loudly.

June looked at Charlotte resignedly. "I share a room with that one... Just try to let it sink in. Voluntarily! I don't quite know what's wrong with me since I've agreed to it..." she sighed and stretched her back.

Charlotte lit up in a smile. "Ha, you're right, June-Bug. She's your problem. I can just leave! So, see you at nine. Can you get the crazy person to book a table for us at the regular place?" she laughed and without waiting for an answer, she walked towards the door. As she made a hasty exit, she could hear the whooshing sound of June's rolled-up towel narrowly missing her and hitting the door behind her.

***

"She let her kid do what?! Seriously? Did she leave the shit by the pool without removing it again?" Cecilia, like the other two, was deeply disgusted by the story June had told them.

"Who the hell chooses to behave so aggressively towards other guests? I would have slapped him right across the face if it was me," Maya exclaimed defiantly and clenched her fist in front of her.

"Yes, honey, and then he probably would have wiped the floor with you," June laughed, and sipped her cocktail.

"Very possible, but at least I would have got one good punch in and I'm sure it would feel *so* good!" Maya raised her glass of Strawberry Daiquiri into the air. "Cheers to a wonderful

241

holiday, ladies! I love experiencing this crazy country with you, and *thank God* that this family has gone home!"

Maya met Haci's gaze across the restaurant. He stood by the bar and looked down at their table. When he saw them toasting, he raised his glass and sent her a big smile. His smile caused warmth to spread throughout her body, so she quickly focused on her friends instead.

"I'll probably call it a night soon, ladies," Cecilia said in a tired voice while trying to hide a yawn.

"Yes, I'm also beat today," Charlotte nodded, checking her phone. "It's also past midnight, so I'm ready when you are."

"No, come on, guys! I'm not tired at all! We can't go home yet," Maya exclaimed, looking desperately at the others. "Let's have a few more drinks, okay?"

"No can do, mon ami," Charlotte replied while waving at Haci so they could pay. "I'm flat as a pancake after all the fresh air, and I can already feel the drinks I've had."

Maya looked at June questioningly.

"Maya, I'm not completely unaffected by these strawberry thingies either. I am also voting to go home. Sorry, mouse," June said, looking apologetically at Maya.

"Seriously? I was just in the mood for more drinks tonight, and I'm not tired at all," Maya moaned and sighed loudly.

"But, Maya, you can just stay. You don't have to leave, because we are," Charlotte suggested, looking at her with a told smile.

"No, I have to go with you. I don't want to sit here alone and by myself. It's completely loser-like." Maya rolled her eyes at the bare thought.

Haci came to the table with their bill. "Are you already leaving?" he asked with a slightly disappointed tone, looking directly at Maya.

"Well, the girls are tired, so I guess we'll go back to the hotel," Maya replied in a tone that strongly indicated that it certainly wasn't her choice.

"Oh, perhaps you're not tired yet?" He looked happy. "Then stay. I'll keep an eye on you, and I'll also make sure you get home safely later." He looked questioningly at the others.

"It's okay with us, but only if you *promise* to get her home safely!" June said, looking at him fiercely.

"Of course!" He threw out his arms with a big smile.

"Hello! I'm sitting right here, friends. Do I not have a say in this?" Maya protested. "It's very simple, everyone. I will not to sit here alone and look like an idiot, so let's just leave!"

"No, no, you can just sit with some of our regular customers. Some really lovely ladies who also won't go home until later. It's really no problem at all!" Haci quickly pointed to a table on the opposite side of the restaurant. It was the four women with whom they had shared pickup service a few times.

"Haci, I can't just sit down at somebody else's table. Who says they even want me there?"

Maya got up. "Come on, let's just go, girls."

"Now hold on a minute, okay?" Haci pleaded, hurrying over to the table with the women and talked to them in a low voice. They immediately smiled and turned around to look at Maya. "Please come and sit with us. You are most welcome at our table!" one of them called out. She was wearing big earrings and had a loud laugh.

"See, no problem at all." Haci looked at Maya expectantly.

"I'm not sure..." Maya hesitated and looked at her friends. "What should I do here?"

"Maya, you want more drinks, and you

clearly want to get to know prince Charming a little more. So, what are you waiting for?" June smiled, and both Charlotte and Cecilia nodded agreeingly.

"Okay, but what about the room key and so on? How do I get in later?" She walked them to the stairs leading down to the street.

"Call me on my phone when you get home. Then I'll open for you," June replied with a smile and gave her a little push. "Maya, go. Have fun and tell us everything tomorrow, okay?"

"Okay... Then sleep well and see you tomorrow!" she smiled a little nervously while waving goodbye to her friends as they entered the waiting minibus.

"Come, come," Haci's eager voice came from behind her.

He took her hand and led her to the table with the four women. "This is Anna, Ingrid, Julia and Jaqueline. We have known each other for many years. Ladies, this is my good friend Maya. It's her first time in Turkey, so be nice to her," he winked at them as he placed a chair at the end of their table and told Maya to sit down.

"I'll just get you a drink, on the house, okay?" he whispered in her ear while letting his hand rest on her neck for a moment. The heat from his hand made her stomach turn around. In a good way.

He walked up to the bar, leaving her alone with the four strangers. All of them looked at her curiously.

"Hiya everyone. I think we've shared a bus a few times, haven't we?" Maya asked to break the ice.

"Yes, that's right!" The lady with the dark hair, who Haci had presented as Jaqueline, smiled at her. "Welcome to our table!"

"So, where are you from?" asked the woman with the earrings and laughter, who was apparently named Anna.

"I'm from Denmark. Just outside Copenhagen, if you know where that is?" Maya replied, looking around at them questioningly.

All four ladies looked at each other, and then started laughing. "Wh... What's going on?" Maya asked, confused.

"*Well*," Anna replied with a big smile. "What a coincidence. So do I!"

It took Maya a moment to understand that the lady spoke Danish to her.

"Really? What a small world! I had no idea you were Danish. I've only heard you speak

English, so I assumed you were from somewhere in the UK," Maya exclaimed, dumbfounded.

"We're a well-assorted group here, so we usually speak English together so everyone understands everyone." She pointed around. "Jaqueline is from France, Ingrid is from Sweden, Julia is from England and I am from Denmark. We have known each other for more than... Thirty years, I think."

Ingrid, who understood her Danish, nodded in agreement and explained in English to the others what Anna had said.

"That is awesome! Did you meet each other here in Turkey?" Maya asked eagerly and send Haci a big smile when he returned with another Strawberry Daiquiri.

"Yes, we have all travelled with our spouses in the past and then over the years, we have developed a close friendship." Anna replied with a big smile.

"So are your husbands here as well?" Maya sipped her drink.

"Well, not quite," Anna smiled. "I got divorced many years ago and have been single since then. I still come here several times a year to see my friends, and my arthritis benefits from

247

the heat as well."

She pointed to the slim woman from Sweden, whose hair had only a few grey streaks in the natural blonde colour. "Ingrid's husband Olav is Norwegian, and they live in Oslo. But he has problems walking without aid, so she mostly travels without him." Ingrid nodded and shrugged in a there-is-nothing-to-do-about-it kind of way.

"Jaqueline was married to a Belgian, Yves, and she lives here permanently," Anna continued, pointing to the dark-haired Jaqueline, who raised her glass and toasted in Turkish. "He sadly passed away five years ago, and he was the love of her life. So now she spends all her time with friends and volunteer work around town."

"And then we have Julia." Julia smiled kindly and raised her glass at Maya. "She was previously married to an English man, but she got divorced about fifteen years ago when she fell for a Turkish man, Onur. She and Onur got married a few years later, but unfortunately Onur died in a car accident a few months after the wedding." She lowered her voice. "Unfortunately, he had a bad habit of drinking and driving at the same time. It cost him his life and broke Julia's heart. Since then, she has chosen to only have lovers and has given up on everything love-related," she finished, sending Maya a knowing smile.

Maya's drink went down the wrong pipe, and she reach for a paper napkin while coughing loudly. "Okay, so you can just do that or what?" she stammered, not really sure herself what she meant by that.

"Yes, yes, off course," Anna exclaimed and quickly translated into English to the others what they were talking about. All four ladies let out a loud laugh and nodded in agreement.

"For example, you and Haci," Anna continued in Danish, winking at Maya.

"What do you mean? Nothing is going on with Haci!" Maya felt her cheeks blush and looked around to make sure he hadn't heard them. To her relief, he was standing at the other end of the restaurant, talking to some other customers.

"Well, I'm sorry, my mistake, then. You could have fooled me, though," Anna winked again and send her a cheeky smile.

"Are you married, Maya? Or in relationships with someone back home in Denmark? Anna asked, looking at her curiously.

"No, I'm single," Maya admitted. She was not sure how she felt about this conversation.

"Okay, so you're single, you're an attractive woman, and Haci is, undoubtfully, into you. I'm pretty sure that you think he's cute, too. So why not?" Anna asked curiously.

"Um, why not what?"

"*Hanky Panky*!" Anna yelled a little too loud, and the ladies at the table began cackling. "They also call it Jiggy-Jiggy in this country, but it means the same," she added a little quieter.

For the second time, Maya almost choked on her drink and had to ask for a new napkin.

Anna continued to speak, unaffected by Maya's coughing.

"Well, just in case you choose to be with him or someone else, allow me to offer some advice. Just so you don't make the same mistakes that many others have made... Yes, that includes some of us around this table."

Ingrid translated continuously, and the ladies giggled like teenagers.

"Well, I'm always ready for some good advice," Maya replied, and decided to just surrender to the madness that was apparently the norm on this holiday.

"Okay, my first piece of advice is to figure out exactly what you want," Anna started, looking visibly excited to pass on her knowledge.

"What I want?" Maya was confused again.

"Yes, what do you want? Do you just want to have sex or do you want *good* sex?" She looked at Maya expectantly.

"Well, then I think maybe I'm going with good sex," Maya giggled, shaking her head in disbelief.

"Good answer! No woman should ever settle for mediocre sex," Anna replied firmly, and the other ladies loudly agreed with her when they had her words translated by Ingrid. "Our motto is this: We don't take off our clothes unless we can be sure that the sex is at least an 8 out of 10s scale!" she added with a big grin.

Maya burst out laughing and could almost imaging that slogan on a t-shirt.

Anna continued: "If you're going to have good sex, then you have to learn to be selective, okay? You have to be able to see through superficial beauty and all the bullshit-talk many men uses when they are hunting for women."

Maya giggled again.

She had seriously never met women like this. These ladies, in their late sixties, had a way of speaking that was refreshingly blunt. Her mother's reaction would have been nothing short of outrage if she had crossed paths with them.

"It's received, loud and clear. Any suggestions on what to look out for? Or what I absolutely should run away from?"

"Of course I have!" Anna exclaimed proudly.

Haci came to the table to see what was going on. They quickly ordered another round of blended drinks, so he was gone for a while. Maya *had to* hear this out!

"Well, where were we... Okay, when choosing a holiday flirt, there are typically two types here in Cennet. Honestly, this probably also applies to other destinations, but this is the city we have the most experience with."

Maya just nodded and listened carefully so that she could repeat the story as correctly as possible to the others tomorrow.

Anna continued: "First type, and this one is unfortunately the most common one, is the *'Special Price For You'*-type. Avoid this kind at any cost!"

"Okay, and how do I recognise him?"

Anna looked at her thoughtfully. "It *can* be a little tricky. He will typically try to shower you with a lot of compliments. He will most likely be a really nice and charming guy, and he can make you feel like the *most* amazing woman in the world in no time. There are many reasons why this type of man is a waste of your time, but I can list the most important ones."

She counted on her fingers while talking: "It's guaranteed that he will oversell his 'goods', he will never deliver what you have been promised, he will always have a disappointingly short 'life-span' and last, but not least, in a worst-case scenario, he can cost you a trip to the doctor!"

"Okay, that really doesn't sound very attractive. So, what is the second type like?" Maya dabbed her eyes with a napkin that was now soaking wet.

Anna leaned slightly toward Maya. "The opposite type is the complete opposite, and unfortunately there are not many of them. You can usually recognise them for being true gentlemen and respectful. They don't try to change your mind by force when you've said no to something, and they would never ask for drinks or money from you. But," she added with a clever smile, "all this is not enough. You also need to make sure it's a man who's either been married or been in a long-term relationship."

Maya looked at her, confused. "Why is that?"

Anna exchanged knowing glances with the ladies around the table, who all nodded in unison and giggled.

She almost whispered to Maya. "Because then he is 'trained' properly and knows what a woman like. In this group of friends, we call this type *'Turkish Delight'*, and he is the closest you get to a good-sex-guarantee in Cennet!" she finished triumphantly while laughter erupted again around the table.

"Oh my God, this is fantastic," Maya stuttered. "I don't know if it will become relevant at some point, but thanks for the advice, anyway!"

At that moment, Haci came to the table with their drinks. He, like everyone else in the restaurant, had heard their many fits of laughter and therefore asked curiously what they were laughing at.

"Nothing, my friend," Anna replied in her most innocent voice. "I just told sweet Maya here about Turkish Delight, that's all," she added, making everyone around the table laugh uncontrollably again.

"Okay?" Haci looked very confused.

"Haci, my dear. Can you get us a round of tequila shots? Then you're an absolute star!"

254

Anna smiled at him, while strongly indicating that she would not tell him anything.

Haci hurried to take the order and then walked away from the table, shaking his head.

When they finally left the restaurant, it was almost four in the morning. For the last hour, it had been just their table, Haci, and the chef Ramazan.

It had been a really lovely night for all of them. The restaurant had played music at a low volume, they had talked and laughed, and they had many, many drinks. But not Haci. He had only had one or two, as he had promised to get Maya home in one piece.

The young guy in the minibus had gone home hours ago, so Haci called a taxi for the four cackling women who were still having a party. It had been like herding cats to get all of them to walk in the same direction simultaneously. But finally, Haci had succeeded, and with much noise and laughter, the taxi drove off with the fabulous four.

"What about me?" Maya asked, and was a little confused when Haci asked the driver to only drive the ladies home.

"You are my personal responsibility," Haci replied, sending her a big smile. "Come with me,

I'll drive you home myself." He grabbed her hand and led her to the left of the restaurant, where there was a narrow passage to the street behind.

Along the wall facing the neighbouring restaurant stood a row of open and very smelly bins. Three scooters were parked next to them.

Haci walked up to the first one, got on it, and told Maya to sit behind him.

Maya looked at him sceptically. "So... Where are you hiding the helmets?" she asked with a slightly slurred voice. It was a challenge for her even to make her eyes stay focused.

Haci laughed. "Maya, we don't need helmets. We will be at your hotel in five minutes. It's not necessary."

"Hmm, I'm not *quite* sure that's how it works..." She looked at him sceptically.

"Beautiful woman, I promise to drive carefully and slowly, okay? You can just hold on to me really tight all the way," he added with a cheeky smile.

Maya rolled her eyes and trudged over to him. With some difficulty, she sat up behind him. "I'm only doing this because I trust you, and I'm both drunk and tired, and I miss my bed." She slapped him on the arm when she noticed he laughed at her. "Hey, don't laugh at me! It's not funny!" She tried to sound annoyed, but her words struggled to come out of her mouth in the right way, and she giggled at herself.

"*Whatever*... Just drive me home," she sighed and held on to Haci so tightly that he could hardly breathe.

Chapter 25

Charlotte lay for a moment with her eyes closed, trying to remember the dream she had just before she woke up. She could no longer remember the details, but it had been something about everyone around her disappearing into thin air.

She could still feel the knot in her stomach from being left alone. As she rubbed her eyes, she also discovered that her cheeks were wet with tears.

Resignedly shaking her head, she reached for her phone, seeking a dose of reality. Snap out of it! It's just your subconscious that cleaned up something!

Kenneth had sent her a video a moment ago, so she got up and tiptoed out of the bedroom without waking Cecilia. She put the kettle on and played the video while the water was boiling. It was filmed during dinner last night, where Kenneth and the kids proudly showed that they had made homemade lasagna and made a lovely table. It ended with them waving to her, while shouting that they were looking forward to her return in a few days.

She watched the video four times, and each time their smiling faces made her miss them even more.

When the coffee was done, she sat on the balcony, enjoying the quiet morning and the sounds of the city waking up.

Her mind kept circling back to Kenneth, and with each thought, a wave of nausea crashed over her, reminding her of the pain she may have caused him.

Charlotte hurried to push the feeling away again. She knew it was almost time to put the cards on the table, but she honestly didn't know how to do it. She had almost confided in her friends on Monday when they had had been drinking and June had revealed her crazy secret. But the atmosphere had been so good afterwards that she got cold feet and didn't go through with it.

Charlotte emptied her cup and, with a thoughtful look on her face, she went inside to make another cup of coffee.

She suddenly remembered an incident in the kids' kindergarten when the girls were little. At that time, she was travelling a lot with her work. Something she had always loved, and it had done wonders for her career. On that particular day, she and Kenneth had picked up the girls together, something that happened very rarely.

Kenneth had overheard a conversation between Charlotte and the extremely harsh kindergarten leader, Vigga.

Vigga had informed Charlotte that she could see in the system that Charlotte was not the one to pick up her kids the following week. And she was wondering if this meant that Charlotte once again prioritised her work over her children.

With a sharp voice and a condescending look, Vigga had added, that Charlotte really should take in to account that children of that age were very sensitive. And that perhaps she should think about whether this focus on her own needs was actually a good idea?

Kenneth's usual friendly smile had disappeared in a heartbeat, and he had coldly asked Vigga if she by that meant that *he* couldn't take good enough care of *their* children?

Vigga's words stumbled out in a fidgety, stammering manner as she insisted that was not at all what she meant.

Kenneth had then asked her if their children were showing any signs of not functioning well? Because then someone had forgotten to tell him!

Vigga had quickly denied, and even added that they were well-functioning and well-behaved children. With a cautious smile and a dismissive hand gesture, she had tried to end the conversation with that.

Kenneth had no intention of letting her off the hook that easily, and had asked her straight up what she meant then. Since she found it necessary to comment on the fact that Charlotte was not always in charge of the pickup. And that if this, in fact, was a genuine concern, why no one had ever said anything when it was *him* who couldn't pick up? Vigga's face turned red with embarrassment as she shook her head, unable to muster a response.

In a sharp tone, Kenneth made it clear that he only accepted written messages and comments about their children from now on.

He emphasised that any further unfounded complaints about him, Charlotte, or their children would lead to him file a formal complaint questioning her leadership, her professional abilities and her as a person.

Charlotte had never seen him so angry before, and she had been both surprised and wildly turned on by it.

Kenneth himself had been a little embarrassed afterwards, as he did not usually speak like that to other people. But he had reacted to someone attacking his family, and he *was* genuinely angry at Vigga's blunt remarks, which were clearly more about her own personal beliefs than real observations about their children.

In reality, their children were used to Charlotte travelling with her work, and Kenneth had always been good at covering as both mom and dad when she was away. That didn't mean she didn't care about her family. She was just well aware that she was both a better mother, a better wife, and a better person if she could also have something that was only hers. Incidentally, Kenneth was just as competent as she was to take care of their family.

Charlotte had been extremely proud of her husband that day, even though he had been very harsh in his tone towards Vigga. He really stood up for her and for their family. Therefore, she knew she could share everything with him. She also knew she would soon have to pull herself together and talk with him about the current situation. "Sometimes it's just not that simple," she muttered to herself.

She drank the last of her coffee and relaxed while looking at Cennet. The city was getting more and more lively as time got closer to eight. She could hear Cecilia's alarm beeping and being muted. However, it didn't sound like she was getting up, so she probably snoozed.

A worried expression flickered across Charlottes face.

Cecilia could be very pedantic. That was not a secret. Through all the years of friendship, the others more relaxed manner had made her better at coping with attention, noise, and their occasionally childish behaviour. She would usually just roll her eyes at them, and that was it.

But something was off with her now. It wasn't all the time, but there had been some episodes that registered on Charlottes radar. For example, she seemed more disapproving than she normally was. It almost felt like she didn't have the energy to be inclusive or overbearing with other people.

Charlotte had noticed that, out of nowhere, Cecilia's eyes would well up, causing her to worry and ask if she was alright. Cecilia had just smiled and explained that her hay fever was acting up, making her eyes water. A few times, June had looked at Charlotte strangely when Cecilia had been particularly pedantic, especially towards her. The knowing glances they exchanged indicated that they were both thinking the same.

But when Cecilia didn't say something, it was kind of difficult to do anything.

She could hear Cecilia's alarm go off again. This time, Charlotte could hear her turning off the alarm and after that, the sound of her footsteps as she dashed off to the bathroom.

Charlotte got up and went inside to put more water over.

They just had to wait for Cecilia to open up. In the meantime, she could only help her by making sure that she started the day with a pleasant cup of coffee.

Chapter 26

"Hey, are you done yet? I'm about to pee in my pants!" A voice came from far away, along with some loud knocking sounds.

Maya grunted with her eyes closed. Her body ached, and she felt disoriented and dizzy.

As she came to life, she noticed she wasn't in her bed. The next thing she noticed was, that the floor below her was cold and that she was hanging on to something hard.

She opened one eye ajar. The light was bright, and a stabbing pain ran through her head. Oh God, that was a mistake, she thought, and hurried to close her eye again. She took a deep breath through her nose and instantly regretted it.

Oh, good God! Toilet smell. Right up the nose! She could feel the nausea rolling in her stomach and in her mouth, the saliva ran. With great effort, she lifted her head from the uncomfortable toilet seat, only to have her stomach revolt and expel its contents in the same direction they had entered.

"Hey, *Drunk-Betty*, if you're dead, could you please just roll aside, so I can come in?" June's voice sounded again from the other side of the bathroom door.

Maya grunted and wiped her mouth with some toilet paper. Then she cautiously got up and for a moment she had to lean on the edge of the sink with her eyes closed, as her internal organs felt like they were swimming around in a rough sea.

"Two seconds, then it's available," she muttered with a hoarse voice, turning on the tap. She splashed ice-cold water on her face and for a moment felt almost alive again. But only for a few seconds. Then the cooling sensation disappeared and she could feel her inside burning and stomach rotating again.

She glanced in the mirror and grimaced. "Jesus Christ," she whispered, rolling her eyes. This caused her headache to explode and she let out a low whaling sound. She was only wearing panties and bra and clearly hadn't cleaned off her makeup from last night. "Great. I look like a raccoon on crack, and with a breath that could undoubtedly cause plants to wither. In the neighbouring city," she mumbled and wrinkled her nose. She grabbed her toothbrush and slowly started brushing her teeth.

She managed to unlock the door at the same time. It was quickly opened ajar, and a bottle of water was handed to her. "Here, you'll probably benefit from drinking this. I have also found some Aspirin. They're on your bedside table." June giggled. She didn't even try to hide her enjoyment.

"Thank you," Maya whispered, and with some difficulty unscrewed the lid off the water bottle and took a sip. Then she fully opened the door and slowly sauntered out of the bathroom.

"Bloody hell!" June exclaimed and laughed even more. "You look like something Freddy has dragged in!"

Maya looked at her with a scowl. "*Shut it*, June. I feel worse than I look, and I can't handle anything right now!" she complained. "What time is it?"

"It's almost half past nine. The rest of us are going down for breakfast. Do you want to come along or ...?" June asked while looking up and down at her doubtfully.

"Oh my God, no. Food... I can't do anything with food right now. I feel like puking just thinking about it," Maya moaned and walked towards the bedroom. "I just need to sleep some more, so I can feel better."

"Okay, no problem," June chuckled. "We're just going to be by the pool today anyway, so come down when you're alive again. We'll bring your towel and save you a sunbed."

"Fino bandino, good night," Maya mumbled as she quickly swallowed the pills June had laid out for her. Then she lay down in her bed with the sheet over her head and fell asleep again.

***

"Is she awake up there?" Charlotte asked during breakfast.

"Hmm, difficult to say. She was up briefly, but went back to bed again... Or, again and again. I'm not sure she even made it to bed last night, or if she went straight out to sing into the big white microphone," June replied and shrugged.

"What do you mean?" Cecilia looked a little confused.

"Well, she came home at... I think it was almost half past four. More than half-baked and in an excellent mood." June took a bite of her toast with jam. "Uhm, you have to taste this homemade jam with cherries. It's really delicious!" she smacked her lips with pleasure and nodded appreciatively.

"And she was talking about the ladies and something about Turkish Delight, I didn't understand. I think she had also been driven home by Haci on a scooter," she continued, taking a sip of coffee. "So, I told her to park the storytelling until today, when I'm actually awake," she laughed.

"Okay, it sounds like she had a really nice night then," Charlotte said and started slicing a tomato.

"Yes, it sounded like it, and apparently also with many drinks. Because when I woke up, her bed was untouched, and she didn't answer when I called. It wasn't until I tried to get on the potty that I realised where she was." June giggled. "I helped her back to life just long enough to send her back to bed, so I could pee."

"It's not a good idea to get so drunk when she's alone." Cecilia sounded worried.

"But she wasn't alone, Mammi. She was with Haci and those ladies," Charlotte laughed and winked at her.

"Yeah, I know, but still. I just hope she's okay."

"Cille-mouse, she's okay. She just has a gigantic hangover because she forgot that she's not twenty-five anymore. Or maybe she just preferred to sleep on the toilet last night. Who knows?" June joked. "We'll probably get that cleared up later. She'll come down when she wakes up."

**

Maya woke up with a startle. Her dreams had been a mess that made little sense. It had felt like being trapped inside a rotating kaleidoscope.

She lay completely still, trying to reconnect with her body in stages. There was no way in hell she dared to *just* get up. That, she knew from experience, would be a terrible strategy.

The headache was still there, but it was not as sharp as before. She slowly turned over on her back. For a few seconds, all organs felt as if they were liquid and therefore splashing around inside her. But a moment later, they calmed down.

Her mouth was insanely dry, so she lifted herself up a little, reached for her water bottle, and took a sip. She let the now lukewarm water wash around in her mouth and sank it.

Her stomach began to growl, and she started to feel a little hungry. Maya smiled with relieve. It was always a good sign that she was craving food.

She looked for her phone on the nightstand,

but it wasn't there. She sighed resignedly. "Well, then there's no way around it. The ultimate test. I need to get up," she mumbled to herself.

She slowly swung her legs over the edge of the bed and sat for a moment with her eyes closed while her insides fell back into place.

Then she slowly opened her eyes and looked down at the floor. Out of the corner of her eye, she noticed that a large bruise was forming on her knee. She gently pressed on it and flinched. "What the hell have I been doing?" she sighed and carefully got up on her feet.

She flinched again, when the headache suddenly exploded like a burning metal band tightened around her head. She closed her eyes and rubbed her temples until the pain went away.

Maya gently opened her eyes again and walked slowly into the living room with her water bottle in her hand. She couldn't immediately see her phone lying around, so she checked her bag from the night before, and sure enough. There it was.

She sat down heavily on the couch with her eyes closed and slowly exhaled. She tried to remember what had happened the night before. She giggled at the thought of the older ladies' advice and felt slightly embarrassed by her own behaviour on her way back to the hotel.

She remembered herself screaming, *'Born to be wild!'* repeatedly into Haci's ear all the way up the mountain. At one point, she had also been on the verge of falling off because she forgot to hold on. When they reached the hotel, he had pulled her in close and had in a low voice said that she was amazing.

She had cheekily agreed with him, and he had just laughed out loud at her drunk confidence.

He had then, with a more serious expression on his face, asked if he could kiss her, and she had whispered yes. His lips were so soft, and his kiss almost made her legs turn to jelly. They were both breathing a little faster when he slowly let go of her.

"Will I see you tomorrow?" he had asked with a soft voice.

"Yes, probably," she had replied with flushed cheeks, trying her best to appear more sober than she was.

He had waited until she had reached the reception area before he left. She had waved at him as he drove away in the dark - and then she had stumbled up the stairs and hurt her knee. She remembered now. Maya glanced at the bruise again and shook her head in dissatisfaction over her own clumsiness.

On the way up to the elevator, she had called June, who had answered fairly fast, and she had opened the door for Maya with her eyes almost closed.

Suddenly, Maya remembered something more. She quickly checked her Messenger and sure enough. About half past four Haci had sent her a message saying goodnight, that he had enjoyed their kiss and that he was looking forward to seeing her again.

She could see that she hadn't answered him. It had probably been around at the same time, her stomach started to turn around and the world was spinning. She must have thrown her phone in her bag instead of taking it with her when she had run to the toilet to puke. She also vaguely remembered struggling to get her dress off in the small bathroom. She looked around. The dress hung on a chair at the dining table. June must have picked it up for her.

She looked at the time. Shit, it was almost half past one!

It might be about time, she pulled herself together and got her makeup cleaned off. She should also remember to write back to Haci and then she would meet the others by the pool.

Chapter 27

"Bloody hell! Looks like someone has finally risen from the dead!" June hollered, as Maya dragged herself across the pool area about fifteen minutes later.

She was wearing sunglasses and her hair was up in a messy bun. Her smudged makeup was removed, and she had taken a quick shower. However, everyone could still clearly see that this was a hangover-stricken person.

"Sshhh, why are you shouting so loud?" Maya whispered to June, scowling sourly at Thor and Lulu, who laughed while playing with a football in the pool.

"Okay, maybe someone should have slept another hour on the other side?" Charlotte suggested with raised eyebrows.

"Are you okay? Is there anything you need?" Cecilia asked, looking at Maya worriedly.

Maya tossed her bag on the ground next to the sunbed, the others had kindly put her towel on, and sat down with a grunt. "Yeah, I'm okay. I'm just tired and have a headache and I'm getting hungry," she sighed.

"The rest of us already had lunch, but can we order something for you? Hey, let me pick up a menu for you," Cecilia said helpfully and hurried up to the bar.

"It's good that we have Mammi with us, huh? She always takes such good care of us," June whispered, and smiled at Cecilia, who looked like she was ordered something from Mr Chippy.

"Yes, she's gold," Charlotte nodded, while taking a sip from her water bottle.

Cecilia returned from the bar. "Here's a menu, and I've provided some cold to drink for all of us". In her hands was a tray with four ice-cold Cola Lights and four pink straws, which she placed on one of the small tables.

"Cecilia, I don't think you realise how much I love you right now!" Maya whispered. She immediately grabbed a can and almost inhaled all of its content through the straw. "Oh my God! It's better than sex... At least as I remember it..."

"Okay, so we're guessing that nothing happened yesterday? I'm just saying that this colourful bruise on your knee could suggest otherwise!" Charlotte looked at her with a teasing look.

"No, no, he was a total gentleman and drove me home as he had promised you. The knee has nothing to do with him, and everything to do with me and my inability to climb stairs while intoxicated," Maya replied with a grimace.

"So, nothing happened at all?" June used a tone of voice that indicated that she didn't quite believe her.

"Well... Nothing big, anyway," Maya tried to avoid it with an innocent look.

"Spill it!" June laughed and pointed at her. "You mumbled something when you came home last night. Something about Haci and his scooter, and also something about a kiss. So don't come here with your bullshit. What happened?"

"Okay, we kissed, but that was it!" Maya quickly replied, while rolling her eyes over the others' teasing hoots. She began studying the menu again.

"Okay, but is he a good kisser, then?" Charlotte asked curiously.

"Yes, he's an excellent kisser. Now, can I please get some peace to choose some food? I'll tell you all in a moment. I just have to get something in my belly so I don't hurl again."

"Okay, very nice mental picture, Maya." Cecilia wrinkled her nose.

"Just be happy that you didn't see her when

she almost came crawling out of the bathroom this morning, Cille-mouse," June replied dryly. "It was such a horrifying vision that I would actually *prefer* to see her vomit here by the pool instead!"

"Yes, yes, I wasn't my usual charming self, I'll admit that," Maya agreed with a loud laugh. "But just hand me a cheeseburger with chips and I'll be all right again!"

While Maya ate her food, she told the others about her night out.

"Okay, let me get this straight... These ladies still have lovers when they're here?" Cecilia looked puzzled. "Even if they're *that* old?!"

"Cecilia, your downstairs regions don't fall off because your birth certificate has a specific number," June took a sip of her soda. "Shit, it's already lukewarm. Does anyone else wants more soda? I'm heading up to Mr Chippy," she asked the others. Both Cecilia and Charlotte declined, but asked for water instead.

"Yes please, just keep it coming," Maya burped, slapping her stomach lightly. "Ah, there's nothing like Cola, fat and salt to recover on," She leaned back against the backrest of the sunbed with a satisfied look on her face.

"But very interesting theory about the two

types of men here. I wonder which one Haci is?" Charlotte continued and looked a little teasingly at Maya.

"He must be in the right category, right," Cecilia promptly replied. "He's a gentleman, sweet, and well-mannered, *and* he's behaved nicely towards you, hasn't he?"

"Absolutely perfect behaviour, at all times," Maya nodded. "There must be something correct about the ladies' theory. Just look at Gio from the beach. He has not once asked you what you want. He has just assumed that you were interested in him, and on that note. Is he still contacting you?"

"Yes, he still writes every day, and I answer briefly." Cecilia looked down at her hands.

"Why don't you just not answer him if you are not interested in him, anyway?" June, who had just come back from the pool bar, interjected. "You don't owe him anything."

Cecilia shrugged. "I don't know... Maybe I find it a little rude not to answer?"

"Cecilia, you are never obliged to answer anyone if you don't want to, and right here you have a very good reason. You didn't ask for the contact!" Charlotte said with a firm voice.

"No, I know. But it's okay. He's harmless..." Cecilia looked over at Maya, trying to change the subject. "So, have you made any plans with Haci, then?"

"No, not yet. When we said goodnight, we just said see you," Maya replied. Then she put her hands on her belly. She made a grimace and quickly sat up. "I'm sorry guys, but I think I have to leave you now. My stomach apparently doesn't agree with my recovery technique."

She stood up rapidly and suddenly started sweating heavily as well.

June quickly retrieved the key from her bag. "Here, if you want to go to the room?"

"Nope, I won't make in time!" Maya exclaimed. With her buttocks clenched hard, she was half-running towards the stairs leading up to the pool's toilet and shower.

Quite some time went by before Maya, with a relieved expression on her face, came walking down the stairs towards the sunbeds.

"Whew, that was way too close to disaster," she laughed and sat down on her sunbed. "The moment I sat down, my butt literally created a nuclear explosion!"

"Why do you always have to be so explicit with your toilet habits?" Cecilia sighed. "'s like, all I hear about on this holiday is everybody's faeces, stomach problems and accompanying smells."

"Then you might want to consider shifting your focus, because we have talked about many other things. Today, for example, we've talked about both puke *and* retirement sex!" Maya teased. Cecilia shook her head resignedly, when Charlotte and June started laughing.

"But if you want a topic change, I have a good story for you. I took it with me back from the toilet, just for you!" Maya added in a slightly lower voice and giggled.

"Only you can get spontaneously diarrhoea, be gone for twenty minutes, and then come back with a story," Cecilia sighed. "But okay, let's hear it."

"Okay, I come out of the bathroom and, first of all, I'm relieved that no one is waiting in line. Because, holy cow, that was bad... I think I must have had a dead animal in my stomach, judging from the smell!" she smirked and looked teasingly at Cecilia.

Cecilia rolled her eyes again, but said nothing. Charlotte and June giggled. "Okay, do you remember that night, when we talked about how Henning and Bjarne can be so tanned when all they do is sitting in the shade at the bar?"

The girls nodded. This had been a mystery

that had come up during dinner the other day, and neither of them had had a logical explanation.

"Okay, so just before, when I left the toilet, I glanced into the shower. You know, the one next to the toilet? Bjarne was there. With a two-litre cola bottle. That he was freaking pouring all over himself. On purpose!" She looked around at the others excitedly.

"Okay, that's super weird. But what does that have to do with their tan?" June asked, confused.

"I asked him that too!" Maya laughed.

"No, Maya, seriously. Did you ask him?!" Cecilia covered her mouth with her hands and looked completely mortified.

"Yes, of course I did! Seriously, Cille-mouse, you can't bathe yourself with Cola in an open shower and not expect questions, can you?" Maya argued, and both Charlotte and June nodded in agreement. Cecilia still looked shocked.

"Well, what did he answer?" Charlotte asked excitedly.

"He told me that the sugar in the cola helps him tan. He simply pours Cola all over himself a few times a day, and then he sits out in the sun for just fifteen minutes, and that's it!" Maya concluded with a laugh.

"I'm sure that method is not something the World Health Organisation would ever approve!" Charlotte looked puzzled.

"No, that's guaranteed! However, I also doubt that Mr and Mrs Leather-skin cares about that kind of thing. If it works, it works." Maya shrugged.

"Some people are downright mental!" Cecilia shook her head and leaned back on her sunbed.

"Did you expect anything else from this place?" June smiled and got up, not expecting an answer, and went into the pool. The other three just enjoyed the sun for a while without saying anything.

It wasn't long before June came back with her wet body dripping on the tiles. She sat down on the edge of her sunbed and looked curiously at Maya.

"Hey, Maya. You quite elegantly avoided our question about Haci, and turned the attention into Cecilia's stalker, earlier... But seriously, what's the plan?" she asked with a big smile, and both Charlotte and Cecilia looked at Maya curiously.

"I don't know yet..." She sat up and looked at June with a slightly doubtful look. "He's super sweet and lovely, and I find him very attractive. But..."

"But what? If you are attracted to him and he's attracted to you, what's the problem?" June looked at her questioningly.

"But that's just it... I can't quite figure out what's going on..." Maya sighed. "Okay, I'll be completely honest here, and that's kind of awkward for me, so be nice, okay?" She looked around at the others, a little uncertainly.

June, Charlotte, and Cecilia moved a little closer.

"Okay. You know, I've been single for quite a few years now, and you may have noticed that my dating life has been at a standstill. This standstill is due to the fact that my sex drive has been completely turned off. As in non-existent. I have simply been dead from the waist down. And I haven't had anything remotely resembling sex in almost three years, so..."

She looked at the others anxiously.

"Okay, it's pretty crazy that it's been completely gone," June replied first. " I knew you were taking a break from men. But I just assumed that you... Maybe gave yourself a good time, when needed? Just like she does." She pointed over to Cecilia.

"Okay, June, but we're not talking about me now, are we?!" Cecilia whispered. Her cheeks flushed, and she looked uncomfortable.

"It's completely natural to use sex toys, and I just happen to know that you once bought a Rabbit after seeing it in *Sex and The City*. I just assumed Maya handled it the same way." June looked teasingly at Cecilia, who blushed all the way down to her chest, but said nothing.

"No, all my lust and passion has been all gone," Maya continued, shaking her head resignedly. "But now... I don't know... It's as if 'things' have started to stir up a bit again... You know, down there..."

"Maya, that's great for you!" June looked happy for Maya. "Sex is great, and if your Mr Haci is ... What was it, the ladies called them? The Turkish Delight type, then it's a win-win situation!"

"Yes, I know you're right, but there's also the fact that he's younger than me. A lot younger." Maya looked down at her hands.

"Nonsense!" June interrupted. "He's a grown man, and you're a grown woman. As long as everybody's boundaries are respected, it's all hands on deck! So to speak."

Maya nodded, agreed to June's points.

June continued on, "Are you going to get married and have kids with him? No, so what's the problem?"

Maya started to laughed. She loved it whenever June started her "*Live your life the way YOU want*"-speeches. And June was really on fire right now!

"Fuck what others think! They don't pay your bills nor live your life. And so what if some indifferent people are frowning over your life choices? Look, some people will always have an opinion about what you do and say, and no matter what, you can't please everyone, so why try? Live that life you want, and up the ass with the rest!" she finished, slightly out of breath and completely red in the face.

Maya gave June a roaring applause.

"Okay, let's switch gears, ladies," Charlotte laughed. "I will obviously use less dramatic rhetoric than June, but I basically completely agree that you are always allowed to say yes to the good things in life. Even if it doesn't exactly fit into what society might expect from a woman our age. Your life is your life, and it's only your business."

"Maybe you're right. Maybe I should just jump into it." Maya stared thoughtfully into the air. Then she looked over at Cecilia, who hadn't really said anything. "What do you think, Mammi?"

Cecilia sighed and looked away. "I'd rather not say anything, Maya. You have to choose yourself what you want to do."

"And I will. But I'm still curious about your opinion," Maya pressed on.

Cecilia sighed again and thought for a moment. "Okay, but you're not going to like it," she replied, looking seriously at Maya.

"Okay, but just bring it anyway."

"Well, then... Personally, I think this is a bad idea. Haci has seemed both sweet and nice, as I also mentioned earlier, and apparently a good flirt. But going from flirting to having sex with him is a big step, in my opinion."

"Why is that?" Charlotte asked curiously.

Cecilia threw out her arms: "Because she doesn't know him! None of us know him. We've known him for less than a week, and he could basically be a serial killer!" She added in a slightly lower voice, "I just don't understand why you don't want to get to know people better before you choose to be naked together... After all, you have to take care of your reputation as a woman as well. If you just sleep around with everyone, you can quickly come across as cheap and easy..."

"Now, I never!" June interrupted. " Cecilia, darling. I am well aware that you see the world a little different than the rest of us. But I would never have taken you for someone who shames women because they have a sex life!"

"I don't!" Cecilia protested.

"Yes, you do!" June interrupted again. "This whole discussion about cheap woman vs. male stud is *so* outdated. Seriously. It must be buried right now! If anyone has a problem with whom I'm sleeping with, that's exactly what it is. Their problem! It has nothing to do with me. Period!"

Cecilia looked completely startled and was lobster red in the face.

June took a few deep breaths and got a grip on herself. "Sorry, Cille-mouse, I didn't mean to rip your head off. You are, of course, allowed to think what you think," she said in a disarming tone. "I just wish for you that you would try seeing the world a little wider. You're missing out on *so* many good things, and I just wish for you to have a full life, too. And honestly, I don't think Maya is slutty at all by shagging once every three years!" she concluded with a small laugh.

She stood up and walked over to Cecilia,

pulled her up and hugged her. "Are we okay?" she asked. Cecilia nodded and gave her a small smile, but she remained silent.

"So, the majority of the votes go to Hanky-Panky? I'm kind of happy about that." Maya smiled as they all settled back into their sunbeds. "Because, frankly, I'm so horny right now, that I'm even considering taking a ride on Mr Chippy!" she added with a giggle, causing the other guests at the pool to turn at the sound of her friends' loud laughter.

Chapter 28

"Ladies, I'm going up to the room to call home. I have promised my boys to make a video call so they can see the view from the balcony. I'll be right back afterwards, so does anyone need me to bring anything from the room?" June asked while looking around at the others.

Maya waved dismissively, half asleep from her sunbed, and Charlotte also declined the offer.

"If you could bring my other book down with you, that would be great! I just finished this one." Cecilia rummaged through her bag for her book, which she gave to June, along with the keys to her room.

"No problem, where is it at?" June asked, while pulling her dress over her head and putting her sandals on.

"In my nightstand drawer. It should be fairly easy to find." Cecilia smiled at her. "Thank you, June, you're a superstar!" she added, sending June an air kiss.

"Yeah, yeah, whatever. See you in a minute," June laughed and walked toward the hotel's entrance.

June decided to start with the book, as she didn't want to forget it, and headed to Cecilia and Charlotte's room first.

She locked herself in and went directly into the bedroom. "I wonder which side she sleeps in?" she mumbled to herself. Both nightstands were empty, so there was nothing to give a June a hint.

She opened the drawer of the nightstand on the left. There was a charger, a couple of women's magazines, a computer and a pack of sanitary pads. "Oh okay, this must be Charlotte's side," June whispered, and was just about to close the drawer again when she saw something strange. She picked up Charlotte's package of pads and looked at its contents. She had seen correctly.

With a wondering look, she put the package back in the drawer and closed it. She hurriedly swapped Cecilia's books in the other nightstand, locked herself out again, and went to her own room to call home.

When she got back to the pool, she handed the book to Cecilia, who immediately started reading it. Maya was now firmly asleep, and a low snore came from her half-open mouth.

June lay down on her sunbed next to Charlotte.

"Hey Charlotte, I was wondering about something..." June said casually and in a low voice.

Charlotte looked up from her book. "Yes?"

"Um, I was just in your room getting Cecilia's book, and I hadn't been told which nightstand it was in," June continued, "so I opened the nightstand drawer on the left side first. Which must be yours?"

Charlotte blinked a few times and straightened up a little in the sunbed. "Yes, and?" she replied, and a flash of uncertainty ran across her face.

"Well, I kind of stumbled over your pads." June made quotation-marks with her fingers, when she said the word pad. "I was just wondering if you had bought something wrong by mistake or what?" June looked at her questioningly. "Cause the packaging was regular pads, but the content were Tena pads?"

Charlotte swallowed visibly a few times and had lost all colour in her face. "No, it's not a mistake. It's mine," she replied in an almost inaudible voice.

June had a surprised look on her face, but

then she began to smile. "What the hell, princess, have your lady parts become leaky? I thought only older ladies used pee pads. And I know that we're not that young anymore, but *come on*! We still have many miles in us!" she added with a laugh that quickly died down as she saw tears welling up in Charlotte's eyes.

"Oh no, honey, what's going on?! I was just teasing..." June stammered and hurried to sit up, so she was facing Charlotte. "I'm pretty excellent at putting my foot in my mouth today, aren't I?" she muttered, shaking her head at herself.

Charlotte also sat up. She took a few deep breaths and regained control of herself.

"I... I've struggled to keep it hidden, but maybe I should have just told you from the beginning..." She then sighed. She blinked away her tears and threw out her arms in resignation. "It's true, June. I've lied to you all along. I don't have my period right now. But I've become so leaky that I don't dare to go anywhere without those ... Tena pads."

June tightly grasped Charlotte's hands, looking at her with a serious expression. "I know you all too well, Charlotte, so now I want an honest answer. How long have you been keeping this all to yourself?"

"For over a year," Charlotte muttered, looking

very uncomfortable.

"Okay, and I'm guessing you didn't tell Kenneth either?" June continued in a calm voice.

"No, I... I've been too embarrassed about it. I couldn't bear if he would find me unsexy, June. Or if I accidentally peed on him while we... You know... It would be so... *humiliating!*" Charlotte whispered in a low voice, staring at the tiles beneath them. "I've tried everything from Kegel Exercises to visualisations to a gadget you have to sit on, which I found online. Nothing has worked for me. So, there's only surgery left." She looked at June again. "The most stupid thing is that I *have* talked to a clinic, and the procedure is relatively small with little downtime. But I won't do something like that without involving Kenneth, and then we're back to the fact that I can't bring myself to tell him."

She shook her head again and looked defeated. "The worst part is that I've rejected his advances so many times now, that he must think I don't want him anymore. And I really still want him," she said with a trembling voice. "I still love him so much! But until this gets resolved, I'll keep avoiding it every single time."

June thought for a moment and cleared her throat before she continued. "Okay, look. I understand that this is really shameful for you, and yes, it's definitely a super uncool situation." She took a firmer grip on Charlotte's hands and looked her directly in the eyes. "But Cha Cha, and I mean this in the best way possible... You'll *have* to tell him! It's not fair to have him thinking that you don't want him anymore. It's devastating to your relationship, and you two are truly made for each other!"

"I know. I just don't know how he's going to react to this..." Charlotte replied and looked down at her hands.

June lifted her chin back up. "Charlotte, darling. Kenneth loves you more than life itself! He has always caught both you and your relationship if something has happened. He's going to do that here as well. That's guaranteed!" She smiled, pointed to her very limp upper arm, and added, "If not, then I'll personally come for him with my guns!"

Charlotte couldn't help but laugh and shook her head as she exhaled. "You're right, I'm just going to pull myself together... Wow, I feel twenty pounds lighter!" She looked gratefully at June. "Thank you for reaching out to me. I've really struggled with how to tell you guys about this. And I have had serious stress in my brain about how to keep explaining shorts by the pool and beach for the rest of the holiday," she laughed with relief.

"What's that about your shorts?" Cecilia, who had only heard the last sentence, suddenly asked curiously.

"Well, I think Charlotte has something to share with the class, but let's wait until later so she doesn't have to repeat herself," June smiled and looked at Charlotte encouragingly.

Charlotte smiled and shrugged. "You're right. I have to start somewhere, and why not with someone who is always on my side... I'll tell it all during dinner tonight, Cille-mouse," she smiled, and lay down with her book again.

Chapter 29

"It's going to be exciting to try a different place tonight, huh?" Cecilia shouted to Charlotte, who was brushing her teeth in the bathroom.

Charlotte rinsed, dabbed her mouth gently, so she didn't ruin her makeup, and joined Cecilia in the living room. "Yes, we will see if it's as good as Lezzetli." she smiled while pulling a tight dark blue dress over her head. "Can I get you to zip me up?" she asked as she wiggled the dress into place over her hips. She turned her back to Cecilia.

"I hope it's a good place when they actually recommend it at the reception," Cecilia said, while zipping up Charlotte's dress with a brisk gesture of her hand. "Surely they wouldn't recommend a crappy place?"

"Well, it probably depends on whether the place is owned by a cousin or something, you know," Charlotte smirked and winked at her.

It was Alican himself who had recommended them to eat at *The Castle* and he had booked both a table and pickup service for them.

When they came out of the hotel a little before nine o'clock, there was already a minibus waiting. The driver, a polite young man who smelled strongly of cheap cologne, politely lent them a hand getting onto the bus.

They were dropped off almost down at the marina in the other end of town. It looked amazing now that all the lights were turned on both along the promenade and out on the boats.

"Welcome to The Castle!" said a loud voice behind them in English with a heavy Turkish accent. They turned around, and a smiling middle-aged man stood behind them. "Come, come with me!" he continued in an excited tone, eagerly leading them up the stairs and into the restaurant.

The place was three times the size of Lezzetli, and it was teeming with guests and waiters. Alican had apparently asked for them to be treated extra nicely, because there was a table reserved for them right next to a larger area that was cleared of tables and chairs. "Maybe it's a dance floor?" Charlotte whispered to Maya. "I could use a little dancing soon," she added thoughtfully.

Just like the rest of the tables in the restaurant, their table was decorated with a white tablecloth, dark blue folded napkins, fresh flowers in a white vase, and lit candles to create a cosy ambiance.

But there was also a red rose on each plate as

well as rose petals scattered all over the table. This was just on their table.

Two young waiters ran around them, pulled out chairs, and moved them back into place when they had sat down. They openly discussed among themselves, in Turkish but with telling hand gestures, who should take the most care of Charlotte. Charlotte tried to ignore it, but looked very uncomfortable.

June, Maya and Cecilia found it hilarious and quickly agreed that they were mostly surprised that nothing like that had happened until now on this holiday.

"It must be because we haven't been to so many places that you've been spared," June said, flipping through the menu, which was the size of a smaller phone book. "Well, I'm blown away here. Have you guys figured out what you want?" she asked the others, looking completely lost.

"I think, I will try a Steak Diana," Maya replied, closing her menu. "I've never tried it before, but it sounds delicious."

"I'll go along with that," Charlotte nodded, placing her menu on top of Maya's. "Here, you get my menu. Then *you* can hand it over to our waiters..." She looked at the others with an annoyed facial expression and almost hissed out though her teeth "and I'm just letting you all know right now... If that sweaty guy presses his penis up against my arm one more time, I'm going to scream. And it's not out of pleasure!"

The sweaty waiter heard them laughing and took it as a sign to rush back to their table. He again positioned himself very close to Charlotte's chair. June tried to call him over by asking about the differences between two dishes on the menu. However, he was reluctant to move and answered June's questions across the table in a disinterested tone of voice.

The man who had received them when they arrived suddenly came to their table. And the waiter immediately rushed over beside him.

He introduced himself as Khalid, and he told them that he was the owner of the restaurant. He had been friends with the hotel owner Alican for many years, and when Alican sent guests to his restaurant, they were *always* particularly well received.

He barked an order to the waiter, who quickly pulled a notebook out of his pocket.

"Have you ordered drinks yet?" he asked kindly.

When they said no, he cast a brooding look at the waiter, who blushed and looked down at his feet. It was obvious that he had not done his job properly and that the error was noted on Khalid's inner notepad.

"I apologise for the wait, dear guests. Zeki here will *immediately* take your drink order, and right afterwards he will take your order for the food. If you need anything, just ask for me," he smiled at them, but angrily whispered something in Turkish to Zeki, before he left the table with a polite nod to the girls.

Zeki hurried to bring out his most professional attitude as they ordered beer, wine, and soda. It wasn't long before he returned with their drinks, a basket with a large inflated loaf of bread in it, and a plate with small bowls filled with delicious dipping for the bread.

He quickly explained that the bread was called a balloon bread and that it was something all guests got at the house's expense.

Then he got ready to take their food order.

"Wow, what a shift in behaviour," Cecilia whispered to Charlotte.

"Yes, that's how it is when the boss is watching." Charlotte nodded towards the bar, where Khalid was keeping a watchful eye on his employees, and right now Zeki in particular.

Just as the food had been served, the lights

suddenly dimmed, and extremely loud Turkish folk music poured out of the speakers.

All four looked at each other in wonder and grimaced.

"Well, great sound level, anyway," Maya laughed and took a bite of her food. With a big smile, she rolled her eyes in pure joy. "*Oh my God, guys,* this tastes amazing! Perfect food choice." She nodded over to Charlotte, who looked at her questioningly and showed with her hands that she couldn't hear her.

A small group of young men, dressed in what must be Turkish traditional clothing, came running in and started dancing to the music. A moment later, a group of young women entered with similar clothes on.

For the next fifteen minutes there was folk dancing as entertainment for the food, and although the music was far too loud and shrilly for the girls' taste, the show itself was entertaining enough.

After the folk dance, a beautiful young woman entered. She did not look Turkish, like the dance troop before. Her music's volume was a little more moderate, and they could now talk to each other if they talked loudly. The woman was dressed in a very tight, silver-shimmering, semi-transparent one-piece suit, which left little to the imagination. She proved to be an incredibly skilled contortionist, and she could twist and bend in the most amazing ways.

"Wow, imaging to be so flexible," Maya sighed enviously and applauded excitedly as the woman once again almost turned herself inside out. "It must have taken years to become so skilled," Cecilia nodded while taking a bite of her food.

"Well, I just know that from my angle I can almost see all the way up her fanny when she's spinning around," June shouted with a cheeky laugh.

"For God's sake, June. Just look away then!" Charlotte, who had taken a sip of her wine, coughed.

"It's kind of hard when it's right there in front of my face. Right behind that very thin fabric!"

"We can't take you anywhere, can we? You're not behaving nicely!" Cecilia laughed, shaking her head at their conversation.

"*Who cares*," Maya exclaimed and rose her glass. "Who wants to have nicely behaved friends when it's much more fun to hang out with those who aren't," she toasted, emptying her wine glass. "Is there by any chance more vino?"

"Well, I wonder how long this entertainment

is going on." June looked at her watch. "It would be nice if we could also talk a little without having to shout."

At that moment, the contortionist took a bow and left the floor to great applause.

A moment later, rhythmic oriental music roared out of the speakers, and a beautiful dark-haired belly-dancer came gliding out onto the dance floor, moving her hips and shoulders to the rhythm of the music. She shimmied around the restaurant, in and out between all the tables. Here and there the guests stuck money bills into the bra and waistband of her brightly coloured outfit.

The table next to them was occupied by two elderly couples from Denmark. The two ladies and one of the men watched the show with great curiosity, while the other man had his eyes glued to the food menu.

When the belly dancer came to the couple's table, she danced inciting for some time in front of the reading man, who didn't seem to notice. Much to the amusement of both his own table and the surrounding guests. Finally, his wife poked him and laughingly asked him to look up. Right then, the man found himself face to face with the belly dancer's bosom.

The man stared directly into the moving

cleavage for a moment, blinked a few times, and then shrugged. "Connie, I don't really care. I'm hungry and would rather have a cheese sandwich than that!" he proclaimed loudly to his better half, and continued to browse the menu.

The belly dancer, of course, did not understand the conversation, but the intention was clear. So, she gave up and danced on to another table.

"Oh my God, that's the best thing I've heard in a long time." Maya sobbed with laughter. "It goes straight into my brains catalogue of great real-life stories. That was epic!"

The other three were also laughing so hard that none of them immediately noticed when the Turkish music stopped and was replaced by a parade of really old pop songs.

A moment later, all the waiters were gathered on the floor and started dancing a rehearsed routine to the songs. It looked somewhat half-hearted, and at least half of them looked like they'd rather be somewhere else than here.

"Okay, when they get to the waiter-entertainment, that must be the end, right?" June asked, looking hopeful.

"Yes, you would think so, but let's see. This *is* Turkey," Maya laughed while toasting with

304

Cecilia.

The waiters started walking around the tables and dragging the guests to the dance floor. Before long, there was a large crowd of men and women following the same dance moves as the waiters showed them.

'Charlotte's Fan Club', as Maya had dubbed the two waiters from their table, both stopped by several times to invite her to dance. She refused each time, and the waiters didn't look thrilled when June and Maya signed up to dance along instead.

Cecilia pulled out her phone and started filming them. "My God, this is funny," she giggled. "None of them know the steps, but they have a good time, anyway."

The crowd of guests finished the dance-session by moving around the entire restaurant in a long line. When they reached their own table, Maya and June deserted, and sat down laughing and gasped to catch wind.

"Holy shit, that was fun!" Maya exclaimed and took a big sip from her water glass.

"Yes, but it's pretty obvious that none of us are twenty anymore." June coughed and pulled out a cigarette.

"Well, those things are probably not helping

either," Cecilia interjected, nodding towards her pack of cigarettes.

"Yeah, yeah, whatever. Take care of your own wine, and stay out of my guilty pleasures, please," June waved her off, but also smiled and winked at her.

The waiter Zeki suddenly stood at the table again and now he wanted Charlotte to dance with him to the slow music that was playing. She again declined.

Only a moment later, the other waiter came strutting to their table with his chest pushed forward. He winked confidently at all of them. Then he smiled broadly, took Charlotte's hand, kissed it, and invited her up to dance. She declined yet again, pulled her hand back, and turned to her friends, whom she was just about to tell her secret.

The waiter looked slightly annoyed and with an angry movement, he jerked her chair away from the table.

Charlotte quickly stood up and moved away from him. "I said no. Please respect my answer!"

He grabbed her arm and tried to drag her with him. "Calm down, it's just one dance. You can do that. It's just one dance, right? Come on!"

June got up, and she looked like a

thundercloud. Maya and Cecilia looked at each other across the table.

"Uh, I'm so bombed out, I don't have any popcorn right now," Maya whispered while she giggled.

Cecilia looked horrified. Fires raining from the sky could easily be the consequence of disrespecting June or anyone else's boundaries.

"Hey, you. Let go of her. Right now!" June pointed directly at the waiter.

"Relax, it's just a dance. She will just have one dance with me. She will be back in a moment," he replied with a dismissive expression on his face, still with a firm grip on Charlotte's arm.

"I'm telling you right now. If you don't let go of her this instance, this is going to be an extremely ugly experience for you!" June had stepped right up to him now.

The waiter looked down at her condescendingly and laughed scornfully, but he still didn't let go of Charlotte's arm. Charlotte looked around a little desperately, caught Khalid's gaze, and waved him over.

The waiter started cursing at June in Turkish, when Khalid popped up and stood right behind him. He did *not* look happy.

"Imran!" Khalid shouted and slapped him on the back of his head. "Let go of her arm immediately! What the hell are you doing?!"

Imran turned pale and quickly let go of Charlotte. Then he sent June a furious look and turned to Khalid with a disarming smile.

"Of course, boss, of course. We were just kidding, weren't we?" he quickly said and looked questioningly at Charlotte.

"No, we didn't! I said no several times, and you didn't respect my answer. So, no. We weren't kidding, and we didn't find it amusing!" Charlotte replied in a harsh tone, looking at him angrily.

Imran looked at Charlotte even more furiously than he had at June. Then, he uttered something in Turkish to her with a hiss, which was clearly offensive based on Khalid's visible response.

Khalids face first turned pale, and then he turned fiery red. "Imran, up to the bar with you and wait for me there. Don't you dare to move until I am back. Is that understood?!" he hissed out between his teeth, and they could see that Imran swallowed nervously a few times.

"But, uncle, I..." he began to said.

"Now, Imran, go!" Khalid interrupted. There was no doubt about his tone of voice. If Imran said one more word, it would be his last.

Imran scowled at them and shuffled up to the bar. He sat down on a bar stool and, with a sour expression on his face, pulled out his phone.

Khalid cleared his throat and shook his head. "Dear guests, I sincerely apologise for the behaviour of my nephew. I hope you can forgive him. He is new here at the restaurant and he doesn't understand... Well, anything really," Khalid muttered, looking resigned. "But when your older brother asks for a favour, then..." he added with a shrug. "So, to make up for this unfortunate experience, I would like to offer you a cocktail at the house's expense. Free choice on the drink menu!" he smiled and asked waiter Zeki, who had just started clearing their table after dinner, to get a menu for them.

Zeki immediately let go of what he had in his hands and ran up for a drink menu. When he returned, he gave it to Khalid without saying a word and then proceeded to clear their table. He clearly wanted to avoid displeasing the boss, like Imran did.

The girls had softened a little after Khalid's apology, which had seemed sincere. They quickly agreed to accept his offer, and they all chose a *Sex on the Beach*. Khalid gave the order to Zeki, who again ran off immediately.

"Again, ladies, I apologise one more time. If you need anything, just come and find me, okay?" Khalid smiled kindly before marching up to Imran at the bar.

"Okay, I'm really happy, that I'm not Imran right now," Maya said with a mischievous smile. Then she pointed at Charlotte. "So, we're just going to bring you along every time we want free drinks. That's neat," she laughed. "We just need to activate 'Charlotte's Fan Club', and we're good to go!"

"No thanks, Maya. I'd rather not be around those types of people!" Charlotte rolled her eyes. "You just know that someone like him has a hard time understanding a no in all contexts," she added with a shudder.

"But then it's good that we have you, June. Our very own private bodyguard!" Cecilia clenched her fists and pretended to fight the air.

June also started laughing. "Yeah, okay, calm down! But really. My piss boils over when I get in contact with such a dickhead. Consider the number of men out there who still believe women exist solely for their benefit. I mean, really?! What year are we in?!" She shook her head resignedly.

At the same time, Zeki arrived with their drinks. He just put them at the end of the table, not looking at Charlotte or any of the others, and then he hurried away again.

Maya's phone beeped. The message was from Haci.

"Hey guys, Haci asks if we'll come to Lezzetli when we're done here?" Maya asked and checked the time.

"I'll pass today. Tomorrow is our last whole day here, and I would like to arrive at the beach before noon," Charlotte replied. Cecilia nodded in agreement. "Yes, me too. It's the last chance to get some summer sun this year, so I'm also voting for an all-day beach trip tomorrow."

Maya looked questioningly at June, who thought for a moment. "I know you want to see Haci, but I'll go back to the hotel with the others. I missed a whole day in the sun when the rest of you were on a boat trip, so I'm a little behind," she said apologetically. "But hey, you can just go there by yourself?"

Maya sighed. "No, you're right. Would I like to see him? Yes. But I also want to go to the beach with you without a hangover, and I'm kind of cured after today."

"What is he saying?" June asked curiously as she watched Maya write back and forth a few times.

"He's off at midnight tomorrow, so he asks if

we want to go out for some drinks on our last night? He has a favourite bar he wants to take us to." she looked happy.

"Absolutely, we can do that. We are leaving in the afternoon from the hotel on Saturday, so that shouldn't be a problem." June nodded and looked questioningly at Cecilia and Charlotte, who quickly agreed.

The phone beeped again, and Maya's cheeks turned red.

"Something tells me we haven't got the whole story yet." June pointed to Maya. "Spill it! Are there love in the air?" she asked curiously.

"Um... Maybe..." Maya replied hesitantly, but with a smile. "Well, he has asked if I'd like to spend the night with him tomorrow when the rest of you go back to the hotel."

"Uuuhh, so maybe now you can join the Slutty McSlut club, too?" Charlotte looked teasingly over at June.

"Come inside, my friend. There's room for a lot here in the clubhouse!" June sang to a homemade tune. "But don't look around too closely, it's probably a bit dingy," she finished and laughed loudly at herself.

"June! That's just gross!" Cecilia exclaimed and shook her head resignedly.

Chapter 30

"Uh, I'm going to miss this." Maya stretched and made herself more comfortable on the sunbed. "I could easily just lie here for the rest of my days and roast in the sun while listening to the waves."

"I think, I'd be bored if nothing else were to happen at all. But for a week, it's okay," Charlotte replied, applying more sunscreen to her arms. "It's sharp today. Feels like the sun burns holes in my skin. Remember to put on a lot of sun lotion, you guys," she added and squinted up at the cloudless sky.

"Hey, isn't that supposed to be Cecilia's line," Maya asked, teasingly looking at Cecilia, who laughingly flipped Maya off.

"Well, well, well! Someone has picked up some bad habits during this holiday, huh?" Maya stated with a big grin. "What's next? Are you going to start swearing like a dockworker, like June does?"

"You have to howl with the wolves you're surrounded by," Cecilia replied and shrugged nonchalantly.

A loud snorting grunt came from June's sunbed, followed by a loud yawn.

"Oh my, I think the bear is alive again," Maya giggled.

"Who the hell are you calling a bear?" June grumbled with a tired tone. She reached for her sunglasses on the white plastic table next to the sunbed with her eyes still half closed.

"Ha, *that* job position can only be claimed by you. Mainly because you growl like one!" Maya exclaimed with a big grin and winked at her.

"What the hell are you talking about?" June asked, confused, pulling herself up into a sitting position. She still didn't look fully awake.

"I think that Maya may be suggesting that you are a ... Loud sleeper. Is that a fair way to put it?" Charlotte asked the others.

Maya nodded in agreement. "Well, that would definitely be one way to describe it... You could also say that you sound like an old rusty tractor with solid engine problems, but, hey! If Charlotte's words make more sense, peace be upon it." Maya innocently threw out her arms.

June looked at her resignedly. "You can just go right ahead and stop with your bullying. I am well aware that I snore a little bit. But it's not as bad as you make it out to be, okay?"

She yawned again and looked wondering at Maya, who now frantically rummaged through her bag.

A moment later, she pulled up her phone and with a cheeky smile she started looking for something on it. Then she let out a loud "Aha!" and triumphantly held it out to June.

"Evidence A!" she shouted with a smug look on her face.

June looked at her incomprehensibly. "What am I supposed do with your phone?"

"I want you to grab it with your sweaty little fingers, and then you have to press play," Maya replied in a teasing manner.

June took the phone out of Maya's hands with an annoyed movement and pressed play.

Maya had turned up the volume, and a loud snore, mixed with a symphony of giggles, erupted. The sound made the nearest sunbathing guests look their way to see what was going on.

"What is this...?" June opened her eyes wide when she realised that the recording was of herself on the plane. The more she saw of the recording, the redder her face became. It was difficult for the other three to figure out whether or not it was out of anger. Fortunately, it wasn't long before June exploded in an infectious fit of laughter that once again made those around them look at them in wonder.

"What the actual... Oh! My! God! This is hilarious!" she hiccupped with laughter and handed Maya her phone back. "Now it makes sense why half the passengers smiled at me when I woke up." She wiped her eyes repeatedly with her sundress. "But girls, that was just on the plane, and I was dead tired that day. It's not like that otherwise, is it?" June looked at Maya questioningly. "Surely you would have said something now that we share a room?"

"I'm sorry to disappoint you," Maya replied, still dying with laughter. "But I've slept with earplugs every single night. Well, except the night I slept on the toilet, of course," she added with a shrug. "But yes, otherwise I wouldn't close an eye!"

"Oh my God, that is really not sexy!" June shook her head and giggled to herself. "Why the hell haven't Bo said anything to me about it?" she added, looking dumbfounded.

"He probably is afraid to do so. Last time you tried to fix something about yourself, you became *Miss Sexuella Galore*! I'm sure he wouldn't take the chance of messing your other end up too!" Maya screamed with laughter at her own words.

"Your comment should offend me, but you're probably right!" June stood up from her sunbed. "Okay, enough talk about my un-charming sleeping habits. Who wants to get in the water?"

"Actually, I want to join today," Charlotte smiled and got up as well. The others looked at her in surprise. "Don't make a big deal out of it. I just need to go to the bathroom first and throw away... You know..." She nodded tellingly down towards her shorts.

"Yes, good thinking. It's a poor strategy to go diving with it on, if there's a chance that *SS Tena* is bobbing around on the surface afterwards," Maya commented dryly, causing the other three to burst out in laughter again.

Charlotte came wading out to the others a few minutes later. She let herself sink into the cool water with a satisfied sigh. The sea was calm today and they could see the sandy bottom clearly. Small, silver-glistening fishes swam around their legs when they stood still.

"By the way, Gio has arrived," she said while turning to Cecilia. "I bumped into him up at the cafe and he said you'd written and told him that we would be here today?"

"Uh, we need to hear a little more about that," Maya, who floated by in the same moment, said. "June, come here, we have juicy gossip!" she

317

called after June, who had swum a little further out.

"No, really girls, there is no gossip here!" Cecilia sighed resignedly. "He wrote this morning asking what we were going to do today, and I replied that we were going here. That's all."

Charlotte looked surprised. "Okay, the version from him is more that you had asked him to come and see you, even though he had the day off today."

"What?" Cecilias cheeks turned red. "Charlotte, that's not true! You can see the messages, if you want... That man is such a liar... How annoying is this?!," she exclaimed furiously, casting an angry glance towards the beach.

"Don't worry, hunny-bunny," Maya quickly tried to smooth things out and swam over next to her. "We know you're not lying. By the way, who cares what that douchebag says? It doesn't matter!" She lay down to float on her back again with her eyes closed.

"Yes, I know... But I get really annoyed when I get accused of doing or saying things, that aren't true," Cecilia muttered and crossed her arms.

"Mammi, breathe! You're on holiday, it's our last full day, and you simply can't let such a bell-end ruin our good vibe!" June was serious. "Up the ass with him. He doesn't matter in any contexts." She pointed at Maya while looking at Cecilia. "I promise you that if you lie down for just five minutes and relax like Maya does, you'll forget all about him!"

"Yep. Having some adipose on your body has its advantages," Maya replied without opening her eyes. "You get a much better flow ability."

Suddenly, a loud shriek sounded from Cecilia. "Oh my God, something touched my legs! I saw something oblong and dark swimming by me! Nope, I'm done bathing for now. I'm heading up!" she squealed in a high-pitched voice and hurried out of the water.

"It's probably just Gio who send out a slimy feeler," June giggled.

Maya laughed so hard at that thought, that she accidentally submerged her head underwater. She quickly got on her feet again, while coughing heavily.

"Maybe it's not a bad idea to get up now so we can dry before lunch," Charlotte suggested. Maya and June nodded in agreement and began wading ashore.

Before they got up, Gio had already settled on Cecilia's sunbed. He immediately started talking about how busy he was at the moment and how much work there was in being the owner of Star Beach. He also strongly indicated that Cecilia should almost take it as a compliment that he came running to see her, because he was actually off today.

Cecilia looked at him with confusion and tried to protest at the statement that she had asked him to come. He completely ignored her comment and kept talking.

"Shit, that dude really likes to hear himself talk," Charlotte whispered to June while rolling her eyes.

"Yeah, we'd better make sure she's okay. He's a bit of a bully right now, and she's really not good at speaking up," June whispered back. Then she cleared her throat loudly.

"Hey, Cille-mouse, if you need help teaching this dude how to scuba dive without a breathing mask, let me know, okay?" she said with a loud voice, in Danish, looking innocently at Gio.

Cecilia started giggling, and for a moment Gio stopped his rambling.

"What did she say?" he asked with a smile that didn't reach his eyes.

"Oh, nothing. She just asked if I would like to have lunch in half an hour and if I would like to have something to drink now," Cecilia quickly replied.

"Yes, *Gio Badio*, can we ask for four Cola Light?" Maya asked with a big smile.

"Hey, lady! My name is Gio, not Gio Badio." Gio's voice was ice cold.

"Alrighty then," Maya replied. She didn't look at him and she didn't comment on his tone of voice. "As long as we can still ask for those Cola Lights..." she added, still with a big smile.

Gio looked at her furiously, but managed to gain some control of himself. "Your friend is very rude!" he muttered lowly to Cecilia, looking very aggrieved.

"No, no, Gio, she's not rude. She's just making fun with you. It's okay," Cecilia tried to smooth it out.

"It's not funny to make fun of people's names," he grunted while rising abruptly from Cecilia's sunbed. "I'll order your sodas and then I'll leave. I'll find out if you'll be able to see me later. Maybe we can meet up tonight if I'm not too busy. I'll let you know later," he quickly announced. Then he stomped away from the girls and toward the restaurant.

Cecilia looked at Maya and started giggling. "Wow, you really stepped on his toes!"

June sat up with an annoyed expression on her face. "Seriously, how self-important can a person be?! It's not funny to make fun of people's names!" She very accurately imitated Gio's voice and attitude. "If it doesn't take more than that to make you *that* angry, then living in your world must be really exhausting!" she added, shook her head and leaned back in her sunbed with a resigned motion.

"I also like how he, once again, twisted the story to be about him trying to see if he could fit you in." Charlotte seemed impressed. "Very elegant spin on the story of you two."

"Now hold on! There is no *us* here! He's just too much! I can't deal with a guy like him and I'm definitely not going to do anything with him!" Cecilia emphasised.

"Speaking of sex, did any of you hear something last night too?" Maya asked in an excited tone, completely ignoring Cecilia's protesting comments that there was no speaking of sex here!

Charlotte sat up abruptly. "Yes, God yes! I had completely forgotten about that," she exclaimed as she swung her legs over the edge of the sunbed. "I was up peeing at around four o'clock, and at first I thought there was some animal outside, grunting!"

June looked questioningly at her: "And *what* animal was that supposed to be, sweetie?"

"Well, there are wild pigs in this country, and in some areas, they wander the streets at night, digging in people's vegetable gardens. I suppose they could be grunting in the meantime," Charlotte explained, looking over at Cecilia. "Wasn't that what you told me?"

"Yes, it's true," Cecilia nodded as she accepted the drinks, they had ordered from Gio. It wasn't him who delivered them, and he was nowhere to be seen.

"Yeah, I heard that sound, too. But when a woman then suddenly moaned loudly and exaggeratedly, as if she was making an adult movie, it wasn't hard to guess what was really going on!" Maya added.

"Seriously, was it *that* loud?" Cecilia looked outraged.

"Oh yes!" Maya continued, with delight in her voice. "And it was damn entertaining! All within a few minutes, I got to hear a whole lot of funny stuff. First it was some sounds like someone got their ass slapped. Then a woman's voice screamed something along '*Harder, harder*' and

323

directly after that, a man moaned and panted; '*I'm coming, I'm coming*'. Then I heard a woman who sounded really disappointed, might I add, saying '*Really?!*'. Less than five minutes later, I heard a door open and close, and then a shower was turned on."

"You're right. It can't have been more than 3-4 minutes in total from the starting grunts to the final grunts," Charlotte agreed. "By the way, it sounded like it was happening just under our rooms. Do we know who lives there?"

They others shook their heads.

"But we have to investigate, then! We can't go back to Denmark without finding out who wakes the rest of us up with bad sex in the middle of the night!" Maya took a sip of her Cola.

"Oh my God, how disappointing it must be to experience Wanker-Sock-Sex," June shook her head and got up to adjust her sunbed.

"What the hell is Wanker-Sock-Sex?" Maya asked, looking over at Charlotte and Cecilia, who both shrugged.

"Wanker-Sock-Sex?" June answered, as she clicked the back of the sunbed to the right level with some difficulty, "That is when a man almost uses the woman as a masturbation-sock." She sat down on the now completely flat sunbed and took a sip of her soda before she continued. "By that I mean that the whole sex-scenario is only about him. That the goal for him is to ejaculate as soon as possible.

So basically, it's masturbation, just with another human being instead of a hand or a sock. As in *Wham bam, thank you, mam!* Where the woman, of course, are allowed all the orgasms she wants. If she takes care of everything herself afterwards, obviously, since most women wouldn't be able to get anywhere in just three minutes."

"Is anyone seriously doing that?" Cecilia looked genuinely surprised.

"Yep! I know you haven't been out shaking your tail feathers that much. But let me just tell you, that the really good experiences, are far between!" June emphasised. "You'd be amazed at how clueless some guys are about women's bodies, so they just rush to finish before you notice how terrible they are. Which is a stupid strategy, really." She looked over at Maya, who nodded agreeingly.

"Well, I've kept my downstairs boutique closed for the last couple of years, as you all know. But I can still attest to the fact that good sex is not on the shelves of all the supermarkets, I have shopped in, before that. If you get my

325

drift... But enough about other people's boring sex lives, I'm hungry. Are you ready for lunch, ladies?" Maya asked, ignoring June, who complained that her timing was less than perfect, because she *just* got her body placed in a horizontal position.

Chapter 31

"June, did you bring any tweezers with you, I forgot mine!" Maya yelled from the bathroom.

"No, but let me just ask Charlotte, she probably has a pair. Two seconds!" June yelled back.

Maya heard muffled voices from the balcony, and a moment later, Charlotte's tweezers were handed to her.

"That's great, thank you!" she replied with relief, while taking the tweezers out of June's hand.

"Aren't your eyebrows in place?" June asked loudly from inside the bedroom as she got dressed.

"Well, yeah, but..." Maya replied with a small laugh. "It's... Well, this is fucking unsexy, but sometimes I get these black hairs on my chest that get quite long. Just now, when I put on a bra, I noticed one that had escaped my usual laser eyesight," she sighed. A moment later, she screeched in agony "God damn it, you little mother-fudger!"

She walked into the bedroom, laughed. She rubbed one of her boobs while making a silly face.

"Shit, I think this one had long roots!"

June nodded understandingly. "Yeah, that's not something you see on the cover of women's magazines every day, is it? This thing about long black hairs starting to grow in strange places on women... It's like this big secret that many women's hair is out of control during menopause. As for myself, I have a few black hairs on my chin that pop up every once in a while. Really annoying and stiff as hell. So, obviously, these little buggers have to go immediately, when I notice them."

She sent Maya a curious look. "So, are you ready for tonight and for... Whatever is going to happen?"

Maya looked at her with a confident look and tallied:

"I've shaven everything that needed to be shaved. Every nook and cranny have been washed thoroughly. I've covered myself in a nice body cream. I've put on my nicest underwear, and I've found my most flattering dress as well. All that's left is some light makeup, drying my hair, and packing my toothbrush."

"Okay, you go girl! Good self-confidence, Mau Mau!" June said appreciatively, giving her a small spontaneous round of applause.

Maya stopped smiling and sighed resignedly. "Well, if you buy the act, he probably will too."

June looked questionably at her.

Maya sighed again and threw out her arms. "Do you seriously think that in less than a week I can go from being tired of my appearance to loving myself completely?"

Her voice went up a few octaves, and the words were now pouring out of her: "The answer is no, June! Yes, I like myself better when I'm tanned, and yes, it also helps to do all these things like putting on nice clothes and makeup to feel more attractive. But that doesn't mean I'm totally cool with the fact, that I maybe have to take of my clothes in front of another human being tonight. Not to mention that I haven't had sex in years, June! What if I have forgot how to do it?!" She had a panicked expression in her eyes.

"Maya, will you please breathe slowly and get yourself under control? You're almost hyperventilating," June said calmly while pulling her over to the couch where she sat her down.

She grabbed a shot glass and poured the very last drops from the vodka bottle into it. "Here, drink this and you'll feel better."

Maya emptied the glass, blinked a few times, and forced herself to take some deep breaths. June just sat next to her without saying anything.

"Are you feeling better now?" June asked softly a moment later.

"Yeah. Jeez, June. I guess, I kind of went off the rails there for a moment, huh?" Maya looked embarrassed and hid her face in her hands.

"Maya, I understand that you are nervous. But you have to trust that if Haci has chosen you, it is because he likes what he sees. Also, if you change your mind along the way and don't want to share sheets with him anyway, it's no worse than saying good tonight and then go home at the same time as the rest of us," June reassured her.

Maya looked at her and nodded. "You're right. This is so stupid!" she sighed, rolled her eyes and got up. "I think I just panicked for a moment. Thank you for catching me before I disappeared down the rabbit hole!"

"Anytime, Maya." June also got up. "And now you really need to move your ass, because we'll get picked up in just twenty minutes!"

June waited until Maya had disappeared into the bedroom before she tiptoed over to Maya's handbag. With a sneaky smile on her face, she placed something in the inside pocket and zipped it up afterwards.

She'll be happy about my gift later tonight, June thought to herself and went out onto the balcony for a cigarette while she waited for the others.

***

Their last dinner was amazing. Haci had suggested they let him put together a meze menu. "It's the same principle as with Spanish tapas," he explained. "It's just called meze here in Turkey. It consists of a lot of small delicious dishes with Turkish specialities that you can sit and enjoy with a glass of wonderful wine."

Everything was incredibly delicious, and all four of them agreed that the food in Turkey where one of the things they would miss the most, when they returned to Denmark.

"So, where are we going?" Charlotte asked with a half-choked voice as they were all crammed into a taxi around midnight. Cecilia sat on June's lap and it was getting uncomfortably hot in the back seat.

"I'm thinking, I will take you to my favourite place, *The Golden Donkey,*" Haci replied. "It's a really nice bar. They play both old and new music, the drinks are great and also I know the owner, so we will get a good discount."

He couldn't help but chuckle when June hollered that in that case, it was also *her* favourite bar in the whole world, too.

The taxi dropped them off almost down by the city beach, and a large sign with a smiling gold-coloured donkey adorned the façade. "Yes, that looks about right," Charlotte said while nearly tripping over the curb.

"Do we have to put some training wheels on you today or what?" June giggled while almost stumbling up the stairs to the bar herself.

"I just think that both of you need to stop consuming more alcohol," Cecilia chuckled and took them both by the arm so they wouldn't have to spend their last night at Cennet's local emergency room.

The Golden Donkey consisted of a somewhat worn dance floor surrounded by a lot of tables and chairs. At the back of the room, along the entire back wall, was the well-stocked bar. All fixtures were kept in golden and black nuances.

The tables and the dance floor were already packed, but Haci led them through the dancing guests and pointed to a vacant table. On the table was a Reserved sign with Haci's name on it.

"Your guy is well connected," June laughed and playfully elbowed Maya. "This is God damn VIP again! Just the way we like it!" she added, looking appreciatively at Haci, who had already walked up to the bar.

They sat down around the table, and Maya made sure to sit at the far end with a free seat next to her.

A moment later, Haci came back with the drinks menu, which he placed on their table. Then he sat down next to Maya with a big smile. "Hey Maya," he whispered. "Is it okay if I hold your hand?"

She nodded and slowly let her fingers merge in between his. She could feel her whole body responding to this very simple touch, and a deep sigh escaped, a little too loudly, between her lips.

"Are you okay?" June asked, a little worried.

"Yeah, yeah. Just a little stomach ache. It just needs to be danced away, I think," Maya quickly deflected and smiled at Charlotte, who was handing her the drinks menu.

There were over a hundred different cocktails

on the menu and everyone at the table had a hard time choosing. Finally, Charlotte closed her eyes and stuck her finger down somewhere random. "Okay, whatever I point at, I'll take. It all sounds good and I can't choose, so *here goes*..."

Haci smilingly shook his head at them and decided on a beer instead.

Their *Spicegirls* cocktails had only just been put on the table when Rick Astley's "*She wants to dance with me*" roared out of the speakers. All the girls went up with a loud squeal and stormed out onto the dance floor.

Haci sat back laughing, but refused to join in. Maya came back when the song was over, while the other three stayed out on the dance floor.

"So, Rick Astley... You really like him, huh?" Haci asked with a smirk.

"No, no. We don't just really like him," Maya corrected him with a raised index finger. "We *love* him!" she laughed and waved her arms around.

"Oh, how I've missed being out dancing!" Charlotte shouted into the ear of a laughing Cecilia while letting her hips rotate skilfully to a Ricky Martin track.

"I can't keep up!" June gasped, when she laughingly sat down again after half an hour.

She reached for her glass and took a large sip. "Oh my God, this is so good!" she smacked her lips and drank the rest of it. "I'm going up to the bar. Do you need me to bring anything?" she asked Maya and Haci, who both shook their heads.

Maya didn't want to drink too much today. She wanted to be fairly clear in her head for later.

The others sent each other tellingly glances during the night. It was perfectly fine that Maya focused on Haci. She needed a good experience with a man, and he seemed to be able to give her just that.

As two o'clock approached, June, Cecilia and Charlotte were getting quite tipsy, and they were all just sitting and enjoying themselves around the table.

Cecilia had her phone in her hand, but suddenly she looked searchingly around the room. Then she waved towards the dance floor, and someone squeezed through the crowd and headed for their table.

"Hello, ladies." It was Gio. He seemed very self-important and over-confident while nodding around the table. His gaze stopped at Haci, and for a moment, he looked startled and annoyed. But he quickly managed to put his face in the usual smooth setting again. Then he unenthusiastically shook Haci's hand and sat down on the opposite side of the table next to Cecilia.

June looked wondering at Charlotte and whispered. "What's going on here? Did she invite him or what?"

Charlotte shook her head and whispered back. "No, he just wrote her a minute ago and asked where she was, and you know Cecilia. She's always overly polite, so she told him we were here and now he's shown up." She looked over at Cecilia. "She doesn't look super excited about it, though..."

June shook her head. "Let's give him five minutes, and if he's still here, and she still looks uncomfortable, then he has to go." Charlotte nodded and looked at her watch. "He gets to ten over, and then it's enough."

Undeniably, Cecilia did not look thrilled. Gio had been writing all evening, and she had tried to ignore the beeping coming from her phone in her bag. But she was raised to treat other people properly, and ignoring someone's messages really wasn't a good behaviour. So, on a mixture of guilt and the many drinks she had consumed tonight, she had finally answered him about fifteen minutes ago, and had told him where they were at.

He hadn't answered right away, but had just written a moment ago that he was here.

She could feel her cheeks getting warm, and a new and strange mixed feeling shot through her body. It was equal parts excitement and red flags. She was therefore very conflicted when he sat down next to her. She could easily see that he was handsome, and he could also be charming sometimes. She also still felt a little flattered that he had chosen her. But he was also arrogant and a player-type, and she constantly had the feeling of being in a room with a hungry shark when he was there.

She had never felt this way before and didn't know how to deal with the situation.

So, she would let him start out their conversation, and then it would go to show, if he had different sides than the ones she had already seen.

"Did you have a good night?" Gio asked, moving closer to her. He smiled invitingly at her and put an arm around her waist.

Cecilia stiffened, and she looked at him uncertainly. "Um, yes, it's been nice," she stammered while looking down at her hands. "Wonderful food and drinks at Lezzetli, and then Haci has shown us this nice place."

"That's good, that's good," Gio replied disinterestedly, and immediately changed the subject. "Well, I was thinking... Let's just sit here with your friends for maybe fifteen minutes, and then we can leave, okay?" He ran his hand up and down her back.

"Um, no, why would we do that?" she asked slowly. She looked at him, clearly confused.

Gio looked at her, annoyed. "What do you mean by why? That is why I have come here, isn't it? After all, you wrote to me where you were, so I could come and pick you up, so we can be together tonight, right?" He starred at her with a strange look on his face.

"Please don't touch me without permission," she said in a low voice while she removed his hand from her waist.

Gio glared furiously at her. "Why are you removing my hand?! Ah, okay, you're one of *those* girls. One of those who plays with men. Promise them things and then won't do anything anyway," he almost hissed. He clenched his jaw.

Cecilia looked at him stunned. "What? I... Surely, I have not promised you anything? You asked where I was, and I just answered you!" she replied, visibly shaken. She could feel her face and chest turning red.

"Yes, you did!" Gio hissed again, pointing furiously at her. "You've talked to me and acted like you wanted me. You sit there and get me completely turned on, and then suddenly you don't want to have sex with me after all? What the hell are you going to do about that?" he asked furiously, apparently expecting an answer.

Cecilia didn't know what to respond to his frenzied outburst and therefore just looked at him, speechless.

Gio mumbled something in Turkish to her in a mocking tone, got up with a forceful movement, and furiously left their table.

Meanwhile, on the other side of the table, Haci had been watching them. "Do you know this guy?" he asked Maya with a worried look as soon as Gio sat down at the table.

"Well, know and know... He owns Star Beach, where we have been a few times. We have met him there. He's obviously very interested in Cecilia," Maya explained while taking a sip of her drink. "Do you want to taste it?" she asked, pushing her glass towards him.

"No, no, it's okay... Did he seriously tell you he's the owner of Star Beach?"

"Yeah, he told us that he owns the place and that he is a very busy man," she quickly replied, and continued to sing along to the music.

Haci sighed resignedly. "Maya, listen to me for a minute," he then said and smiled as he turned her face and caught her eyes. "That guy is *not* the owner of Star Beach. I know the owner. He lives in a completely different city and he only comes to Cennet a couple of times a month to keep an eye on his investment," he added. "That guy is just an ordinary employee trying to make himself sound more important than he is."

Maya shrugged.

"Hmm, maybe I've misunderstood him, then. To be honest, I don't listen much when Gio speaks. He really talks a lot. Especially about himself!" She rolled her eyes.

Haci now laughed even more. "Just a moment... Did he say his name is Gio?"

Maya now looked a little annoyed. "Yes. Short version of Giovanni... Haci, why do we keep talking about Gio?"

"Maya, have you ever met a Turkish man named Giovanni?"

"No, but he's not entirely Turkish," Maya explained. "He's half Italian."

Haci now laughed so much that he couldn't breathe. Maya looked at him and shook her head, irritated.

"What? Why is it funny?"

"Maya, sweet darling. That guy there is not Italian. Not even half!" he coughed and took a sip of his beer.

"Okay, and how do you know that?" Maya replied, a little offended.

Haci cleared his throat and took her hands. "I'm so sorry, beautiful, I shouldn't laugh. And I'm not laughing at you, I promise! I laugh at him and his ridiculous lies."

When Gio got up from the table, they all looked questioningly at Cecilia, who just shrugged and shook her head.

Haci whispered in Maya's ear: "That guy's name is Fetullah, and he's not half anything at all. I know this because we come from the same village and I know his family. Believe me when I say that he is *not* a good person. He will say anything to get in the ladies' pants."

His laughter ceased, and he looked at her with a serious expression.

"Maya, you have to warn Cecilia about him. I like your friends. They're nice people with good hearts, and he's really not!"

Maya looked at Haci, stunned.

"Seriously?" she stammered.

"Guaranteed," Haci nodded, looking up at the bar. "Just keep an eye on him up there."

Maya turned so that she could discreetly see 'Gio', who was now aggressively flirting with a pretty woman in a red tight dress. The woman appeared to be the same age as themselves, and she had been sitting alone at the bar for the past hour.

Less than a minute later, 'Gio' was standing with his whole tongue down her throat. His hands had a good hold on her breasts, which he massaged with vigorous movements.

Maya poked June, who sat next to her, without missing even one second of the show.

"What's up, Maya?" June asked. Then she looked in the direction Maya was pointing at. June let out a gasp. "What the actual fuck?! What a... Yuck!" she exclaimed so loudly that both Charlotte's and Cecilia's attention quickly turned in the same direction.

Maya broke her stare and looked worriedly at Cecilia, who was sitting with a very surprised expression on her face. "Are you okay, mousy?"

she yelled over the music.

"Well... Honestly, I had just refused to go home with him, so..." she replied loudly, shaking her head resignedly. "But I didn't realise he was going to jump on the next moving object less than ten seconds after..."

June looked furiously over at 'Gio', who had now climbed halfway up the lady's lap. He rubbed his crotch rhythmically on one of her thighs while he stuck his tongue into her ear.

"God damn it! I'll rip his balls off!" She got up and was about to walk over to him when Cecilia stopped her.

"Hey, it doesn't matter. But I think I want to go home now. I'm feeling exhausted, and I'm honestly completely filled up with, let's call it experiences." With a tired look on her face, she grabbed her bag.

"Okay, that's fine with me. It's also almost half past two, so it is probably a good idea, anyway," Charlotte nodded and drank out.

"I'm going to the toilet and then I'm ready to go," June quickly responded and started moving before anyone could stop her. She marched past 'Gio' without looking at him, to the toilets located behind the bar. On the way back to their table, they saw her quickly whisper something in the ear of the lady in the red dress. June sat down with a triumphant look next to Maya and stared expectantly up at the bar.

The lady in the red dress had now thrown 'Gio' off her and was in a loud voice, trying to get him to stay away from her.

"*What* did you say to her?" Maya whispered to June, with an impressed tone in her voice.

"Well, I just told her he had just cost my friend over 100 euros on antibiotics. Just to get rid of the crabs, he had 'gifted' her during sexy times," June giggled. "And that I knew he didn't have the money to be treated himself, so enjoy!"

Meanwhile, 'Gio' had figured out that June had something to do with the whole mess and marched furiously over to their table.

"Why are you saying to that woman that I have... insects in my dick?!" he yelled in frustration and clenched his fists again and again.

"Listen, I don't know what you have in your little radish, Gio-Boy," June replied, cold as ice. "But I do know what you don't have *on* it. The poor lady there!" She pointed to the woman who, in that exact moment, almost ran past them while frantically wiping her mouth with a whole

344

pile of wet wipes.

'Gio', red-hot with rage, stepped all the way to the table and raised his hand toward June.

At the same time, Haci jumped up and started speaking Turkish in a very loud voice. 'Gio' tried to retaliate, but Haci quickly stopped him and looked at him furiously. Finally, 'Gio' gave up. Before he stormed out of The Golden Donkey, he shouted some short and angry Turkish words to June, followed by a few not-so-nice hand gestures.

Haci turned to Maya and the others and smiled strainedly. "I'm so sorry that you had to experience this. He's just a terrible person."

"It's okay, Haci, it's not your fault. I'm just glad you were here to stop him. So, thank you for that," Maya smiled and took his hand.

"Maya, we're leaving now. I think there's taxis right outside so we don't get into more trouble with that idiot." June got up.

Maya looked at Haci, smiling. "They're on their way home now..."

"What about you? Are you on your way home too?" he asked with a crooked smile.

"Well... It depends on whether I have other options. What do you think I should?" she whispered and send him a flirtatious look.

Haci pulled her close and kissed her softly on the lips. "I think that tonight, you should be mine," he whispered back.

"Okay, now we're *definitely* leaving!" June laughed, and dragged Charlotte and Cecilia with her. "Maya, write us and let us know where you sleep tonight. And remember to take notes, okay? We want every sexy detail tomorrow! Oh, by the way, I have put a small gift in your bag, in the compartment that you never use. Take a look when you are alone. Have fun!" she shouted in Danish as they walked out, leaving Maya alone with Haci.

Chapter 32

"So, now what?" Maya asked, when she suddenly became very self-conscious.

Haci also looked a little shy, but said that they could go to his house. He lived only ten minutes away on foot.

She nodded and let him lead her out of the bar and into the street. He stopped when they got outside and turned to her. "I'll take good care of you, don't worry," he whispered, pulling her close to him and kissing her softly again.

The music and noise of all the bars in the area faded behind them as they walked, hand in hand, up the winding streets. They didn't say much along the way, but it was okay. Maya was overwhelmed by all the sensations that flew through her body right now and that had been away for so long.

He stopped when they reached a slightly worn, white, three-story building. On the black iron railings of the balconies, blankets and clothes hung to dry, and it was clear that this was an ordinary residential complex and not a hotel.

"Here we are," he pulled her towards the entrance door and up the stairs to the 2nd floor.

He looked at her a little apologetically as he unlocked the door to his apartment. "It's a fully furnished rental home, so don't have too high expectations for the décor," he smiled as he opened the door and put a hand inside to turn on the light.

Maya entered curiously and looked around.

The apartment was not big and all the fixtures looked old. The kitchen consisted of a row of cupboards on one wall in the living room. All the doors hung, and one was missing completely.

"It... looks fine..." she began, but couldn't help but look somewhat sceptical as well.

Haci laughed. "It's all right, Maya. I know it's not very fancy. I have just rented it for the season, so I only need a bed, a shower and a place to store my clothes."

"Oh okay, that makes sense," she nodded. At least it was both clean and tidy, and that wasn't always a given with men who lived alone. That much she remembered from her dating days. Maya looked around, feeling a little confused. "Where's the bedroom?" she asked and smiled uncertainly at him.

Haci shrugged. "This is all. I don't really need a separate bedroom when it's just me. I only have this one."

He turned to an old sofa bed with a hideous bright-green plastic-like fabric. He reached under the couch and unfolded it with a quick movement of his hand. Maya was relieved to find that the ugly plastic side was now facing downwards and that the sleeping side was covered with normal soft fabric.

He walked towards her with a cheeky smile.

"So, is that good enough for you?" he asked, pulled her in and kissed her gently.

"Yeah, that's perfectly fine," she smiled. She laid her head back and looked up at him, letting her fingers slide through his short hair. He closed his eyes for a moment and smiled blissfully. He let one hand slide up to her neck and buried his fingers in her hair. "I love your hair. It is so... Red and curly. It's really beautiful. Just like the rest of you," he whispered, and let his hand slide slowly down her back.

He gripped her hips a little firmer and pressed his lower body against hers while kissing her deeply.

"You are so amazing. How can you be so amazing?" Haci whispered with wonder in his voice while slowly letting his tongue wander up her neck and up to her earlobe.

Maya could feel her legs almost disappearing

under her. *Oh my God!* I completely forgot what it's like to be so turned on that you can barely handle being in your own body, she thought, before also feeling something else. She had to pee!

"Um, wait. Hang on for a moment," she mumbled and pulled out of his arms.

"What? What's wrong? Did I do something wrong?" Haci looked completely startled, and Maya couldn't hold back a little laugh. "No, no, you are... Absolutely perfect, so far," she winked and send him a look, she hoped was sexy.

"But I have to borrow your toilet for a moment, and maybe we could turn off some lights as well?" she smiled and looked up at the cold fluorescent light on the ceiling, while shielding her eyes. "Soft light is just better at our age, isn't it?" she joked, and Haci laughed agreeingly.

"Okay, go to the bathroom. I'll bring out the romantic vibe in the meantime."

Maya grabbed her bag and hurried towards the toilet.

The bathroom looked just as worn as the rest of the apartment, but it was equally clean and tidy. Maya turned around to lock the door and discovered that there was no lock on it. She briefly felt the panic spread, but chose to kick the feeling away again with a shrug. "I can't do anything about it anyway, and if I want to have sex with Haci, I have to pull myself together," she muttered to herself, trying to sit as far out on the edge of the toilet-seat as possible so he couldn't hear her pee.

She quickly removed the tight cotton shorts, which she had to wear when wearing a dress and bare legs underneath. They were far from sexy, but just really necessary if she didn't want her inner thighs to chafe. "Well, that's what you have to struggle with, when you have thick thighs," she sighed to herself. She shrugged as she rolled up her shorts like a sausage and placed them at the bottom of her bag.

She looked scrutinising at herself in the mirror and sighed again in resignation. The light in the bathroom was just one powerful halogen spot that only illuminated her from above. So, besides the fact that she could now see every wrinkle and impurity clearly, the location of the light source also made her look like she had deep, dark circles under her eyes.

"Jesus Christ, I look like a junkie in this light," she muttered and shook her head resignedly.

"Did you say something to me?" Haci's asked from outside the door.

"No, no, I... I just talked to myself a little," Maya replied quickly, feeling slightly embarrassed.

"Okay?" His voice sounded a little confused. "Would you like something to drink? I don't have many choices, but I can offer a beer or some water?"

"No thanks, it's okay," she replied as she removed some dry mascara from under her eye with her index finger.

She was just about to step out of the bathroom when her phone beeped. She checked it right away. It was a message from June:

Hey your slutty potato!
Remember to write where you are so we know where to send the police to look for you, if you don't show up again. Ha ha!
And now go and have a great night!
We look forward to hearing all about it!
N.B. Remember to check the pocket in your bag! ☺

Maya had completely forgotten June's cryptic message about the pocket in her bag, so she hurried to check it. She started giggling to herself. In the pocket were five condoms with rippled texture, 'for her pleasure', and the guidebook that Cecilia had bought, but had refused to use in public.

June had put a receipt from Migros on the sex-commands page, acting as a bookmark, with her own writing on the back: *Now there's no excuse for horrible sex!* Beneath was a drawing of a smiling, erect penis.

Maya's giggle turned into a half-stifled laugh, and she swiftly stuffed her phone, the drawing, and the guidebook back into her bag's inner pocket. She put the condoms in the large compartment so she could easily get to them.

She dried her eyes and hands and got a hold of herself before she stepped out of the bathroom and into the living room.

In the meantime, Haci had turned off the ceiling lights and had instead pulled out some artificial candles. It was set up on the side tables around the sofa bed and on the TV bench. We had also made the bed, and it looked way comfier now. Haci himself had taken off his shirt and was now squatting in front of the small fridge that stood on the floor of the kitchen area.

Maya stopped in the middle of the room and looked at him curiously. She wasn't into really buff guys who spent all their time in the gym, but she wasn't into very skinny guys either. They always made her feel short and fat by their physique alone. She was mostly into guys who were either a bit on the chubbier side or naturally robust.

Haci had a slender body-type, but his shoulders and arms looked strong, showing that he was used to physical labour. Maya bit her lip as she felt an expectant quiver running through her body.

"Have you decided what you want?" she asked curiously as she stood behind him and glanced into the open refrigerator.

"Yes..." He replied as he got up. He closed the door to the refrigerator and quickly turned to her. "You... I want you..." In one smooth motion, he put his hands on her buttocks, pulled himself close to her, and pressed her up against the wall while kissing her passionately.

Maya felt as if the inner volcano that had been dormant for years was now exploding, causing her brain to melt down. All her previous insecurities and nervousness about herself and her body disappeared like dew before the sun.

She had never experienced anything so enticing in her entire life, and she could do nothing but indulge totally in the flames of Haci.

Chapter 33

Maya woke up with a startle and was completely confused about where she was. It took her a moment to recognise the hairy arm around her waist, and then she remembered the amazing night they had together.

Her body warmed at the thought of Haci and the things they had done.

She smiled tiredly and, without pulling completely out of his arms, reached for her phone to check the time. It was already half past nine.

There were a lot of messages in their chat, primarily from June, who had written with increasing concern both last night and this morning.

Maya grimaced when she realised, she had forgotten to write about where she was staying. She quickly replied that she was alive and well and that she was very sorry for her forgetfulness. But that she had a good excuse, because her night was steaming hot, and that she would be back at the hotel soon.

June immediately wrote back that she was

relieved to hear that she did not have to go out and find her body buried under a cone-bearing tree up in the mountains. Then she announced that she, Charlotte, and Cecilia would stroll into town after breakfast to buy some gifts for their families. But that they intended to have lunch at the hotel at two o'clock, and that they expected Maya to be ready with juicy details by then.

Maya giggled at June's message and wrote back to ask when they had to be out of their rooms. She had packed nothing yet and was wondering how stressed she should prepare to get later on.

June replied she could take it easy. Charlotte had asked the front desk last night and had been told they could just keep their rooms until they were picked up at four. Maya sighed in relief and put her phone back on the nightstand. Immediately, the arm around her tightened, and Haci pulled her close to him.

"Mmm, you're not leaving yet, are you?" he muttered as he slowly kissed her between her shoulder blades.

"Haci, I have to leave today, so I'll have to get up soon," she mumbled, intertwining her fingers between his.

"I know, but can you wait half an hour? Then I'll drive you to your hotel," he whispered while slowly letting his hands explore her body.

"Okay," she whispered with her eyes closed. "But only for a moment... I..." Her words disappeared into a murmur, and she again let herself drift away on the waves of desire.

***

It was a quarter to eleven when Maya insisted, she had to go back to the hotel immediately. Haci accepted somewhat grudgingly, but he was also well aware that there was no way around it.

They both got dressed, and Maya quickly brushed her teeth before walking down the stairs and out into the street.

The street was alive with activity. The complete opposite of the previous night's silence. Outside Haci's building, two old men were playing cards at a small table. An old lady with a scarf was carrying shopping bags full of veggies, and a bunch of little boys played with a ball up against the house wall.

Haci nodded and greeted them all, and they greeted him back.

Maya suddenly felt self-conscious about still

wearing yesterday's black dress and her makeup being a disaster. She felt very exposed here in the bright daylight and hid her face slightly as they walked past the two older men who were grinning at them.

"Oh my God, how embarrassing!" Maya exclaimed and looked extremely uncomfortable. Haci stopped in front of his scooter and unlocked it. "What do you mean?" he asked, genuinely surprised, and turned to her.

"You! Me! Us! Me in this dress! This entire street now knows what we've been doing last night!" she whispered with red cheeks. She shook her head at herself. "That's just so fucking embarrassing!" she added shamefully.

"Hey, hey. Breathe and calm down a little!" Haci hugged her. "Now be honest... Have you regretted our night together?" he asked with a cheeky smile.

"No, no, of course not, but...".

"Okay, but then why do you care what they know or don't know?" he interrupted while waving his arms dismissible. "We're both single and we can do whatever we want, right? I have no regrets, Maya. You are a beautiful and amazing woman, and I feel very lucky to have got to know you." He smiled and gave her a quick kiss on the lips.

She sighed and looked at him resignedly.

"Well, it's too late to do anything about it now, anyway, so what can I do but accept it, right?" she replied with a shrug, but she still looked a little ashamed. "Just drive me back to the hotel, okay, Haci?"

"As you wish," he nodded. Then he started the scooter while helping her up behind him.

Neither of them said anything as they drove through the winding streets, with Maya hiding her face against his back all the way up the mountain.

He drove past the hotel and stopped the engine a little further on. "I don't want you to feel any more awkward, so I'll say goodbye to you here, and then I'll drive another way back."

"Good thinking, thanks for that". Maya smiled and let her hand slide caressingly down his arm before she got off the scooter. Then she stepped forward, gave him a hug and a quick kiss, and stepped away again.

"Thank you for a wonderful night, Haci. It was perfect. *You* were perfect. It was just what I needed. Just forget my outburst before. I regret nothing. I just overthink things sometimes." She shrugged a little reluctantly.

Haci lit up visibly, and a content expression

spread across his face. "If you're happy, then I'm happy, Maya, and I really enjoyed our night together, too."

Then he took a deep breath and started his scooter again. "I'd better go. Take good care of yourself, say hi to the girls and get home safely to Denmark." He sent her another warm look before driving further up the street and disappearing.

***

An hour and a half later, Maya had showered and packed most of her things. It made things way easier that June's stuff was already packed away, and she sent her grateful thoughts a bunch of times on the way.

She glanced at the clock. It was only a quarter to one, so she might as well go down and get some sun until the others came back.

With just her phone, a book, and sunscreen in a bag, she walked down to the pool and settled into a sunbed, exposing only her legs to the sun.

She waved to Gert and Nora, who were soaking up the sun at the other end of the pool area.

Lulu was floating around on an air mattress wearing big pink sunglasses and a matching bikini. With a sharp voice and her phone in hand, she directed Thor around so she could get the perfect holiday photo for her Instagram.

Maya tried to concentrate on her book, but was distracted by Lulu's constant commanding voice. It didn't help that Thor seemed more and more like someone who would rather drown her than shag her.

"I'll give that relationship a maximum of three months. Then he has either kicked her out of his life or is on the cover of a newspaper, arrested for murder!" Maya mumbled to herself.

A few minutes later, Thor apparently decided enough was enough and marched out of the pool with a highly irritated look on his face. He put headphones in his ears and lay down on the sunbed with his eyes closed.

Lulu looked at him in surprise, and for some time she continued to float around on the air mattress, while she still yelled at him to get back on "set". But Thor apparently had no intention of giving in this time and remained demonstratively lying down, not responding to her demands.

Finally, with an irritated movement, Lulu let herself slide into the water, swam over to the stairs and stomped straight up to him and ripped one of his earphones out of his ear.

"Hello, don't ignore me, Thor!" she said in a

loud voice.

Thor just shrugged, took the earphone out of her hand, and inserted it back into his ear.

Maya giggled. She was somewhat impressed. "Uh, it takes *balls*, that move. Are you sure that's the right way to go, Thor-darling," she whispered to herself, catching sight of Gert and Nora, who were watching the scene with just as much amusement. They exchanged a quick wave and a shrug and smiled in agreement across the pool.

For a moment, Lulu looked like she was going to hit him. But she apparently decided that wasn't the way forward. Instead, she hastily packed up her things and stomped back towards the hotel.

"Your move, Thor. What do you do now?" Maya whispered, lurking over the edge of her book.

A few minutes passed. Then Thor sighed deeply, got up, packed his things, and moseyed in the same direction as Lulu.

After disappearing into the hotel, Maya looked over at Gert and Nora. "Oh, that won't be fun to fix," she said, laughingly pointing the way Thor had gone.

"Don't worry. Give them twenty minutes and

they'll make completely different sounds," Gert exclaimed with a big laugh. Nora slapped him on the upper arm and shook her head. "Gert, that enough! Stop talking!" she said indignantly, but laughed at the same time.

"Jesus Christ, they've been like this all week! They argue, they make up and they have sex. That's just how it is!" Gert replied so raptly that Maya couldn't hold back her laughter.

"Are you girls leaving today?" Nora tried to change the subject.

"Yes, we are getting picked up at four. What about you two?" Maya asked curiously.

"No, we have one more week. We always travel two weeks if we can. It's good for our old bodies with all this warmth," Nora replied and turned to pat her husband on the back. "Shall we have some lunch, old timer?" she asked cheekily and picked up her bag from the ground.

"I never say no to lunch with such a hot potato." Gert winked lovingly at his wife.

They walked hand in hand up to the pool bar. Maya's eyes followed them and a warm feeling spread within her. "Look at that. That's the dream relationship, isn't it?" she whispered and smiled to herself. Then she looked at the clock. Half past one. The others would be here soon.

Her stomach rumbled, and she was feeling starved.

She lost herself in her book again, but fifteen minutes later, her concentration was interrupted by a shouting voice. "Woo-hoo, Mau Mau. Are you feeling fresh today?" followed by an implied loud laughter. Maya lowered her book with a smile. Charlotte, Cecilia and June stood grinning at the reception entrance with a lot of shopping bags and waved to her.

She nodded and waved back at them.

"We're just going up with our bags, then we'll come down," June shouted. She wasn't waiting for an answer, but followed Charlotte and Cecilia into the reception.

Chapter 34

Maya spent the wait putting the book away and sat down by a table under the canopy in the pool bar. She chose a location at the very back so no one could hear what they talked about during the meal.

A few minutes later, the girls were back and came laughingly to the table.

"I completely forgot that you have our room key," June explained, "so my purchases are currently stored in room 408."

Maya accepted the menus that Mr Chippy handed out while the others sat down.

"I can't decide," Cecilia complained. "It's the last chance for lunch here at the hotel. What should I choose?"

"*When in doubt, pick the cheeseburger,*" Maya replied with a smile, folding her menu together.

"Is that a real thing or what?" Cecilia looked confused.

"No, it's just a little saying we have in my family." Maya shrugged. "There's no science behind it. We just really like cheeseburgers, that's all..."

"It's true. You really have to have a very special talent if you can ruin an ordinary cheeseburger so much that it's completely inedible," June nodded. "I'll go along with it."

When Mr Chippy arrived a moment later, everyone had agreed on a cheeseburger with a Cola Light.

"What the hell, June? Aren't you going to have a beer with your food today?" Maya commented with a smile.

"Nope. My head was a little tired this morning, and now that we're going home, I'm thinking I'd better keep both hands on the non-alcoholic steering wheel," June replied with a grimace.

"Speaking of hands on something." Charlotte looked at Maya excitedly. "I think our girl here has a story to tell?"

All three looked at her expectantly, and Maya smiled.

"First of all, thank you for the gift, June. I didn't need it because he had everything under control regarding our safety precautions. But thanks for the thought, anyway," she laughed and nodded over to June, who smirked and winked at her.

Maya continued with a giggle: "I will not tell you all the details. That would be a little weird, okay? But I can say this much... When he pushed me up against the wall and whispered how sexy I was, I almost fainted!" she whispered and giggled again at her own words.

"Uh, nice! So passionate!" June nodded with an appreciative look.

"Big, medium or small?" Charlotte asked with a smirk, ignoring Cecilia's indignant gaze.

"Hey, turn your voices down a bit, guys! No need to let the entire pool area know what I've been doing, okay? But let's just say he had nothing to be embarrassed about..." Maya whispered, and Charlotte and June giggled loudly. Cecilia shook her head and rolled her eyes, but she didn't say anything.

"So, all in all... Turkish Delight or Special Prize For You experience?" Charlotte whispered back with an excited expression on her face.

"Well... Let me just say that he managed to make me really, really happy. All over the place..."

"Not bad, not bad," June nodded again appreciatively.

"... Three times," Maya added. She laughed and hushed them as they started cheering loudly.

"Okay, definitely a Turkish Delight experience," Charlotte said as she dried her eyes with a napkin from the napkin holder. "I'm so happy for you! Not only do you really deserve it. You seriously also needed a little shake-me-up!" she teased and laughed even louder when Maya agreed with her without hesitation.

"Well, we also have some gossip here from the hotel," June interjected as she leaned over the table and lowered her voice.

"Okay, get this... When we got home last night, the Egg Divider was standing here at the pool bar talking to Mr Chippy. The bar was almost completely dark, but we could see them in the light from the pool. They were standing very close to each other. She giggled every time he said something, and he kept touching her hair," she said in a low voice and stopped when Mr Chippy came with their order.

She continued after he left. "Charlotte talked to Alican at the reception about our check-out, as you already know, and he asked about our holiday and so on. So, it probably took at least five minutes before we could go to our rooms. Just as we are about to get into the elevator, we hear the Egg Divider ask for her room key..." June looked at Maya excitedly.

"Yeah, and?" Maya looked puzzled.

"She lives in 307!" June exclaimed excitedly and giggled loudly.

"So ...?" Maya looked at her with an incomprehensible look.

June sighed and shook her head. "Jeez, did Haci fry your brain completely last night or what? Think again! Add things up, Maya! The room below us + flirting at the bar + horrible sex. What does it add up to?" she asked again, waiting for the penny to drop.

"June, what are you even talking about? I ..." Maya stopped herself, and they could see the gears turning. Then she started smiling. "Oh my God! Now I understand! Mr Chippy and the Egg Divider are knocking boots, and now we know he's a Special Prize For You man! Wow! How disappointing it must be for her! Just think of all the work she's put into that flirting!"

Suddenly, they realised Cecilia was no longer a part of their conversation. She sat with her phone in her hand. She looked concerned.

"Hey, Mammi, is everything okay?" Maya had instantly stifled her laughter.

"Yes, yes, it's just my dad who wrote a minute ago. He's a little worried, but I'm sure it's nothing," she replied and put her phone down on the table with the backside up.

"What's nothing?" Charlotte asked and looked at her uncertainly.

"Oh, he can't get hold of my mom right now. She doesn't pick up her phone when he calls, so..." she replied and took a bite of her burger.

"So, is everything okay or what?" June asked and looked seriously at her.

Cecilia brushed it off with a big smile. "Yeah, yeah. She probably just turned it off, or she has it on silent. My dad is a little silly sometimes, so just forget about it."

June and Charlotte glanced at each other, clearly not buying Cecilia's explanation. But both chose to shrug their shoulders and leave it alone for now. Maya sat and smiled by herself, not noticing anything. Her thoughts were occupied with the night's experiences.

Chapter 35

"We're going to... Gate 228," Charlotte said as she put her boarding pass back in her bag while looking at the direction overview in front of them. "This way," she said and turned left with the others hot on her heels.

"Hey, isn't Cecilia more quiet than usual?" Maya whispered to June while trying to keep up with Charlotte's brisk walk. "She has hardly said a word since we left the hotel, and she also keeps a little to herself right now," she added and pointed discreetly to Cecilia, who was indeed walking with a distance from her friends.

It had only been them and the young couple, Thor and Lulu, on the transfer bus. They had apparently become good friends again since the trouble in paradise earlier. At least they sat wrapped around each other all the way, and Lulu swiped through the holiday-photos on her phone while making exciting sounds.

"Well, that *is* a little weird," June whispered back and observed Cecilia, a little worried. "Maybe it has something to do with her mother?" she suggested, looking questioningly at Maya.

Maya shrugged doubtfully. "Maybe... But she

told us it was nothing. Of course, she may have lied to us..." she added thoughtfully, but then shook her head dismissively. "That can't be it, June. You know how she feels about lies and omissions... She explodes in seven directions if people are reckless with the truth."

"Yes, that's true, of course, but something's up with her..." June thought for a moment, then stopped abruptly and grabbed Maya's arm. An overweight man in a business suit, and with a phone to his ear, crashed right into her. He sent them an annoyed look as he head-shakingly walked on.

"Well, excuse me," June laughed, while childishly sticking her tongue out at him as he looked back at them. His head turned almost blue with anger, as he walked towards his gate with a scowl.

"Well, what a sourpuss."

She began to move forward again. "Where did I come from? Oh Yeah... Maya, what if it's about something completely different?" June stood on the automatic conveyor belt that was placed at intervals throughout the hall. "What if it's about that dickbag, "Gio"? What if she was actually interested and then got treated in that disrespectful way?"

Maya considered it for a moment, and then

nodded. "You may be right... But in that case... Haci told me some things about him last night that I haven't told the rest of you yet. Maybe she needs to know that his behaviour isn't about her?"

"Yes, maybe that's not a bad idea," June nodded and stepped off the conveyor belt. "Hey, gate 228 is right there, and there's a food stall right across from it!" she exclaimed excitedly and dragged Maya over to look at the food selection.

Prices were on the expensive side, but June still bought four sandwiches and four bottles of water, so everyone had a snack for the flight.

Charlotte and Cecilia were already waiting on the benches around the gate when they arrived, and they were glad that June had thought of them as well.

June cleared her throat and sent Maya a knowing look. "Hey, Cille-mouse, are you okay? You seem a little quiet today?" she asked gently.

Cecilia looked at her and smiled. "Yes, I'm perfectly okay. I'm just a little tired after last night, and I'm not too fond of flying, so..."

"Okay, that's fine too. I... We just thought we wanted to make sure it wasn't about... Anything else?" June looked at her questioningly.

Cecilia looked a little confused. "No, what would that be?"

June looked over at Maya. "Well..." June began.

"Okay, Cecilia, I'm just going to put it all out on the table," Maya interrupted. "You are not to blame for all that shit with him 'Gio'! Just so you know! Haci told me his name isn't Gio at all. He's not even half Italian, and he's lying about being the owner of Star Beach as well, so he's the one who's an idiot, not you!" He doesn't deserve you *at all*. He is truly a miserable, miserable person!" The words poured out of her so quickly that she almost became a little out of breath.

"Wow, wait a minute. What did you say?" Charlotte looked shocked. "What's his name then?!"

"His name is Fetullah. He is 100% from Turkey, and he is just a regular employee at that beach club! Everything he had said was to make him selves more interesting, and to get with the ladies. So disgusting!"

"How *crazy* to be such a big liar!" Charlotte whispered to herself while shaking her head.

"Cecilia, are you okay?" June asked gently, and with a gesture of her hands, she got the others to stop talking.

Cecilia looked petrified. "So, let me understand this," she whispered, slowly turning her head towards Maya. "You knew all this about him without telling me? Wow, you're really a good friend, Maya!" She shook her head with a disbelieving expression on her face.

"What?! No, I... What?" Maya exclaimed, looking confused. "Mouse, I was told all of this while you were talking to him last night, and you yourself rejected him before I could say anything. When did I have the chance to tell you?!"

Cecilia glared at her. "Wow, I'm so disappointed in you. Nicely done, Maya," she hissed. Then she got up and sat down a few rows further away.

Maya also got up. "What's going on, Cecilia? Why do you get so angry with me?" She was confused and tried to go after her. Charlotte pulled her back down on the seat and shook her head.

"Hey, let her steam off," she whispered and shook her head again. "I'm sure she'll be okay again. Just let her take it all in."

"Take what in?" Maya whispered, frustrated. "I have done nothing wrong here, Charlotte! For fuck's sake, I don't have a time machine so I can go and tell her the truth before even I know it!"

Charlotte nodded. "I totally agree, Mau Mau. I'm also not entirely sure that this outburst is really about you. She has been *off* several times on this holiday. Now let's just see if she doesn't calm down soon."

June moved over beside them. "I agree with Charlotte, Maya. You won't get anything out of her now. There may very well be more to this outburst. But either way, she's tired from yesterday, stressed about having to fly, and probably also *pissed at* herself for being attracted to such an... ass-hat!" June snarled, making Charlotte and Maya giggle.

"Ass-hat?! Is that really the only description that came to you? I have to say I'm a bit disappointed with your creative ability right now." Maya looked at her teasingly.

June sighed and leaned back in her chair. "Yes, well, when I'm running on too little sleep mixed with litres of alcohol from yesterday, this is what you get." She looked towards the gate, where some airport employees were getting ready to let people onto the plane.

"It's time, ladies," she said a moment later, as the loudspeaker above their heads crackled and announced that boarding was now open. Cecilia walked past them and lined up by herself.

"Is she seriously going to be like that all the

way home?" Maya looked at the others with frustration.

They both shrugged. "I don't know, babe. But I'm thinking we'll just leave her alone until she warms up again, okay?" June whispered, slinging her bag over her shoulder, and walked over to the line.

Cecilia had luckily got a window seat on the way home, as she quickly shut herself in behind both a sleeping mask and some headphones. June took a seat next to her so Maya wouldn't have to sit right next to someone who refused to talk to her. Charlotte was, once again, seated on the opposite side of the aisle.

Maya looked worriedly at Cecilia as the plane took off, but to her surprise she saw no reaction. Perhaps the others are right. Maybe she's just tired, she thought to herself and settled down with her book.

None of them said much on the ride home. All were exhausted, and Maya went to sleep after only half an hour in the air.

Charlotte had pulled out her computer so she could get an overview of what tasks had piled up while she was away.

She chuckled at her own naivety. Thinking

she could get some work done during the holiday was clearly a misjudgement. That had not happened at all! She had enjoyed herself too much with the others to think about work.

Despite Cecilia being rather weird this week and completely unreasonable today, this has been the most insane and hilarious experience she's had in ages.

She had a worried expression on her face as she thought about Cecilia's outburst at the airport again. It was so far away from her normal behaviour.

She gave her three friends a warm look from across the aisle. These were some of the most important people in her life, and she wouldn't trade them for anything in the world.

Chapter 36

"Where did Cecilia go?" June asked, confused. She looked around.

They had been let off the plane in Copenhagen Airport a few minutes ago. Maya and Charlotte had exited first and were waiting for June and Cecilia just outside the gate.

"I can't see her," Charlotte replied and stretched her neck as she looked around.

"Well, she was right behind me a moment ago," June checked her phone at the same time. "There isn't any network yet, and I don't see her here. Maybe we should just go. We're going to the same place, anyway, right?" she suggested with a shrug.

Maya sighed. "I don't want this holiday to end in such a strange way. Especially when I have done nothing wrong," she said with a tired voice, and walked after the others towards the passport control.

"No, that's understandable," Charlotte nodded and smiled encouragingly at her. "I wonder if she just went ahead?"

"Hey, I think I can see her." June pointed a little further ahead in line.

"Yeah, that's her. Then everyone is located," Charlotte nodded in satisfaction. "She'll probably just wait for us on the other side."

But when they got through the passport control, there was no Cecilia to be seen.

Maya looked both disappointed and frustrated as they made their way down to the baggage claim. "Guys, I understand nothing! Is she just going to leave by herself or what?"

June and Charlotte didn't respond, but shared a worried expression.

They made it to the baggage carousel, and surprisingly, the luggage was already coming out.

They could see Cecilia standing by herself a little further ahead. One of the first suitcases that came through was hers. She pulled it off the baggage belt and started walking towards the exit.

Charlotte, Maya, and June looked at her in astonishment. But after only a few steps, she stopped again, looked around, and caught Maya's eye. She then pointed over to the nearest wall as if to say they could meet there.

Once Maya, Charlotte, and June's suitcases arrived, they all headed towards Cecilia together. Maya felt angry and wronged, and was dead-set on, that a huge apology was necessary if things were to be fixed.

However, Maya quickly forgot all about it when she saw Cecilia's eyes welling up.

"Cille-mouse, what's wrong?" she exclaimed worriedly, but Cecilia stopped her with a gesture of her hand.

"I... I would like to say something before I leave... And without interruption..." She smiled a small, uncertain smile and took a deep breath to calm herself.

The other three looked at each other, confused, but then nodded without saying anything.

"I'm sorry that I acted so strangely today, and maybe also sometimes on this holiday as well. I know this has been a stupid and unnecessary end to a fantastic holiday." She smiled warmly at all of them, but the smile quickly disappeared again. "I think I owe you all an explanation for my behaviour. Especially you, Maya. I was super unreasonable earlier about all that stuff with 'Gio', or whatever his name is. In reality, I really don't care about that nobody. I owe you a big apology, so... I am so sorry, Maya! You're not an awful friend. It has nothing to do with you at all," she added quietly.

Before Maya could respond, Cecilia continued with a trembling voice, "All this drama on my part are actually rooted in something else. That something else is also why it was really important for me to have all of you come with me on holiday this fall."

Maya gasped, and tears flooded her eyes. "Oh my God. Is it cancer? No, Cille-mouse, it's not cancer, is it?"

"No, no, it's no such thing! Don't worry," Cecilia quickly replied. Then she quietly added, "It's not me personally."

She sighed and took a deep breath. "Okay, you know I mentioned earlier today that my dad wrote he couldn't get hold of my mom? And also, that I said she probably just forgot to turn on her phone?" she continued.

All three of them nodded.

"Okay... So, it's not the first time my mother has gone missing like this, and it won't be the last," she said in a very low voice, and grief shone through every word. "My mom has developed dementia, and it's a really aggressive version... We don't know how much time she has left." The last sentence was almost whispered, and a sob escaped from her.

"Oh no, mouse." Charlotte hurried to pull Cecilia into a warm hug. June and Maya looked at each other, stunned for a moment, and they could easily read each other's minds: *Fuck! Fucking fuck! Poor, poor Cecilia!*

They quickly put their arms protectively around both Charlotte and Cecilia. Shielded behind the arms of her friends, Cecilia let her tears flow freely for the first time in a week.

They stood like this for a while until Cecilia had regained control of herself. They only let go of her when she assured them, in a half-choked voice, that she was okay.

Maya pulled out some handkerchiefs so that all four could dry their eyes and blow their noses.

Cecilia took a few deep breaths. "This is why it was so important for me to travel with you all this year. I just knew this trip would reconnect us."

She looked determined at them. "You are my chosen extended family, and I *will* draw heavily on your support and friendship in the near future. Consider yourself warned," she said with a little smile.

Maya began to sob again and unfolded her

crumpled napkin slightly to dab her eyes once more.

"Of course, Cecilia, we are here when you need it. Night and day. You just let us know!" June responded in a firm voice. She was always the best at dealing with big emotions and could find her way back to the more comprehensible version of herself faster than the others.

Charlotte cleared her throat and got her voice under control. "Always, mouse, always. We've got you. You're never alone, okay?" She reached out and squeezed Cecilia's hand.

"Me and Mr fatty are always ready if you need some company! Just let me know and I'll come racing with the cat-carrier!" Maya promised solemnly, making Cecilia smile.

Her phone suddenly beeped, and she hurried to look at it. "Oh, thank God, there's a connection again," she exhaled in relief and her eyes filled with tears again. "It's my dad. They have found her safe and sound while we flew home!"

"That's good, mouse!" Charlotte replied and looked at Maya and June with relief.

"He writes that she had walked down to Lidl to shop. They recognised her and contacted my father when she showed up in just her dressing gown and slippers. She's home now and he's just outside in the arrivals waiting hall. He's waiting for me, so I have to hurry out there," she added, looking at them apologetically. "I'm sorry to just drop a bomb like that and then leave you." Her eyes welled up again.

"Cille-mouse!" June cut through. "The waterworks have to stop now! Go! Get out to your dad, and then go home and give your mom a big hug. We'll figure it out ourselves, okay? Off with you!" June ushered her towards the exit.

"You are the best. I love you all! We'll talk about it soon, okay?" she waved and disappeared into the swarm of people leaving the baggage area.

Maya, June, and Charlotte looked at each-other, clearly shocked.

"Jesus Christ... I did not see that coming," Maya said in a low voice while staring into space.

"Hey guys?" Charlotte turned to the others. "The time ahead is going to be so insanely hard for Cecilia. We have to make an agreement right now. That we'll make sure to catch her at all times, no matter what, okay?"

"Of course, that goes without saying," June replied a little wonderingly, but Charlotte interrupted her.

"Yeah, you would think so. But I also know that some of us have not always been there when needed. Because life got in the way. But that's no excuse!"

Then she looked directly at Maya. "Maya, I know that you, if anyone, were standing alone, and that no one really caught you when you fell. I promise you this. It's never going to happen again, okay?"

Maya looked at her in surprise. "I... Um... Okay. It's received, loud and clear," she replied with a crooked smile.

She didn't want to contradict Charlotte, because it was absolutely true. Only Cecilia had been there completely when Maya's life collapsed around her. Unfortunately, that was not enough. Cecilia was, without any doubt, the best and most loyal friend in the world. But it's impossible to get useable advice from someone who had tried nothing bigger in life than changing job positions. And that was even at the same workplace she'd been at since she was very young. The lack of a frame of reference fell short when it came to Maya's downfall. However, she had long since forgiven them all, and it was no longer something she felt sick to her stomach about.

June looked ashamed. "Yeah, me too. What

Charlotte said," she added with a smile and an apologetic shrug.

Maya cleared her throat, grabbed her suitcase, looked at the other two, and smiled. "Well, with all taken care of, should we try to find the exit?"

"Can we have a smoke before we head down to the train?" June asked and sounded very much in need.

"Off course! As long as 'we' really means 'you,' it's all good," Maya laughed.

All three of them walked through the exit gate into the arrival hall and further out the revolving door. Out in the fresh air.

"Well, I guess it jacket-time again," Charlotte said with a resigned voice while rummaging through the front pocket of her suitcase.

"I'm telling you, girls!" Maya turned to them. "I have had the best holiday with you all! Even if the end was a little... sad. I really had so much fun and it was just what I needed in my life. I would like to propose right now that we make this a new established tradition. One trip every year. With sun, drinks and a lot of good food, and fun experiences together. What do you say?" she asked excitedly.

"I'm in!" June quickly agreed. "Maybe I can

even stick to my plan about *not* sitting around eating chocolate roulade every night."

She patted her stomach. "Well, not because I'm buying that nonsense about the *perfect body*, you know that. It's only because it took me months to find a bikini I actually like, and where I don't look like a ham in tight strings. I will not ruin that small victory by increasing my junk in my ... Well, everything!"

"What a beautiful mental picture I got there," Maya sputtered with laughter. "Is it okay with you if I don't print it out?"

"You know what, June, that reason is as good as any other." Charlotte coughed and wiped away tears of laughter. "I'm also in on that plan. I've really enjoyed myself, and it's been a long time since I've felt so free!"

Maya stopped laughing. "What about Cecilia? I wonder if she's in on it too?" she asked hesitantly.

They all stood in a moment of silence.

"Maybe we should wait and see how it all goes and then leave it up to her?" June suggested.

"Yeah, it's probably a good idea to let her manage it herself. Well, Kenneth has arrived now, so I'll just mosey right over, so I can get picked up in the parking area. See you, girls!" Charlotte shouted as she waved and walked across the pedestrian crossing.

"Ah, that was just what I needed," June sighed contentedly, extinguished her cigarette butt on the ground and threw it in the nearest trash can. "Shall we go?"

Maya nodded and grabbed her suitcase.

"Do you have something to eat at home? I'm getting a little hungry again, and that sandwich was hours ago," June said thoughtfully as they walked towards the subway. "Uh, I would *love* a cold Coke before we pick up the fat boy and I turn my car towards my home!" she sighed. "What about you?"

"No, I'm not craving anything," Maya replied thoughtfully.

Then she giggled and added. "Well, maybe some Turkish Delight!"

Did you enjoy your trip to Cennet?

Then you are most welcome to share your thoughts on: amazon

Want More Turkish Delight?

Then keep an eye on my social media ...

Because Turkish Delight 2 is in the making!

I'm expecting to release the girls into the wild once again around late summer/fall 2024.

In the meantime, may you have the best summer of your life!

Best regards

Anjelica Søndergaard
26. marts 2024

About the author

- Lives in a cosy townhouse in the suburbs outside Copenhagen with four lazy, and somewhat chubby, shelter cats.

- Was over 40 years old before she figured out what she wanted to be when she "grew up". (Spoiler-alert: It's an author! ☺)

- Has always done things in her own way, and has chosen a life where travel, career, introspection, and personal freedom plays the main characters.

- Has never really grown up, (according to the conventional norms), and she still loves playing computer games, costume parties, cocktails with colourful umbrellas and dancing until the early morning.

- Loves dark humour, quirky people and tall tales with a passion!

- Have not yet met a person who did not have at least one interesting story to tell.

Social Media and Contact

Sign up for my newsletter and/or read reviews, news and updates:

Webpage: www.turkishdelight.dk/english
Instagram: @turkishdelightdk

Contact me on:

E-mail: kontakt@turkishdelight.dk

Printed in Great Britain
by Amazon

47823702R00229